THE STORY OF THE REFORMATION

THE
STORY OF THE
REFORMATION

✠

William Stevenson

John Knox Press
RICHMOND, VIRGINIA

Library of Congress Catalog Card Number: 59-10517

✠

FOREWORD

I feel greatly honored to have been invited to write a few words by way of introduction to a book at once so useful and so eminently readable as I believe the present volume will be found to be. Mr. Stevenson is a friend and near neighbor of my own, and I have long been impressed by the breadth of his knowledge and the accuracy of his scholarship. There are many things about which he could have written with equal acceptance, but there are two reasons why I am particularly happy about his present choice of subject.

First, it is so timely. The Church of Scotland and its daughter Presbyterian churches throughout the world are this year celebrating the four-hundredth anniversary of the triumph of the Scottish Reformation. It was in May 1559 that John Knox returned to Scotland, and my old teacher, A. R. Macewen, writes in his standard *A History of the Church in Scotland* that "The year which followed the arrival of Knox is the most important in the history of the Scottish Church and the Scottish nation," and further that "No year of Scottish history has been so important for other nations."

I understand that other volumes appropriate to this quatercentenary are being prepared and these, as is natural, will be mainly concerned with the Geneva-Calvin-Knox tradition. But there is room also for a fresh, succinct presentation of the whole Reformation movement, Lutheran and Anglican as well as Calvinist, such as will meet the needs of the general reader; and my second reason for welcoming Mr. Stevenson's book is that it offers us exactly this. The whole story is there, vividly told in the shortest possible compass, and I know of no other publication that is quite like it. May it recall many to the riches of their heritage.

JOHN BAILLIE
Principal-Emeritus
New College
Edinburgh

✠

AUTHOR'S PREFACE

My aims in writing this book were modest. The first was to provide a readable and (it is hoped) popular history of the Reformation for the general reader. The Protestant Reformation is an immense subject. For original work the specialist finds that he must very greatly narrow the field, and there are many admirable books dealing with various aspects of the subject. But it seemed to me that at the present time there was lacking a short, simple book narrating the story of the Reformation as a whole. The present volume aims at supplying this need.

My second object was to stimulate interest in the Reformation movement. We Protestants have entered into a rich and wonderful heritage; but, as happens so often with the best things, we are apt to take it for granted without pausing to consider the price that was paid to make it possible. The story of the Reformation in all the lands is not only a thrilling tale but an inspiration to all who read it. It is my hope that the present volume may serve as an introduction to a great subject and encourage its readers to further study of a glorious episode in history.

I am deeply indebted to the Very Reverend John Baillie for generously giving of his time to read this book and to write a foreword.

W. STEVENSON
Edinburgh

✠

CONTENTS

CONTENTS

1

THE EVE OF THE REFORMATION

✠

A few years ago a pilot flying a jet-propelled airplane breakfasted in London, lunched in New York City, and dined in London, all on the same day. He proved, as not a few have asserted, that it is a small world we live in and a shrinking world. This shrinking process began some five hundred years ago. Before that time the world was the great unknown, and people were foreigners to one another if they lived at a distance of two days' journey, possibly a hundred miles by foot or on horseback.

But gradually a transformation took place. A new dawn was beginning to break, new life was stirring, there was the rebirth of the human spirit in what men have called the Renaissance. It may be described as the transition from the medieval to the modern world. No one can tell whence it came or whither it goeth, for we still live in it. But five hundred years ago, when the Renaissance burst upon the world in all its fullness, life suddenly became an adventure. It was the dawn of a new age when, as one of the German Humanists, Ulrich von Hutten, exuberantly declared, "It is a joy to be alive!"; when, as another has put it, "for an enchanted hour real life had become romance."[1] Paradoxically, the world was expanding and yet contracting. Everywhere its horizons were widening, but simultaneously the means of reaching them were easier and ever more plentiful. If it was an age of discovery, it was also one of far-reaching inventions.

The most famous of the early discoverers was Henry the Navigator, a Portuguese prince born of an English mother. Having sailed out into the Atlantic he turned southward along the shores of Africa, and after forty years of adventurous activity he died in 1460. Then came the great age. In 1487 Bartholomew Diaz rounded the Cape of Good Hope; the next year young Vasco da Gama sailed across the Indian Ocean to Calicut; in 1492 a landfall in the Bahamas was made by Christopher Columbus, an epoch-making event in world history. John Cabot sailed to Cape Breton Island in 1497, Brazil was discovered by Cabral in 1500, and within twenty years—in 1519—Magellan had completed the first voyage round the world. It was an age of wonders, an age too of expectancy. It is said that "every time the guns of Cadiz or of Lisbon greeted a homeward-bound galleon, an inquisitive crowd would gather round the harbour in order to learn of freshly discovered lands, to be told about strange birds, beasts, and men, and to be shown these wonders."[2]

The practical effect of these discoveries was a reorientation of the world. Hitherto the Mediterranean had been the principal trade route to the East. But the eastern Mediterranean was blocked by the advancing Turks, and the discovery of a new route to the East was the commercial problem of the times. This was the reason why Columbus sailed across the Atlantic, not to discover a new world, but to find a new way to the old one. Even when he discovered America, he believed it was part of the east coast of Asia, and he persisted in this belief (it is said) until his dying day. But the significant point is that the Mediterranean was no longer the center of the world: the new center was the western European nations, and the future lay with those lands that were fortunate enough to possess an Atlantic seaboard.

But if a new world was being discovered, a new *universe* was also unfolding to men. It was one of the great moments in history when the Polish mathematician Nicolaus Coppernick, or Copernicus, propounded his theory that the sun was the center of the universe, that our earth was only one of a number of bodies that revolved round it. This discovery, aided by the invention of the telescope, revolutionized the science of astronomy. Copernicus died in 1543, two years after Calvin returned to Geneva from exile and three years before the death of Luther.

Another invention, that of gunpowder, revolutionized the art of warfare and consequently affected political development. The invention of gunpowder was almost comparable with the evolution of nuclear weapons in our own time. By it more people could be killed more easily and more quickly—a wonderful advance in the history of civilization! Of course the men of that time were not so civilized as we are: they had no hydrogen bombs or guided missiles. But even primitive guns primed with gunpowder made a difference. Wars became possible between peoples and nations, and killing became more democratic.

These discoveries and inventions came suddenly on men, all of them within the span of a single lifetime. Almost in a moment of time the physical universe was transformed and enlarged, and this upheaval exercised a profound influence in the realm of the spirit. The old certainties had vanished or at best were matters for inquiry. Men were beginning to question things, spiritual as well as physical, instead of tamely accepting them, and it is of capital importance to keep this in mind as we approach the study of religious reformation.

But the Renaissance was more than physical enlargement: it was also a rebirth of art and of literature. The movement began in Italy, and in art especially the Italians "attained the highest perfection that has been reached by man."[3] It was the golden age of Michelangelo and Raphael, of Leonardo da Vinci, of Perugino, Titian, Botticelli, and of many others, whose works of art are scattered over the cities of Italy and have not been surpassed to this day.

In literature, too, Italy was first in the field. Since the time of Dante in the fourteenth century there had been signs of the new awakening. Greek scholars had begun to settle in Italy and expound the ancient Greek classics. Both before and after the fall of Constantinople in 1453 the flow of scholars increased, many of them carrying their precious manuscripts and instilling in men's minds the desire to study the old Greek masters whose works had been hidden so long from the world. The impelling purpose of these men was not to find out what happened in the distant past; it was to search for beauty, and above all for truth. The critical,

not to say skeptical, spirit of the scholars was but another preparation for a religious reformation.

But still another factor entered in, a decisive factor. Though
there had been critics and skeptics in the past, their words had
comparatively little effect; they were permitted to go so far but
no farther. If they became really troublesome, the authorities had
their own methods of dealing with them, and the troublemakers
were speedily liquidated. But criticism could no longer be stifled
or heresy suppressed because a new medium had come into being.
In 1454, the year after the fall of Constantinople, Pope Nicholas V
proclaimed an Indulgence for any who would subscribe money for
the defense of Cyprus against the Turks, the significant point being that this proclamation was *printed from movable type,* the
earliest example of the use of the new invention of which we have
certain knowledge.

The invention of printing was one of the greatest achievements
the world has ever known. One writer says it "deserves to be put
side by side with the discovery of the new world and of the new
universe."[4] It made literature democratic. Hitherto learning had
been the possession of the few, but now it might be shared by the
many. Books became cheaper and more available, especially the
Bible since early printing was not so much literary as religious.
The first book to be printed, in 1456, by Gutenberg, was the Latin
Bible. Before the turn of the century nearly a hundred other editions appeared. On all sides was printing acclaimed. Archbishop
Berthold of Mainz said that "the clergy . . . hailed it as a divine
art."[5] The old church was slow to see the red light of danger. In
former times the laity knew only those snatches of the Gospels
that were recited in church. But now large numbers of thinking
men had the whole Bible before them; now they were able to read
it from cover to cover and interpret it for themselves. The invention of printing made reformation inevitable. Luther was right
when he said, "Printing is God's latest and best work to spread the
true religion throughout the world."

It is evident, then, that in all these different ways a new age had
dawned. It was an age of travel and discovery, an age of scientific

inventions; it witnessed the renaissance of art and literature; it saw the beginnings of printing. In other ways, too, it was an age of changing horizons. Politically, feudalism was vanishing, Europe was breaking up into nationalities, and there was the growing tendency among secular rulers to throw off the bonds of ecclesiastical suzerainty. Economically, there was within every nation the rise of a wealthy commercial middle class. There was a new consciousness of power and success; for many it was an age bristling with new opportunity. At the opposite extreme from the monied commercial class there were the peasants of Europe whose lot was desperately hard and among whom there were strong undercurrents of revolt. On the eve of the Reformation, especially in Germany, there were bitter class hatred and widespread discontent; and, as Lindsay puts it, "It was into this mass of seething discontent that the spark of religious protest fell—the one thing needed to fire the train and kindle the social conflagration."[6]

Such, then, was the state of Europe on the eve of the Reformation. It only remains to consider the pre-Reformation church. And here the picture is indeed dark. Everywhere in the world new life was stirring, in every direction there was progress, advance, enlightenment; in every branch and department of life men were reaching forward—in all except one only, the church of Christ.

Yet to outward appearances the church seemed all-powerful. Never had it attained such heights of splendor and magnificence, never did its position seem more secure. Centuries before, it had won its battles with its secular opponents, and now unchallenged was enjoying the fruits of victory. Its authority was absolute, an authority it wielded with terrible effect. One recalls the humiliation of an emperor compelled to hold the stirrup for Pope Gregory the Seventh as he mounted his mule; of the proud English King, Henry Plantagenet, who was forced to walk barefoot through the streets of Canterbury and then kneel down for monks to flog him. One remembers the massive support of St. Thomas Aquinas and his pronouncement that only by the possession of faith could salvation be attained, and that the church was the sole repository of the true faith. The old maxim of Cyprian still held:

Extra ecclesiam nulla salus, outside the church there is no salvation; the man cast off by the church is derelict both now and hereafter. The medieval church wielded a power beyond the dreams
of any secular monarch. The Bishop of Rome was the most commanding figure in all Europe. By a single word he could relegate
any man, however exalted, to eternal perdition, and his word
was law against which there was no appeal. The church as a whole
was vested with the same ghostly authority. To the ordinary man
a Latin paternoster was the most potent of spells. If repeated
through, it is said, it had all power in heaven; and if repeated
backwards, it was a charm no spirit in hell could resist.[7] The
church invaded a man's life at every point, and the role of the
priest was decisive. Without his mediation salvation was unat-
tainable. The unbaptized could not be saved, and only the church
could administer baptism; no sinner could be saved without confession and absolution, and only a lawfully ordained priest could
hear confession and speak the word of peace. The church kept a
stranglehold upon the souls of men, with power to open or shut
fast the gates of heaven.

The medieval church, then, all-pervading in its influence,
seemed to stand on strong foundations, built on an impregnable
and enduring rock. But here we must reckon with one of the great
laws of human life. If any power or any institution is to endure
or even to survive, it must be progressive. The real tragedy of the
medieval church is that it failed to move with the times. All
around was progress and enlightenment: here alone was obscur-
antism and stagnation. But it is impossible, spiritually, to stand
still; if there is no conscious advance, there is an inevitable slip-
ping back. It is true of a church as of the individual man. If we do
not deliberately advance, if we fail (as the hymn puts it) to wrestle
"on towards heaven, 'Gainst storm and wind and tide," we drift
down with the stream. That is what happened with the medieval
church. Far from being progressive, far from giving a spiritual
lead, it was retrograde and decadent, corrupt in all its members.

One of the first retrograde steps was taken in 1309 when a
French archbishop was elected pope as Clement V and removed

the papal court from Rome to Avignon. There it remained for seventy years, progressively losing in influence and prestige. Outside France it was suspected by every state in Europe as a puppet of the French monarchy and an instrument to promote French interests, and that in an age of growing national consciousness.

Second, there was the Great Schism of the papacy which lasted for forty years, from 1378 to 1417, and which shocked the devout in every European state. During those years there were always two and sometimes three rival popes, each anathematizing the others and each claiming for himself the supreme headship of the church. It was a scandal to all Christendom and came near to disrupting the unity of Christianity in the West.

But more serious still was the rank corruption of the church, starting at the top and working its way downward through all its orders. The plain fact was that the papacy was now aiming at the political more than the religious leadership of Europe, and it was a fatal ambition. Two centuries earlier Dante had seen how the beneficent power of the papacy was vitiated by the lust for temporal power. Even a pope cannot touch pitch without soiling his fingers. By entering the political arena the papacy was forced to compromise with secular leaders, and the consequence was the gradual secularization of the church itself. In order to uphold its prestige as a political power and to maintain the pomp and magnificence of its court, the papacy was compelled to find new sources of revenue. Hence it was essential to impose new taxations —tithes and annates and procurations and others—so that year by year vast sums of money flowed into the papal coffers. But even greater sums were required and the most corrupt means were employed to secure them. Papal corruption and immorality reached their height with the pontificate of Alexander VI, the infamous Rodrigo Borgia, a monster of all the vices. It was not without reason that Savonarola denounced Rome and its clergy, quoting a common saying of the time, "If you want to ruin your son, make him a priest." Indeed, the Roman scandals were so notorious that in 1499, as during the time of the Great Schism, they once again came near to destroying the unity of the Latin Church.

But clerical abuses were not confined to the papacy: they were rampant in the church as a whole. Laymen bitterly resented the special privileges enjoyed by the clergy. If an ordinary man committed a crime, he was punished by the laws of the state. But if a priest was guilty of the same offense, the law of the land had no power to punish him; he was a sacred person and could be tried only by an ecclesiastical court. The practical consequence was that he often escaped scot-free. For the clergy it was a pleasant law but for all others a source of bitter resentment.

There were other abuses as well. There was *simony,* for instance, or the giving of bribes to secure a clerical office. There was *nepotism,* the appointment of relatives and friends to offices for which they had no qualification. Not infrequently even children were given important posts in order to assure them of an income. As late as 1558 Quintin Kennedy, a Scottish Romanist abbot, thus deplores the corruption of his church: "See we not daily, by experience, if a benefice be vacant the great men of the realm will have it for temporal reward. . . . And when they have got the benefice, if they have a brother, or a son,—yea, suppose he can neither sing nor say,—nourished in vice all his days, forthwith he shall be mounted on a mule, with a side-gown and a round bonnet, and then it is a question whether he or his mule knows best to do his office. Perchance Balaam's ass knew more than both of them! . . . And not only such men have crept into the Kirk by means of some wicked great personages; but thou mayest see daily, likewise by experience, a bairn and a babe, to whom scarcely would thou give a fair apple to keep, get perchance five thousand souls to guide. And all for avarice . . . that their parents may get the profit of the benefice."[8] Another evil was *pluralism,* or the holding of more than one full-time appointment, and hand in hand with this went *absenteeism.* After all, a man can be only in one place at one time; if he holds a benefice in Scotland and another in France, as sometimes happened, he cannot be present in both places. But why should he worry, if he was allowed to enjoy both incomes?

It always came back to the same thing: money, money all the

time, money the root of all evil, money to provide the means of self-indulgence. An English writer, speaking of the priests and their seizure of tithes, says: "They look so narrowly after their profits that the poor wife must be countable to them for every tenth egg, or else she getteth not her rights at Easter, and shall be taken as a heretic." "I see," said a Spaniard, "that we can scarcely get anything from Christ's ministers but for money; at baptism money . . . at marriage money, for confession money—no, not extreme unction without money! They will ring no bells without money, no burial in the church without money; so that it seemeth that Paradise is shut up from them that have no money."[9] Even when a man was dead he still had to pay, or at least his relatives had to find for him a mortuary or death present; if any misguided person refused to pay, he was excommunicated, cut off from human fellowship, and even denied Christian burial.

It seemed that money was the true God, and to gain it even fraud was not discountenanced. J. A. Froude tells us of a chapel in Saxony, where "there was an image of a Virgin and Child. If the worshiper came to it with a good, handsome offering, the child bowed and was gracious; if the present was unsatisfactory, it turned away its head, and withheld its favors till the purse-strings were untied again. There was a great rood or crucifix of the same kind at Boxley, in Kent, where the pilgrims went in thousands. This figure used to bow, too, when it was pleased; and a good sum of money was sure to secure its good-will." It was quite miraculous except for the end of the story. "When the Reformation came, and the police looked into the matter, the images were found to be worked with wires and pulleys."[10] Similar examples might easily be cited. But what must we think of any institution, let alone the church of Christ, that would employ such methods? One of the first and constant duties of the church is to assert the supremacy of the spiritual in human life, to protest against the undue love of material things which has been the besetting sin of every generation. It is to bear clear and faithful witness to the Gospel truth that man shall not live by bread alone. The medieval church signally failed to provide this testimony.

But there were other evils as well. For one thing, the clergy were notorious for their immorality. There was Henry, Bishop of Liége, who according to Milman was "a monster of depravity . . . his lust was promiscuous. He kept as his concubine a Benedictine abbess. He had boasted in a public banquet that in twenty-two months he had had fourteen children born. This was not the worst."[11] But let us draw a decent veil over the rest. It is sufficient to say that this is not an isolated example, and we read of priests spending their nights in conviviality and sin and celebrating Mass the next day.[12] This kind of thing is recorded of the thirteenth century, the so-called golden age of the church: by the beginning of the sixteenth century the situation had deteriorated even more.

Not only were many of the clergy immoral: they were also ignorant. Archibald Hay, writing to David Beaton on the latter's appointment in 1538 as Archbishop of St. Andrews and Primate of Scotland, thus trenchantly puts it: "I declare, as I desire God's love . . . that I often wonder what the bishops were thinking about when they admitted such men [that is, ordinary priests] to the handling of the Lord's holy body, when they hardly know the order of the alphabet." Many priests were unable to read their own language with any fluency; many were even so ignorant that they resented the "New" in New Testament, imagining it was a heretical work by Martin Luther! There was reason for Sir David Lyndsay's satire:

> "No, sir, by him that our Lord Jesus sauld,
> I never read New Testament, nor Auld,
> Nor ever thinks to do, sir, by the Rude;
> I hear friars say, that reading does no good."

Examples might be taken almost at random, but let us think only of this one. In England in the year 1551 Bishop Hooper, suspecting the ignorance of the clergy of his diocese and their hostility to the Reformation, decided to set them an examination, by modern standards an absurdly easy one. The subjects were the Ten Commandments, the Apostles' Creed, and the Lord's Prayer. Of three hundred and seventy-three men summoned, sixty-two were unable to attend because they were pluralists and lived else-where. Of the three hundred and eleven actually examined, only ninety secured a pass mark. One candidate said that the authority for the Creed was the first chapter of Genesis; another had no idea why the Lord's Prayer was so named, but he was willing to believe it was the Lord's because the king had said it was. Those men were not raw students or inexperienced probationers; they were all in full charges, some of them for at least sixteen years.[13] Nor is there any reason to suppose that the clergy of this particular diocese were worse than those of any other in England, or that the clergy of England were less enlightened than those of other Euro-pean countries. It stands against the clergy of the age that many of them were ignorant and unfit for the posts they held.

But if they were ignorant, it almost goes without saying that they were also superstitious. Let us turn for a moment from Eng-land to Germany, the Germany of Luther's childhood and youth. It would seem that there much of the priests' teaching was de-signed to frighten rather than to edify. God was awful in His majesty and unapproachable. Christ too was regarded as a stern Judge whose chief function was not to save but to punish guilty sinners. Sermons and pictures alike portrayed Him in this terrible role. Luther tells us how he used to gaze fascinated at one such picture, utterly terrified at the sight of Christ as Judge. He also, like God, was too awful and too holy to be directly approached, and thus someone must be found to intercede with Him. This person was found in His mother, the Blessed Virgin Mary. In the second half of the fifteenth century Mariolatry or worship of Mary reached its height. But presently Mary herself was regarded as too sacred for direct approach, and so still another intercessor was essential. This time it was the mother of Mary, St. Anna, who became the object of a new and widespread cult. But how compli-cated religion had become! People prayed to Anna who inter-ceded with Mary who interceded with her Son who interceded with God for sinful men. It was fantastic, but that was the kind of superstitious belief on which the souls of men were nourished.

In view, then, of the scandalous abuses of the church; in view of its immense wealth, its insatiable greed, its contemptible deceit; in view of clerical immorality, ignorance, and superstition, is it surprising that there was the growing demand for a purer, more inward personal religion? It was by no means an irreligious age to which the Reformation came, but quite the reverse. The roads were thronged with pilgrims as they journeyed to famous shrines; there was a hunger for the preaching of the Word; devotional literature was more and more widely read. An irreligious age would have been barren ground in which to plant the seed of reformation. The reforming movement achieved success because it came at a time when men's hearts were stirred with deep religious yearnings, when all over Europe thoughtful men felt instinctively that there was something radically wrong with the church and that supreme efforts must be made to reform it. Reformation must come; the burning question was: Could the church reform itself?

Various attempts had been made in the past. First, there was the Conciliar Movement, the calling of general councils. During the time of the Great Schism, when there were more popes than one, a council was called at Pisa in 1409 and another at Constance in 1415. Later, in 1431, a third was convened at Basel. By means of these, much might have been done to silence heresy, to reform the church and give it a proper constitution, but nothing came of the movement: the pope, jealous of his supreme power, crushed all efforts at reformation.

A second attempt to reform the church from within was made by the Mystics, especially by the so-called Brethren of the Common Life. Perhaps the most well-known of these was St. Thomas à Kempis (1380?-1471) whose classic, *The Imitation of Christ,* emphasized the inwardness of religion and pointed out the way to salvation by loving God and imitating Christ. Though the Mystics accomplished little in a practical way, the stress they laid on inner spirituality was a valuable contribution to later reform.

In the third place we may note the names of a few early reformers, forerunners all of them of the Protestant Reformation. In fourteenth-century England there was John Wycliffe, the Ox-

ford don who attacked the Catholic doctrine of transubstantiation, the veneration of saints and their relics, pilgrimages to their
shrines, and Indulgences. He denied the supreme authority of
the pope, emphasized personal piety, and adumbrated what later
became one of the two fundamental ideas of reformed doctrine,
the priesthood of all believers. He stressed the importance of
preaching based on scripture, a scripture made available to all,
and to this end he and his disciples translated the Bible into
English.

One of his disciples, John Huss of Bohemia, was put to death
for holding similar views. In 1415 he was summoned to the Council of Constance on the promise of safe conduct on his way to and
from the Council and at Constance itself. But the fathers of the
church broke their pledged word. He was incarcerated in a stone
dungeon "three feet wide, six feet high, seven feet long," and
then was condemned and hanged, his body being burned. It was a
costly act of perfidy, for as Fisher has put it, "In condemning
Hus to the stake the fathers of Constance roused the soul of a
nation."[14]

Wycliffe in England and Huss in Bohemia were paralleled in
Italy by the somber figure of Savonarola, whom Luther acclaimed
as a proto-martyr of the Reformation. In 1482, at the age of thirty,
Savonarola entered the convent of San Marco, Florence—lovely
Florence with its hundred and seventy churches, its Duomo by
Brunelleschi, Giotto's Campanile, and the Baptistry gates of
Ghiberti which Michelangelo said were "fit to be the Gates of
Paradise." In this lovely city Savonarola spent the remainder of
his life, a second John the Baptist, preaching in the cathedral,
pleading for a return to the purer life of early Christianity, casti-
gating the sins and wrongs of the church and the world, drawing
from the Bible lurid prophecies of danger and woe unless the
people repented. "Listen to me," he cried. "Or rather listen to
the words that come from God. I cannot say other than 'Do Penance!' Come, sinners, come, for God is calling you. . . . O Florence
[like Babylon] you are sitting by the rivers of your sins. Make a
river of your tears that you may purify yourselves in it."[15] It is

related of Pico della Mirandola that when he heard the friar preach a cold shiver ran through his bones and his hair stood on end. For nearly twenty years Savonarola's preaching produced a religious and moral revival, but at last he fell afoul of the Borgian pope, Alexander VI, was excommunicated, and finally put to death on May 22, 1498.

The last forerunners of the Reformation were not so much individuals as a group, the so-called Humanists. They comprised such men as the Italians Lorenzo Valla (1505-57) and Pico della Mirandola (1463-94), who at twenty years of age (it is said) had offered to reply in twenty-two languages to seven hundred questions to be proposed by twenty of the most learned men of the age, if they could be assembled in Florence! France was represented by Guillaume Budé (1467-1540) and Lefèvre d'Étaples (1455-1536); England by Colet, Fisher, and More; Germany by Ulrich von Hutten and the great Hebrew scholar Reuchlin (1455-1522); and Holland by the most famous of them all, Erasmus of Rotterdam (1466?-1536).

Erasmus has been called *homo per se*, a man in a class by himself. He was a nomad all his life and the true cosmopolitan. He was a scholar and man of letters, sought by emperors and kings and the leading men of Europe, rivals all for his good will. He was called the "light of the world"; wherever he happened to be living he attracted the intellectuals of his day. His reputation was international, and not even Voltaire and Goethe in a later age enjoyed so great a prestige in Europe.

From the beginning he set himself to raise the standards of a corrupt church. In his *Praise of Folly* (1511) he lashed its vices and follies. This book was one of the most dangerous that ever appeared. Under the cloak of mockery and derision, clerical abuses were mercilessly exposed so that the urgent need of reform was brought home to the consciousness of contemporaries. But Erasmus believed that the church could be reformed from within. He hoped for a renaissance of religion without turmoil and without too much dogma: without turmoil, for he was a man of peace who hated war and tumult; and without excessive dogma, for he was a moralist rather than a theologian (his patron saint, he said, was the penitent thief because he was admitted to Paradise with little or no theology).

Being a Humanist, he believed (with Protagoras) that man was the measure of all things and self-sufficient; and whereas Luther contended that man was ineradicably bad, Erasmus would have said that he was fundamentally good. All he required was enlightenment, education. To Erasmus, Christianity was little more than a lofty humane morality, and he taught the old Platonic doctrine that men will live the good life if only they know what the good life is. Hence there was the paramount need of education. In many ways man had conquered the world of nature by increasing knowledge: could not religion too be brought within the limits of human understanding? Humanism was the best instrument to dispel ignorance, which to Erasmus was the root of so many evils. Thus his self-imposed mission was to enlighten. Above all, he could enable men to see what Christianity was by bringing before them the very words of Jesus and the Apostolic writers; he could edit the New Testament and so make the scriptures known to all men. That is what he did in 1516, and as he wrote in the preface, he had this one aim: "I wish that even the weakest woman should read the Gospels and the epistles of Paul; I wish they were translated into all languages, so that they might be read and understood, not only by Scotsmen and Irishmen, but also by Saracens and Turks. I long for the farmer to sing portions of them to himself as he follows the plough, for the weaver to hum them to the tune of his shuttle, and for the traveller to beguile with their stories the tedium of his journey." The publication of Erasmus' New Testament in Greek was one of the landmarks of religious history and certainly one of the contributory factors of the Reformation. Later this edition was used by Luther for his German translation.

Humanism was a valuable and possibly indispensable preparation for the Protestant Reformation—in exposing vice, in condemning the uselessness of externals, in stressing the inwardness of religion. But Humanism is not itself Reformation. That glittering ideal of the Humanists—education, enlightenment—is insufficient in the things of the spirit. However highly men may be educated, human nature does not appreciably change, but remains the same in its greatness and littleness, in its hopes and aspirations, and in its ineradicable needs. Men shall not live by education alone. In the last resort not education but religion can nourish the human soul, not reason but faith, and not the works of man but only the grace of God. Humanism stops far short of satisfying the needs of the world, whether it be in the twentieth century or the sixteenth.

It is said that "Erasmus laid the egg and Luther hatched it." But between the two men there lay a world of difference. Luther denounced Erasmus as *verba sine re*, a man of words without deeds, who said much but did nothing; and Luther was right. Erasmus was the student and man of contemplation; Luther was a man of action. Erasmus was a neutral, forever seeking peace and abhorring violence of any kind; Luther was a born fighter. Erasmus played for safety, but safety first could never have brought a reformation. Luther ridiculed Erasmus as one always walking on eggs and never wishing to crush one. Both alike saw the corruption of the church; but while Erasmus would have taken the physician's way of treating it and working for a gradual cure, Luther seized the surgeon's knife and cut it away. He accused Erasmus of caring more for human than divine things, as is the way of Humanism. To Luther himself religion was all in all, the greatest thing both here and hereafter. In the end Erasmus was a man of letters and nothing more; he was a dilettante, compromising and temporizing, with no deep burning convictions. But, as Luther said, "Without certitude, Christianity cannot exist. A Christian must be sure of his doctrine and his cause, or he is no Christian." Erasmus was not of the stuff reformers are made of: the world awaited a stronger, more virile personality.

In this chapter an attempt has been made to paint a picture of Europe on the eve of the Reformation and to indicate some of the factors at work for the cause of reform. Let us note in closing the wonderful way in which God in His providence prepares the world for His great works. There is a vivid illustration in the early centuries when the means were marvelously provided for the spread of the Christian Gospel. There was the universal Empire of Rome to ensure peace and good order; there was a common language, Greek, which was almost everywhere understood; there were the great military roads of the Empire, and the most admirable means of communication by which the missionaries of the Cross might disseminate their message to men. It was then, in the fullness of the time, that God sent His Son into the world. So, too, fifteen centuries later, God provided a wonderful concatenation of circumstances especially favorable for a reforming movement in Germany.

First, there was the political disunity of Germany, itself little more than a geographical expression, where it was most easy to disseminate heresy and most hard to suppress it. Second, there were the strained relations, sometimes open feud, between pope and emperor, and the jealousy and intermittent wars between the emperor and the king of France. It is surely one of the supreme ironies of history that the Protestant Reformation was kept alive, now by the Most Christian King of France and now (incredibly) by the pope himself! Again and again the Reformation might have been suppressed but for the intervention, for political reasons, of these strong champions of Catholic orthodoxy. In the third place, there was the new upsurge of nationalism. Much of Luther's success was due to the fact that he was German to the core, that he, a German, spoke to and for Germans, so that they made his cause their own. And then, lastly, we must again underline the vital importance of the new art of printing. Not only were the writings of the Reformers swiftly and widely circulated, but the German printers all sided with the Reformed party, eagerly publishing their works and declining to publish those of their opponents. We know today the tremendous power wielded by the press, but never was that power used to greater effect than in promoting the Reformation in Germany.

These, then, were some of the propitious factors of the time; but the greatest of all was the Reformed leader himself, Martin Luther. We have already noted how God provides for the great events of history, but He does something more. He not only creates the circumstances, but He also raises up the man for the hour. Dramatically at the crucial moment there appears a Paul or an Augustine, a Calvin or a Knox, a George Washington or a Winston Churchill, men of destiny every one of them. So now in Germany the hour had struck, the stage was set for the entrance of *her* man of destiny, and in the fullness of the time God raised up His servant, Martin Luther.

2

THE REFORMATION IN GERMANY

✠

In the Church of St. John Lateran in Rome there is a famous staircase, the Scala Santa. It is said to have been brought to Rome by the saintly Helena, mother of the Emperor Constantine, and is alleged to be the very staircase our Lord ascended to Pilate's judgment hall and then passed down, condemned, to bear His Cross. The faithful in all ages have ascended this stair on hands and knees, pausing on each step to offer a prayer for the remission of sins. A pleasant, if facile, legend tells that Luther, during a visit to Rome, also began to climb in the approved manner. But when he was halfway up, there flashed across his mind the great truth of scripture that the just shall live by faith, by faith only and not by works or ceremonial observance, and immediately he rose from his knees, walked down the stairs, and swiftly left the church.

It is only a legend and accounts too easily for a change in Luther's outlook that was effected only after years of striving and suffering. But legendary though the story is, it illustrates in a striking and dramatic way what was later to be the dominant principle of Luther's life, the great doctrine of justification by faith, which is fundamental to any study of the Reformer.

The legend also testifies that Luther visited Rome. Here we stand on the solid bedrock of fact, for he actually was in Rome in the year 1511, being then an ardent young man of twenty-eight. His own words describe his emotion and the eager expectancy that thrilled him as he gazed upon the Eternal City. Falling down on his knees he cried aloud: "I greet thee, Holy Rome, thrice holy from the blood of the martyrs that has been shed in thee!" But presently his dreams were rudely shattered. He found in Rome not the city of his devout and ardent hopes but a cesspool of corruption. He was impressed and appalled. As he afterwards said, "I would not for a hundred thousand florins have missed seeing Rome. If I had not seen it myself, I might have been troubled lest I had been unjust to the Pope." Thrilled with eager expectations he had entered the city: he departed from it a sadly disillusioned man. "Adieu! Rome," he said, "let all who would live a holy life depart from Rome. Everything is permitted in Rome except to be an honest man." The scales had fallen from his eyes, though we must not take too literally Lindsay's rhetorical statement that he went to Rome "a mediaeval theologian; he came back a Protestant."[1] It is sufficient to say that Luther's visit to Rome made an impression on him that he never forgot.

Martin Luther was born at Eisleben in Saxony on November 10, 1483, in the same year as the Italian painter Raphael and a few years before Henry VIII of England and Francis I of France. His father, a miner of sturdy peasant stock, was a strict and stern parent, and Martin's early life was somewhat checkered. "I shudder when I think of what I went through," he later said. "My mother beat me about some nuts once till the blood came." At school, too, he could remember painful moments. "I was flogged," he said, "fifteen times in one afternoon over the conjugation of a verb," those being the days when Latin was Latin and an irregular verb no trifling matter. His father intended him for the law, and to this end he was schooled at Mansfeld, Magdeburg, and Eisenach. He was starved and bullied, and like so many school children in that austere age he was forced to earn his livelihood by singing in the streets, begging from door to door for alms and bread. He left school at seventeen and proceeded to the University of Erfurt, called by its inhabitants "the little Rome" because of its many churches and other religious foundations. There he took his bachelor's degree in 1503 and his master's in 1505.

Then came one of the turning points of his life. On July 17, 1505, much against his father's wishes, he entered the Augustinian monastery at Erfurt. Various legends have grown up to account for this sudden decision. One day, it is said, he was out walking with his best friend Alexis, when a thunderstorm came on and a bolt of lightning struck Alexis dead at his feet. Shocked by his friend's death and suddenly conscience-stricken by the thought of his youthful sins, he was constrained to devote himself to a monastic life. Luther himself, however, not by any means the most reticent of men, preserves complete silence as to his motive.

But whatever the cause, this much is certain: during his three years as a monk he was weighed down by the sense of sin and the hopelessness of winning forgiveness. "Oh, my sins, my sins!" was the burden of his despairing cry. On the one hand he saw his own wickedness and the perdition to which he was doomed, on the other the dazzling holiness of God; and it seemed to his morbid fancy that there could be no bridge between the two. There was indeed one bridge—*faith*—for the just shall live by faith; but it was only in later years that he made this momentous discovery. Meanwhile he was told to repent and do penance. And both he attempted to do, valiantly, unceasingly. Before long he was conspicuous for his devoutness and scrupulous observance of all the rules of his order. As he himself put it, "If a monk ever reached heaven by monkery, I would have found my way there also."[2] We can imagine him in his cell, beating his brows in despair, starving himself, flagellating his tortured body, cudgeling his brains to devise some new austerity. He passed long nights on his knees before the altar and weakened his body with lonely vigils, doing endless penance, ever seeking but never finding peace of mind and soul.

For more than two years the struggle continued, till in 1508 he was appointed professor of philosophy at the University of Wittenberg, a new seat of learning recently founded by Frederick, Elector of Saxony, the "Good Elector" who later proved himself so staunch a supporter of Luther and the Reformed cause. In his new post he attracted large numbers of students to the University, and he also began to preach. In 1511 came his business visit to Rome, which we have already noted. On his return to Wittenberg he rapidly became the leading man in the University, gaining also the reputation of being a powerful preacher; and so the years slipped past till the Indulgences controversy flared up in 1517.

We must pause at this point to ask what Indulgences were. A full account is given in the first volume of T. M. Lindsay's monumental work, *A History of the Reformation,* pages 216-27. Here we can indicate only the bare outlines. The practice of Indulgences goes back a full thousand years before Luther's time. In the early centuries, if a man was guilty of a heinous sin he was automatically cut off from the church and its fellowship; and in order to be readmitted he was obliged to make public confession and then to perform what were known as "satisfactions," such as fasting, almsgiving, good works. But even so, there were mitigating circumstances. The man might fall ill and be unable to fast without endangering his health, in which case another form of penance might be substituted. A further step was taken in the seventh century when there arose the practice of commuting the penance into a payment of money; this was virtually the beginning of the system of Indulgences, a scandal to the church long before Luther's time. Finally, in the thirteenth century, three ideas were formulated that changed the whole conception.

The first was the idea of a *treasury of merits.* There was a storehouse filled with the good deeds of living men and women, of the saints in heaven, and with the infinite merits of Christ. They were all in the hands of the pope to dispense, so that sinners might benefit by these accumulated merits and thus have their sins remitted.

The second change was the conversion of the *institution* into the *sacrament* of penance. When a man confessed to a priest he was absolved from all eternal punishment and need only concern himself with the *temporal* punishments to be endured before he reached heaven, to be borne either in this life or in a place of punishment after death, that is, in purgatory. The penance must be duly performed, and it was at this point that a difficulty arose. In allocating the penance required, the priest might inadvertently underestimate the heinousness of the sin, and where then was the sinner placed? He could never be sure that he had given the proper satisfaction or that he would be immune from the agonies of purgatory. It seems as if a real impasse had been reached, but the church was ingenious and had its answer ready. There is no need to worry, it said in effect to sinful men, all you have to do is to draw on the treasury of merits: naturally, you will have to pay something or, when you are dead, your relatives will have to do it. The climax was reached when it was believed that the payment of a few cents would rescue a soul from purgatory and open to him the gates of heaven.

> "As soon as the coin in the coffer rings,
> The soul from Purgatory springs."

The ill-omened Tetzel played on this credulity, in one sermon representing deceased relatives appealing to the living and saying, "Have pity on us for we are in most grievous pains and torments from which you may redeem us with a little alms and you will not."[3]

The treasury of merits, the sacrament of penance, and now the third idea was the substitution of *attrition* for *contrition*. Once again it is unnecessary to enter into details of the theory, but the practical effect was this. The contrite heart was no longer an essential condition of forgiveness: forgiveness might be bought for money and a man enjoy with impunity the pleasures of sin. No doubt this is an oversimplification, but it is what Indulgences meant to ordinary people, unaccustomed as they were to appreciate fine theological distinctions. To them it was the easy way out: to buy an Indulgence or "papal ticket," to perform the penance imposed by the priest, and to escape punishment for sin both here and hereafter.

The circumstances of the 1517 Indulgence are well known. Not for the first time and not for the last, the pope required money, and like many of his predecessors and some of his successors, Pope Leo X was not above using crooked means to achieve his ends. He wanted money to rebuild and embellish the new cathedral church of St. Peter's at Rome, but he pretended it was to wage a holy war against the Turks. In order to raise the vast sums required he set afoot on a large scale the profitable trade in Indulgences. Official sellers were dispatched to the various countries, and to Germany came the Dominican preacher, John Tetzel, "whose name has acquired a forlorn notoriety in European history."[4] It was quite an occasion as he passed from town to town complete with price lists for different sins. For all practical purposes Indulgences were a license for sin, and human nature being what it is, if a man paid the price, he would see to it that he got his money's worth. It was an iniquitous and immoral system, an offense to pious men everywhere and to Luther an utter abomination. Above all it was the complete negation of a truth on which his very life depended and all his hopes of heaven. The problem with which he had wrestled so long and so painfully was: How can a man gain salvation and acceptance with God? By 1517 he had found the answer. He was passionately convinced that good works could never achieve the desired end, that rather is salvation a free gift of God's grace which men receive through the medium of faith. By faith only are men saved and by it alone are they justified in the sight of God. This was the burning conviction that consumed Luther, heart and soul, and now the pope's Indulgence had come to flout the precious truth; an attempt was being made to oust faith by which alone salvation was possible and to supplant it by works which were unavailing. Charged as he was with the cure of souls he could not suffer his people to be thus shamelessly deceived, and in protest, on the eve of All Saints' Day, October 31, 1517, he nailed his Ninety-five Theses to the door of the Castle Church at Wittenberg.

In these Theses Luther insisted on the need of real penitence and contrition. He further maintained that there can be no human mediation between a man's soul and God. No Indulgence can absolve guilt: forgiveness rests not with the pope but only with God. In the Theses themselves there was nothing antipapal, but the condition of Germany was such that only a spark was required to set it ablaze. The Ninety-five Theses struck the spark: the Reformation had begun.

The ecclesiastical authorities at first made light of the matter. When the pope saw the Theses, he smiled contemptuously and remarked, "A drunken German wrote them; when he has slept off his wine, he will be of another mind." As Luther himself put it at a later date, "My being such a small creature was a misfortune for the Pope. He despised me too much! What, he thought, could a slave like me do to him—to him, who was the greatest man in all the world?" If the dispute had been only a religious one, the pope's contempt might have been justified. But the movement stretched far beyond the field of religion: it was political and social as well. There was the resentful feeling all over Germany that the nation was being exploited by Rome and impoverished by burdensome exactions in order to maintain the splendor and temporal dignity of the papal court. Luther's Theses had an unprecedented circulation, being read all over Germany within a few weeks, and Germany was solidly behind the Reformer.

The following year, 1518, was a year of negotiation. In October, Luther was ordered to Augsburg for examination by the papal legate, Cardinal Cajetan, but the meeting was quite unsatisfactory. The legate lost his temper and called Luther "a wretched worm," and Luther, not to be outdone, replied by saying that the other was as unfit to judge in spiritual matters "as an ass was to play on the harp." Luther was never the man to pull his punches! A quarter of a century later, in 1543, when he denounced an opponent as a fool and a maniac, his wife Katie said to him, "Dear husband, you are too rude!" (It may be remarked that Luther married a nun: two of the reasons he gave for marrying were to please his father and to spite the pope! Katie must have been more worthy than beautiful, for as Luther said when the marriage was proposed, "All my friends exclaimed, 'For heaven's sake, not this one!' ")[5]

Luther left Augsburg virtually condemned, but appealing (as he put it) "from the Pope ill informed to the Pope to be better informed." In March of the following year he wrote the pope a submissive letter admitting the authority of the church as superior to all else "save only Jesus Christ, Who is Lord of all."

But this same year (1519) was one of growing tension, and the breach with Rome widened. One event in particular hastened the rupture and opened up an unbridgeable gulf. That event was the famous Disputation at Leipzig between representatives of the University of Wittenberg in north Saxony and of the University of Leipzig in south Saxony, the first protagonists being Carlstadt of Wittenberg and John Eck of the University of Ingolstadt. At length Luther was drawn into debate with Eck, a former friend but now an enemy. Various topics were debated, but the most controversial centered on the question of the papacy. Was it or was it not supreme and divinely instituted? Basing his arguments on history and the Bible, Luther insisted that the supremacy of the Bishop of Rome was of less than four hundred years' duration, that it was unknown to the early church and over the first eleven centuries, and that it was unscriptural. If denial of papal supremacy was the mark of a heretic, all the early fathers of the church were heretics. In any case, if Christ was the Head of the church, a pope was redundant. Again, as we have seen, Luther was convinced that men were justified by faith, and if so they required no mediating priest but were themselves priests unto God. All this seemed to play into the hands of Eck, whose purpose was to drive Luther into admitting that he was a Hussite or at least had Hussite sympathies. It was a most damaging admission. Bohemia was the neighboring state to south Saxony where Hussite propaganda had been specially virulent ever since Huss' death at Constance in 1415. If the Hussite label were attached to Luther, he could be represented as anti-German as well as heretical. Luther was indeed forced to admit that Huss' opinions were not all wrong. No doubt Eck won as a disputant, but his triumph was a kind of Pyrrhic victory, the net result of which was to bring Luther to the forefront and make him a national figure, the champion of German hopes and aspirations and a leader round whom the German people might rally. As for Luther himself, the Disputation confirmed him in his views of the primacy of the Bible, of the church as the society of all believers, and of the papacy as a purely human institution. He also saw with startling clarity that his attack on Indulgences was not so much a skirmish on the fringes as a mortal blow aimed at the heart, challenging the whole system of priestly mediation which stood between a man and direct access to God. Others too came to share his views and his determination, and from then on he was assured of a solid body of support. The Leipzig Disputation between Luther and Eck lasted for ten days, commencing on July 4, not an unfamiliar date in world history!

The following year (1520) saw the publication of Luther's three great Reformation Treatises—in August, September-October, and October respectively—*An Appeal to the Christian Nobility of the German Nation, On the Babylonish Captivity of the Church,* and *On the Liberty of a Christian Man.* In these are set forth the fundamental views of Lutheranism—the harmfulness of the Roman Church to Germany, the reduction of the sacraments from seven to two (baptism and the Lord's Supper), the authority of the Bible, and the direct access of the soul to God without recourse to a human medium.

The first tract, *To the Christian Nobility,* was immediately successful and enjoyed a remarkably wide circulation. It was an appeal addressed to the German princes to unite against Rome and to reform the church. It presented all the German grievances, which may account for its popularity. It asserted that the clergy have no monopoly of spiritual things but that all believers share in them because Christ has made them all priests to God. The ordination of priests and bishops does not render them different in character from laymen but only in the duties they are set apart to perform. The tract then proceeds to denounce the splendor of the papal court with its multitude of officials who are paid out of the revenues of the church. Germany is despoiled to maintain this retinue and indeed contributes more to the Roman *curia* than to its own emperor. Then there were the *annates,* or first year's income from benefices. A century before, the emperor had allowed the pope one-half of these in order to finance a war against the Turks. But as Luther points out, they were never used for that purpose but only to defray papal expenses; and now the payment is demanded as a right. The Germans are fools to allow themselves to be despoiled in this shameless manner. And other exactions are similarly denounced. Reform is obviously essential, and such reforms are urged as the abolition of the temporal power of the pope and the cessation of money payments to Rome, the creation of a national German church, the limitation of the number of pilgrimages, mendicant orders, and holy days, and the repudiation of masses for the dead and the celibacy of the clergy which is a constant source of immorality.

In the *Babylonish Captivity* Luther again denounces abuses in the church but confines himself for the most part to theological and liturgical points. The Babylonish Captivity is the denial to the laity of communion in both kinds. Transubstantiation is castigated as monstrous and foreign to the usage of the church in the first twelve centuries. The Lord's Supper is not a sacrifice offered by the priest but a celebration in which all participate. Convinced as he was of the priesthood of all believers, Luther repudiated ordination as a sacrament; and equally convinced of justification by faith, he dismissed as futile the idea of priestly absolution and penance. There are only two sacraments, baptism and the Lord's Supper. In this tract, too, Luther denounces the Roman Church for interfering with the scriptural laws that govern marriage. The church has no right either to annul marriages or to enforce them contrary to those laws. Divorce he admits as permissible but he himself prefers bigamy to divorce.

The Liberty of a Christian Man is among the most beautiful of all Luther's writings. Emphasis is again laid on the priesthood of all believers which follows from justification by faith. "Nor are we only kings and the freest of all men," he writes, "but also priests for ever, a dignity far higher than kingship, because by that priesthood we are worthy to appear before God, to pray for others, and to teach one another mutually the things which are of God."[6] All that is required of a man is to fear God and trust Him. Everything depends on faith, everything a man does, everything he has—spiritually—comes from faith, and without faith he is spiritually bankrupt. It is faith that makes a Christian man free, "the most free lord and subject to none." "It is clear then that to a Christian man his faith suffices for everything, and that he has no need of works for justification. But if he has no need of works, neither has he need of the law; and if he has no need of the law, he is certainly free from the law."[7] He is specially free to do good works which are only the outward expression of his faith and follow directly from it. As Luther put it in one of his sermons, "You must have heaven and be already saved before you can do good works." Good works do not make any man good: he is justified by faith alone. It is interesting to remember that even in October 1520 Luther could dedicate this last tract to Pope Leo X.

The papal reply was a Bull of Excommunication, the famous *Exsurge Domine,* so called from its opening words, "Rise up, O Lord, a wild boar has invaded Thy vineyard." It reached Wittenberg in October 1520, and on December 10 came Luther's dramatic act of defiance. He took the Bull and publicly burned it at the Elster Gate while students stood round and sang the *Te Deum.* Here was defiance indeed; there could be no turning back. "It is scarcely possible for us in the twentieth century," writes Lindsay, "to imagine the thrill that went through Germany, and indeed through all Europe, when the news sped that a poor monk had burnt the pope's Bull. Papal Bulls had been burnt before Luther's days, but the burners had been for the most part powerful monarchs. This time it was done by a monk, with nothing but his courageous faith to back him. It meant that the individual soul had discovered its true value. If eras can be dated, modern history began on December 10th, 1520."[8]

But now another actor appears on the scene. Luther had defied the pope, who, failing to quell the rebel by ecclesiastical weapons, invoked the help of the secular power. Luther had now to reckon with the emperor, the recently elected nineteen-year-old Charles V of Spain, a true son of Mother Church, an ardent not to say bigoted Roman Catholic. By preference as well as by policy he would have stamped out heresy, but fortunately for the Reformation his hands were tied. Germany was so disunited that the princes largely shaped their own policy; the warlike Turks in the East were a constant menace; and most threatening of all there was France in the West. Though France was loyal to Rome, she was intensely jealous of the imperial power, and French kings and statesmen in order to further their own policy found it expedient to support the Protestants in Germany. In fact, as A. J. Grant writes, "it is hardly too much to say that German Protestantism largely owed its survival to the support of Catholic France."[9] Charles, then, would gladly have suppressed Lutheranism, but for one reason or another he lacked the requisite power. Nevertheless he was an immensely important personage, and this was the man who undertook to deal with Luther.

He summoned him to appear at the Diet to be held at Worms in April 1521. Luther was promised a safe conduct, but that did little to allay his friends' anxiety. Just over a century before, John Huss of Prague had suffered martyrdom by trusting the pledged word of an emperor and the church. Men had long memories: they recalled the treachery of 1415; they knew that when the interests of the church were at stake, promises of safe conduct were not to be trusted too far. "Good" meant what was to the church's advantage, "bad" what was to its disservice. Luther himself was well aware that he was treading a dangerous path; but whatever his faults, lack of courage was not one of them. Go to Worms? Why, certainly he would! "I will go," he said, "if there are as many devils in Worms as there are tiles upon the roofs of the houses." And go he did. His journey was like a royal procession. Crowds gathered everywhere to encourage the man who had taken so heroic a stand and was ready to risk his life for his convictions. Even as he passed up the great hall to meet his judges, a baron in steel armor touched him on the shoulder and said, "Pluck up thy spirit, little monk . . . some of us here have seen warm work in our time, but, by my troth, nor I nor any knight in this company ever needed a stout heart more than thou needest it now. If thou hast faith in these doctrines of thine, little monk, go on, in the name of God." "Yes, in the name of God," said Luther, "in the name of God, forward!"[10]

According to Carlyle, the Diet of Worms and Luther's appearance there on April 17, 1521, "may be considered as the greatest scene in Modern European History." [11] It was indeed a memorable occasion. There was all the pomp and ceremony of an imperial and ecclesiastical court. On an elevated dais sat the emperor, ruler of half the world. Beside him were the princes of the Empire, ministers of state, archbishops and bishops. And these were sitting to judge a poor monk, the son of an obscure miner.

Twice did Luther appear before that august court. He was accused of having broken the laws of the church and of having taught heretical doctrines. Accordingly, he was ordered to "recant and recall." On his first appearance he begged to be given time to consider; but the next day a namesake of his old enemy, another John Eck (he of Trier), demanded without further delay a clear answer to the question: Would Luther recant or would he persist in his heresies? It was then that he made his famous speech, the clarion call of the German Reformation. Refusing to retract anything unless convicted "by the testimony of Scripture or evident reason," he concluded with the words, "Here I stand, I can do no other. God help me." [12]

Now had Luther declared himself and the die was cast. As a consequence he was placed under the ban of the Empire, cut off from human society and with every man's hand turned against him. No one might help him on pain of arrest, no one even communicate with him. He was an outlaw in the sight of men, a derelict in a friendless world.

And yet his predicament was not so dire as it might have been. For one thing the only person who could enforce the imperial ban was the emperor and he was already otherwise engaged—in a war with France. Then Luther had public opinion solidly behind him, and in addition he enjoyed the powerful protection of Frederick the Wise, the Elector of Saxony, without whose help Lutheranism might not have survived. It was Frederick who came to the rescue when Luther was on his way home to Wittenberg. All kinds of rumors began to circulate when Luther suddenly disappeared. Some alleged that in a silver mine his body lay pierced with a gaping dagger wound. All Germany was in a ferment. The truth was that retainers of Frederick had waylaid him and hurried him to safety in Wartburg Castle. There he remained for ten months, allowing his hair to grow over his tonsure, discarding his monkish habit, and masquerading as a knight by the name of Junker Georg. But above all it was in the seclusion of Wartburg that he translated the New Testament into German for the use of plain men and women.

This is not the place to discuss the merits or defects of Luther as a translator. To quote his own words, his aim was "to make Moses so German that no one would suspect he was a Jew." Luther's Bible was the work of a great master of German; it gave Germany a language and was comparable in its influence on German thought and expression with the King James Version of the Bible on the thought and language of the English-speaking peoples. Five thousand copies were sold in two months, two hundred thousand in twelve years. It was a notable landmark in both German history and literature.

By this time it was certain that the Reformation in Germany had come to stay. A few years previously the papal nuncio there, one Aleander, had reported to his master that nine-tenths of the Germans cried "Luther" while the remaining one-tenth cried "Death to the pope." This was a gross overstatement, but in the years following the Diet of Worms the Reformation spread ever more widely and converts came streaming in. Luther himself, after ten months at Wartburg, defied the imperial ban and returned to Wittenberg to preach and write without let or hindrance.

So far we have studied in some detail the coming of the Reformation to Germany, but now in briefest outline we must hasten over the events of the next thirty years. There was first the Diet at Speyer in 1526, when the emperor, handicapped by the machinations of the pope, was forced to make concessions to the Lutherans, even going so far as to permit each state to choose its own form of religion, whether Roman or Lutheran. But three years later a second Diet at Speyer reversed the decisions of the first. The evangelicals protested against the findings and so for the first time were given the name of "Protestants." Next year,

1530, the Diet of Augsburg set itself to end the religious dispute but the conference broke up with nothing settled. At last peace was concluded at Nürnberg in 1532 when the Protestants were permitted to adhere to the terms of the Augsburg Confession, a document prepared by Philip Melanchthon setting forth the principal Lutheran doctrines.

The 1530's saw the deepening of the cleavage between the two religious parties. A Catholic League was formed to be countered by a Protestant League under the leadership of Philip of Hesse, "an event of decisive importance in the history of the sixteenth century."[13] As the years passed by, the membership of the Protestant League greatly increased so that by 1540 Rome had reached the lowest point in her fortunes in central Europe as Lutheranism had attained its highest. In 1546, on February 18, Luther died at Eisleben. He was a man raised up by God for a great work and endowed with remarkable qualities. None could doubt his energy or question his courage. On one occasion when his life was endangered by the enmity of Duke George of Saxony, he would not be held back, as he put it, though it rained Duke Georges for nine days. He was a born fighter whose writings were trenchant and whose words were often caustic. All through his life he was inflamed with a burning love of truth and with hatred of lies and humbug. Religion to him was a practical reality and theology but the means of leading men to the grace of God. He built on fact, not theory. As T. R. Glover has written, to Luther "everything turns on the Incarnation, but the Incarnation does not begin with a doctrine and an abstract noun—it begins with a baby," Mary's child lying in a manger.[14] In many ways he was not what we imagine a saint ought to be, but he was the man for the times without whom the Protestant Reformation would have followed a vastly different course.

A kindly providence had ordained Luther to die before the outbreak of the religious war in 1547. On April 24 of that year the Lutherans, badly led and without any coherent plan, were annihilated by the imperial troops at the Battle of Mühlberg. It was an overwhelming victory but quite indecisive since Lutheranism was now too deeply entrenched to be uprooted. With varying fortunes the struggle dragged on till at last peace was signed on September 25, 1555, the famous Peace of Augsburg, one of the milestones of European history. The most important result was the emperor's surrender of his claims to interfere with the religious affairs of the various states that comprised his empire. The decision of the first Diet of Speyer was reaffirmed, *cuius regio eius religio,* the form of religion to be the choice of each state. The Peace of Augsburg is not to be placed among the great declarations of history. At best it was a makeshift. While the Reformation was legally established, religious freedom was not granted in principle, since Lutheranism alone of the Reformed faiths was recognized. And yet, unsatisfactory though it was, it gained for Germany a much-needed truce from the discords and struggles of the two contending parties. Peace reigned for more than sixty years, from 1555 to 1618. But it was an uneasy peace: rancor and bitterness were deeply embedded in men's hearts, the two antagonists glared at each other with somber and unveiled hostility, all the causes were present to unleash war in the following century, a war destined to last for thirty years, one of the most tragic disasters ever to overtake Germany or Europe. At last in 1648 the Peace of Westphalia, one of the greatest landmarks in modern European history, terminated the ordeals and the anguish of a tortured continent. By its terms, and despite the protests of the pope, religious equality was granted not only to Lutherans and Roman Catholics but also to Calvinists in all affairs of the Empire.

But this lies far in advance of our period, and we may well stop with the year 1555 when Lutheranism reached its high-water mark. In conclusion, let us touch briefly on two topics: first, the limitations of Lutheranism, and second, the legacy it bequeathed to the world.

1. First, then, its limitations. Lord Macaulay points out in his essay on von Ranke that the history of the next fifty years after, say, 1560 or 1565, "is the history of the great struggle between Protestantism possessed of the north of Europe, and Catholicism possessed of the south, for the doubtful territory which lay be-

tween." At first the chances seemed to favor Protestantism, but they gradually receded. As Macaulay strikingly puts it, "Fifty years after the Lutheran separation, Catholicism could scarcely maintain itself on the shores of the Mediterranean. A hundred years after the separation, Protestantism could scarcely maintain itself on the shores of the Baltic."[15] It is even more significant that Protestantism (outside the New World) has never been able to extend its territorial borders. Why has it failed? Why in particular has Lutheranism been so circumscribed?

There were at least three contributory causes. The first is to be traced to the Peasants' War in Germany (1524-25). The seething discontent was neither new nor restricted to Germany. All over western Europe the peasants endured a miserable lot. Burdened with payments to their feudal lord, they were also forced to work for him to the detriment of their own cultivation; tithes and other payments were demanded by the Roman Church; prices had risen steeply. These were the pitiable conditions under which the peasants everywhere existed, and in Germany they were no harder than elsewhere. While the Reformation was in no way responsible for the ensuing revolt, the peasants felt that by its liberating doctrines, its claims for equality, and its attacks on the financial abuses of the Roman Church, it implicitly encouraged the movement. They looked for support to Luther, who was himself of peasant stock and who at first was not unsympathetic. The revolt spread rapidly over a wide area, but lacking proper leaders was swiftly and relentlessly quelled. It is said that all told a hundred thousand peasants lost their lives. And Luther the while did nothing to help. On the contrary, at the height of the carnage he published his notorious tract, *Against the Murdering, Thieving Hordes of Peasants*. In the most intemperate terms he incited the princes to suppress the revolt. "Strike," he wrote, "strike, throttle, stab . . . and remember that there is nothing more poisonous, more hurtful, more devilish than a rebellious man." In extenuation it must be said that Luther always stood in favor of authority and abominated insurrection. When the rebellion was over, he blamed himself for his callous words which must forever remain a blot on his memory and which had a most disastrous effect on the course of the Reformation. The peasants believed that he had betrayed them and were now completely alienated.[16] The part he played in this tragic affair was never forgotten and it severely handicapped his movement in succeeding generations. The first defect of Lutheranism was that it failed to weld the nation into one: it might have been, but no longer was, a national movement.

The second defect was its inability to unite Protestantism. A real opportunity of effecting such a union was lost when Philip of Hesse arranged a conference at Marburg, the famous "Marburg Colloquy," between German and Swiss theologians. Among the delegates were Luther and Melanchthon from Saxony, Bucer from Strassburg, Oecolampadius from Basel, and Zwingli from Zürich. The purpose of the conference was to arrive at a common confession. Agreement was eventually reached on fourteen out of fifteen doctrinal questions discussed, but there was wide divergence on the fifteenth, the doctrine of the Lord's Supper. It all centered on the translation of a simple Latin word of three letters, *est*. Seizing a piece of chalk Luther scribbled on the table in front of them, *Hoc est corpus meum*, "This *is* my Body." The Swiss Reformer Zwingli contended that *est* in this phrase meant "signifies"; not "This *is* my Body," but "This *signifies* my Body." It is clear that two radically different conceptions were involved. To Luther, the Body of Christ was in the elements of bread and wine "as the fire enters into the iron when it is heated"; to Zwingli, the Lord's Supper was in the nature only of a commemoration. Neither side felt it could compromise on this question without sacrificing a vital and fundamental article of its faith. It is hard to see how either Luther or Zwingli could have abandoned his position, and so on this issue the conference broke up in disagreement. We need not question the sincerity of any of the delegates, though the result was a grave disservice to the Protestant cause. At a time when the best hope of success lay in a united front against the common enemy, Rome, it was tragic that the Reformers were unable to agree among themselves.

Lutheranism, then, failed to unite Germany and failed also to unite Protestantism. But there was a third cause that impeded the spread of the Reformation and even deprived it of some of the territory it had gained. This was the Counter Reformation and especially the founding in 1540 of the Jesuits, the Society of Jesus, under the compelling leadership of Ignatius Loyola.

This young Spanish nobleman was a man of dynamic energy, a visionary who yet retained a remarkable grasp of practical affairs. As a professional soldier he was wounded in both legs at Pampeluna in 1521 when fighting against the French. Forced to abandon his military career, a cripple for life, he turned his thoughts to religion and resolved thenceforth to be a soldier of the Cross. He practiced the most severe austerities, studied for seven years at the University of Paris, and in every way sedulously prepared himself for his new calling. In 1540 with the pope's consent the Order of the Society of Jesus was founded. The Jesuits had arrived. Their watchword was the soldiers' virtue, obedience, their avowed purpose "to fight for God under the standard of the Cross and to serve only God and the Roman pontiff, His vicar upon earth." Unquestioning obedience to the pope, unswerving loyalty to the Roman Church, the relentless stamping out of heresy—these were their aims. As the shock troops of the Counter Reformation, a *corps d'élite,* rigorously trained, almost fanatically staunch, they infused a new stream of life blood into the veins of the old church. In 1540 the Society numbered only a handful of members; when Ignatius died in 1556 there were a thousand members and seventy years later more than sixteen thousand. Poland was won back to the Roman fold together with extensive regions in Germany and Austria. In every land the Jesuits ruthlessly fought against the Reformation and everywhere impeded its growth.

2. So much, then, for the limitations of Lutheranism. We pass now to the second point, the legacy it bequeathed to the world, which may be summed up in one word, *freedom.* The challenging dictum of Patrick Henry might well have been spoken by all the great Reformers, "Give me liberty or give me death!" The keynote of the Reformation was freedom, freedom of the

intellect and of the spirit. It shines out in the lives of the Reformers and equally in the doctrines they promulgated. By way of illustration let us think of two of the most vital.

The first is fundamental and underlies every other, the *priesthood of all believers*. It asserts the right of every believer to go straight to God and to find in Him pardon and strength to live. For long centuries the church had denied men this right. Every approach to God was opened up by the church alone, or by the church was shut fast. On the one hand there were Indulgences, which meant in effect that the church could dispense forgiveness for sins. But on the other hand, it could and often did bar all approach to God. For over against Indulgences stood the dire threat of excommunication. A king or ruler, say, offended the pope, and as a consequence his whole domain was placed under an interdict and the ordinances of religion were suspended. As long as the interdict was in force (and it might be for years), no child might be baptized, no lawful marriage be performed, no consolation be given to the dying. No service of public worship was held, no sacrament administered. To the whole nation the church was a closed door; upon thousands of innocent people the blight fell, and the way to God was bolted and barred, since the only means of access to God was the church and its priests. It was to set men free from this ecclesiastical tyranny that the Reformers insisted upon the validity of this basic doctrine, the priesthood of *all* believers.

A second fundamental principle of the Reformation was *justification by faith*. In the medieval church, if a man confessed his sins to a priest, he was absolved and enjoined to perform certain acts of penance. Thus holy living meant the performance of specified rites such as fasting or reciting certain prayers a certain number of times or performing other mechanical acts. Luther himself had made the unhappy experiment and knew its barren futility. Only later did he discover that the promises of God are not thus attained; not by works of penance but by true penitence of heart; not by the multiplicity of mechanical acts but by faith; and not by priestly absolution but by God's free grace. The one essential in men is faith, the strong robust faith to commit themselves entirely to God's mercy and to trust in His promise of redeeming grace. It is God who forgives and God who saves, and thus men are set free from the intolerable burden of working out their own salvation.

The peoples of the English-speaking nations are justly proud of the freedom they enjoy, political and social freedom, emancipation from repression and tyranny. But there is another kind of liberty, even more precious—freedom of the mind and above all freedom of the spirit, both of which can be directly traced to the Protestant Reformation.

3

THE ANABAPTISTS

✙

Standing over the body of dead Caesar, Mark Antony declaimed the famous words:

> "The evil that men do lives after them;
> The good is oft interréd with their bones;
> So let it be with Caesar."

And so in fact it has been, until comparatively recent times, with the Anabaptists of the sixteenth century. History has witnessed many injustices, but surely none more flagrant than the disrepute of a generally pious and godly sect. For centuries their virtues were thrust into the shadows while the spotlight was focused on one disgraceful episode. Later on we shall revert to this, the so-called "Kingdom of God" at Münster, where a band of irresponsible fanatics plunged into a sorry experiment of communism, polygamy, and other antisocial vices. For those excesses of the guilty few, the innocent majority has been condemned. The very name, Anabaptists or Rebaptizers, was a term of reproach and obloquy, a *nomen horribile*. Thus they have been described as "one of the wildest and fiercest sects ever bred within the pale of the Christian Church," "a blood-red spectre which swept across Germany, inspiring riot and rebellion."[1] Or as another writer has put it (but significantly his book was published in 1902), "whenever they momentarily gained the upper hand, they applied the practical methods of modern Anarchism or Nihilism to the professed principles of Communism."[2] Half a century's researches have not been without effect and it would be hard indeed to find a reputable historian of the present time who would think of describing Anabaptism in such denigrating terms.

It cannot be too strongly emphasized that the Münster episode was exceptional and not typical. If a Presbyterian writer may say so without giving offense, the great Baptist churches of modern Europe and America, which ultimately emerged from sixteenth-century Anabaptism, have no reason to be ashamed of their origins. The Anabaptists, far from being evil-doers, ruled their lives by the highest standards, as even their bitterest enemies admitted. Such is the testimony of a Swiss chronicler, who writes: "Their walk and manner of life was altogether pious, holy, and irreproachable. They avoided costly clothing, despised costly food and drink . . . their walk and conduct was altogether humble."[3] Judged by any Christian test, those harried and persecuted men and women came through with flying colors and satisfied every Gospel condition of discipleship. Jesus said: "If any man will come after me, let him deny himself, and take up his cross, and follow me." (Matthew 16:24.) And that is what the Anabaptists did. In the *Chronicle* of Sebastian Franck it is recorded that "they taught nothing but love, faith, and crucifixion of the flesh, manifesting patience and humility under many sufferings." Again Jesus said: "By this shall all men know that ye are my disciples, if ye have love one to another." (John 13:35.) Mutual helpfulness and service were among the most cherished ideals of the Anabaptists. As the *Chronicle* just quoted puts it: they broke "bread with one another in sign of unity and love, helping one another with true helpfulness . . . calling each other 'brother.' "[4] Or again Jesus said: "Herein is my Father glorified, that ye bear much fruit; so shall ye be my disciples." (John 15:8.) This again was one of the most consistent tenets of Anabaptism. Luther had said that we are justified by faith and God's free grace operating in us, and that there can be no justification by our own works. But the Anabaptists claimed that they must so live as to be an example to all, that they must be as the salt of the earth, that their light must so shine before men that they might see their good works. "By their fruits ye shall know them" (Matthew 7:20) is a legitimate test of Christian discipleship. The Anabaptists might have quoted the epistle of James (that "right strawy epistle," as Luther had termed it) and said, "I will show you by my deeds what faith is!" (James 2:18, Moffatt translation.) They laid no claim but only aspired to perfection, and it cannot be gainsaid that they lived outstandingly good Christian lives. Nevertheless, they were persecuted, by Catholic, Protestant, and the secular authorities alike, how cruelly persecuted we shall see as we proceed.

The origin of the Anabaptists has been traced, first, to the periodic uprisings of the poor and oppressed against the more privileged classes, and it is significant that in the early days their numbers were recruited from the peasants in the country and the artisans in the cities. The second source from which they sprang was the medieval Christian brethren who organized themselves into anticlerical bodies. Being free thinkers, they broke with tradition and distrusted institutional religion, fettered as it was by a common creed and ritual. By far the greater part of those brethren were Anabaptists, so called because they insisted on the necessity of adult baptism. Prior to 1524 a number of "praying circles" had come into being in many parts of Europe—in Germany, Bohemia, Italy, Switzerland, France, and the Netherlands. At first they made no move to separate themselves from the church, though they were very conscious of its corruption. But in June 1524 an irrevocable step was taken when the groups sent representatives to meet together at the house of Balthazar Hübmaier at Waldshut, where the historic decision was made to leave the Catholic Church. Further gatherings were held at Augsburg in 1526 and 1527 when adult baptism was recognized as a fundamental principle. Among the early leaders of the sect were Balthazar Hübmaier himself and Hans Denck, both distinguished scholars. The teaching of Denck especially was imbued with a deep mysticism, and among other things he preached the doctrine of the "Inner Word" or "Inner Light," which became a distinctive tenet of the Anabaptist faith.

By the mid-twenties of the sixteenth century, groups were to be found in many parts of Europe; and though they differed from one another in the tenets they held, they might all be loosely termed Anabaptists, sharing as they did the common belief in adult baptism. There were, for instance, the "Zwickau prophets." Readers of the book of Revelation, these men were inspired by apocalyptic hopes and by dreams of the millennium. They envisaged a new Jerusalem and the speedy return of Christ to receive the righteous to Himself and to exact dire punishment on the wicked and unregenerate. Among these visionaries was Thomas Münzer who with Nicolas Storch and Mark Thomas Stübner arrived at Wittenberg at the end of December 1521, while Luther was still immured at the Wartburg. Their quarrel with Luther sprang from the idea that he was not thorough enough. He had made the Bible the supreme rule of faith and life and yet admitted infant baptism which was both unscriptural and unknown in the early church, a "dipping in the bath of Rome," and which was without efficacy or even meaning. Münzer also differed from Luther in emphasizing the importance of the "inner light." The Zwickau prophets believed that they were directly inspired by the Holy Spirit and accordingly that they had no need of guidance from the dead letter of the Bible. If the Bible was indispensable to salvation, God would have dropped it down from heaven, and if its writers were inspired, they were no more inspired than themselves, who had direct access to the truth and held conversations with God Himself. Melanchthon was deeply impressed by the prophets' claims. When they attacked infant baptism, he did not consider their viewpoint unreasonable; even on the question of inspiration he said, "Luther alone can decide; on the one hand let us beware of quenching the spirit of God, and on the other of being led astray by the spirit of Satan." But Luther was not deceived, and returning post haste from the Wartburg he gave short shrift to Münzer and his associates, scorning their fantastic claims and expelling them from Wittenberg. The climax came in 1525 during the Peasants' Revolt. Here was a golden opportunity for Münzer to carry the fight against the embattled forces of oppression and feudal power and to set up his New Jerusalem. But the peasants were completely routed at Frankenhausen, and Münzer, with a number of the insurgent leaders, was executed. Though the enthusiasm he kindled never completely died down, it was at least temporarily damped.

It may be justly claimed that Anabaptism proper began at Zürich, the city in which Zwingli carried out his religious reforms. Even before his arrival, there had been an Anabaptist community. At first they warmly supported Zwingli, but presently they criticized him for the same reason as their brethren in Germany had criticized Luther: he was not thorough enough; he was "a false prophet." It was a fundamental principle of Anabaptism everywhere, and not least in Zürich, that the church was the visible church of professed believers, free alike from state control and state support. Zwingli was unable to accept these views, and in an attempt to reach agreement a Disputation was held (January 17-18, 1525) between the Reformer and the Anabaptist leaders, Conrad Grebel, Felix Manz, and Brother Jörg, nicknamed "Blaurock" or "Blue-coat," and commonly known by that name. The Disputation was entirely fruitless. In spite of Zwingli's urgent appeal for unity, the Anabaptists repudiated the authority of magistrates and pastors alike, and threatened to set up a church of their own. A crisis was reached in the same month, January 1525, when in the house of Felix Manz, Blaurock was baptized by Grebel, the first such instance of adult baptism to be recorded.

This act of open defiance, with other adult baptisms that followed, greatly offended Zwingli and provoked the city fathers of Zürich to retaliatory measures. The Council passed a decree demanding that all children should be baptized not later than February 1, that those parents who disobeyed should be arrested, and that those who had rebaptized should be banished and the leaders imprisoned. Though these harsh measures were rigorously applied, the number of Anabaptist converts increased to an astonishing extent. Among them were Balthazar Hübmaier and Hans Denck, both of whom immediately began to baptize others. From one bucket of water Hübmaier alone is said to have baptized three hundred men and women, thus proving that baptism was administered by sprinkling and not by immersion.

The Zürich Anabaptists repudiated infant baptism as unscriptural and contrary to the practice of the primitive church. They emphasized the importance of godly living, abstained from offices of state, avoided litigation, and advocated a policy of non-retaliation for injuries suffered and of nonresistance when force was used against them.

Soon their faith was put to a cruel test. The exceedingly harsh treatment meted out to the Anabaptists reveals one of the less agreeable features of the sixteenth century, its indiscriminate intolerance. The hand of every man was turned against them— Protestants, Catholics, and the secular power. The religious bodies were offended by the practice of rebaptism. *"Qui iterum mergit mergatur,"* said Zwingli, "Let the man be drowned who baptizes a second time"; and many suffered in this way. In Switzerland the ancient Code of Justinian was invoked for the condemnation of those who rebaptized. Anabaptism has been called the *"bête noire* of all the Reformers"[5] and both Luther and Zwingli were convinced that the misguided enthusiasm of the sect was completely undermining their own work. The idea of a "gathered church" not coterminal with the whole community or district seemed to destroy the conception of both state and church as accepted by Roman Catholics and Protestants alike. The second reason why they were persecuted was that they were universally regarded as disturbers of the peace, almost as the Bolshevists of the times, completely irresponsible and capable of any misdeed.[6] Nicknamed both Ana- and Kata-baptists (the "up and down" Baptists), they were not only condemned as rebaptizers but as red-hot revolutionaries who turned their communities upside down. It is highly significant that when Felix Manz, one of the Anabaptist leaders at Zürich, was flung into the lake and drowned —with Zwingli's approval—the Reformer maintained (it would seem on insufficient grounds) that Manz had suffered not because he was a rebaptizer but because he was a rebel who had disobeyed the decrees of the state. This was in 1527.

Whatever the true reason may have been, a veritable wave of persecution overwhelmed the hapless Anabaptists, and all over Europe they were victimized. In 1527 an imperial decree issued by the Archduke Ferdinand of Austria threatened the death penalty to all the Anabaptists in his domains, and the resultant persecution in Bavaria and the Tyrol was draconic in its severity. Two years later at the second Diet of Speyer both Catholics and Protestants voted that all Anabaptists should die without even receiving an ecclesiastical trial. No penalties were too dire, no sufferings too terrible. The unfortunate victims were not only burned at the stake but were frequently roasted till they died. Even sex was no protection against the avalanche of persecution, and we read of many instances of women buried alive. In Switzerland the common method was death by drowning. The tribulations of this unfortunate sect are thus catalogued by Menno Simons, an Anabaptist leader in later times: "Some they have executed by hanging, some they have tortured with inhuman tyranny, and afterwards choked with cords at the stake. Some they roasted and burned alive. Some they have killed with the sword and given them to the fowls of the air to devour. Some they have cast to the fishes [that is, drowned]. . . . Others wander about here and there, in want, homelessness, and affliction, in mountains and deserts, in holes and caves of the earth. They must flee with their wives and little children from one country to another, from one city to another. They are hated, abused, slandered and lied about by all men."[7] The reader's mind is taken back to the New Testament and to the tribulations of the early days. "They were stoned, they were sawn asunder, were tempted, were slain with the sword . . . being destitute, afflicted, tormented." (Hebrews 11:37.) One of the Anabaptist hymns describes them pathetically as sheep without a shepherd—rendered homeless, exposed without shelter to the elements, creeping into caves or crouching behind wild rocks; trailed by bloodhounds, taken and roped as sheep for the slaughter; chained and thrown into dungeons; hanged, drowned, flayed alive—men and women alike. And yet we read that "they were far readier than followers of Luther and Zwingli to meet death, and to bear the harshest tortures for their faith. For they run to suffer punishments, no matter how horrible, as if to a banquet."[8] The Anabaptists were drilled to *expect* persecutions because they were Anabaptists, but they went "to the stake singing." As Lindsay has put it, their hymns show that life was "for them a continuous Holy War, a Pilgrim's Progress through an evil world full of snares, of dangers, of temptations" until, if they persevered, they should reach the Celestial City.[9]

Such, then, were the sufferings of the Anabaptists. Presently the number of martyrdoms reached the appalling total of tens of thousands. It was only natural that the first casualties were the leaders, whose deaths left congregations without their spiritual guides. This was among the most disastrous consequences of the persecutions, since power necessarily devolved on less responsible men, who led their followers to excesses that were no credit to a sect composed for the most part of quiet, inoffensive men and women.

The stormy history of Anabaptism in so many European countries is repeated in the Netherlands which, according to Professor Bainton, "in the 1530's [were] the greatest center of the Anabaptist movement."[10] Here the persecutions were even more rigorously applied. In 1535 was published a notorious edict condemning to death by burning all who had "seduced or perverted any to this sect or had rebaptized them." Those who recanted were permitted an easier death—they were put to the sword; women were treated even more considerately—they "were only to be buried alive." One of the earliest victims was Jan Walen who with two others was barbarously roasted to death at The Hague in 1527. In 1530 Jan Volkertz and nine of his congregation at Amsterdam were beheaded. Roastings and burnings, drownings and executions became all too common, and a veritable reign of terror set in. This brutality continued during the entire reign of Charles V, and shortly after his abdication when his son Philip II came to the throne, Philip was able to write to his regent, Margaret of Parma: "Wherefore introduce the Spanish Inquisition? . . . The inquisition *of the Netherlands is much more pitiless than that of Spain.*"[11]

One of the early Anabaptist leaders in the Netherlands was Melchior Hoffmann (1498-1543 or 1544), a chiliast or believer in the theory that Christ would return to the world and reign for a thousand years before the last judgment. (See Revelation 20: 1-5.) His followers, called Melchiorites, by their excesses brought discredit to the sect. In 1523, when Hoffmann was imprisoned at Strassburg the leadership passed to the notorious Jan Matthys, a Haarlem baker, of whom we shall hear again when we turn to the infamous Münster episode. In spite of the government's concentrated efforts to suppress the movement, many converts were made, especially in centers like Daventer, Zwolle, and Kampen. But harsher measures were adopted, and soon the Dutch prisons were crammed with arrested Anabaptists. Many of those still at large attempted to leave the country by land and sea but were intercepted and pitilessly driven back. Up to this date the Anabaptists, true to their doctrine of nonresistance, had made no efforts to fight back, but now at the point of desperation they began to retaliate. Every other alternative had been resorted to, but in vain: now they had no option but to take up arms. First they attempted to seize Daventer, and when they failed there, Leyden. In Leyden too they were unsuccessful, suffering horrible losses, and in May 1535 they made an attempt on Amsterdam; but though they succeeded for a time the city was finally reduced. In the same year a number of the citizens, maddened by unremitting persecution, became victims of hysteria, and the streets of Amsterdam witnessed a strange sight. Seven men and five women threw off all their garments as a token that they spoke the naked truth and thus unclothed ran through the streets crying "Woe! Woe! Woe! The wrath of God!" But this, like all else, did nothing to soften the stony hearts of their tormentors. The persecutions were only intensified, and the forlorn Anabaptists were still without their city of refuge.

Meantime, a curious experiment was being tried at Münster, a city in northwest Germany at no great distance from the boundaries of Holland. Münster was under the rule of the Bishop Count Francis of Waldeck who was also a German prince. From time to time there had been uprisings of the citizens, in 1527 and again in 1529 under the leadership of one Knipperdolling. In the six years, 1525-31, the city was further roused by the preaching of Bernard Rothmann, a Lutheran who gradually came to espouse Anabaptist doctrines—the unlawfulness of infant baptism, the common sharing of goods, and generally a return to the standards of living in the primitive church. In a short time the news spread like wildfire, and Anabaptists came streaming into the city from all directions, but for the most part from the Netherlands and nearly all Melchiorites, those disciples of Melchior Hoffmann who, as we have already seen, were chiliasts and looked for the speedy return of Christ to the earth. The Anabaptists had found a haven of rest, where at last they might build a New Jerusalem and set up the Kingdom of God.

The leaders in Münster were Knipperdolling and then two Dutch fanatics, Jan Matthys, a Haarlem baker, and his disciple, the notorious John of Leyden (a tailor). The bishop and his adherents were driven from the city, the ungodly were expelled, all books save the Bible were burned, and a form of apostolic communism was introduced. The Anabaptists were now in full control, but presently were compelled to defend their city against the investing forces of the expelled bishop (April 1534). It was then that Matthys, urged by the crazy notion that he could repel the besiegers almost singlehanded, made a sally with twenty or thirty followers and was immediately cut down. Power now devolved on John of Leyden and until the city fell in June 1535 he ruled like a king. At once began the experiment of living according to the Bible, Old as well as New Testament. All adults must be baptized or leave the city; food and clothes must be shared; in June 1534 polygamy was introduced. John himself, the Brigham Young of the age, was a young man (aged twenty-five at his death in 1535) attractive to women; and he set an example to others. To begin with he took four wives, but later increased the number to sixteen, one of whom he publicly beheaded with his own hand in a fit of rage. Even Henry VIII of England, with a total of six wives was modest in comparison! But John's rule was of short duration, and on June 25, 1535, Münster fell to a combined force of Catholics and Lutherans led by Philip of Hesse and the bishop. The Anabaptist leaders were arrested and tortured, their dead bodies being "placed in iron baskets which hung in the tower of Lambert Church until 1881."[12]

The Münster excesses brought into discredit the Anabaptist movement all over Europe. And yet, as already suggested, it is unjust to condemn the innocent majority for the sins of the guilty few. Soon after the Münster episode, there appeared a leader of a vastly different stamp, Menno Simons (born 1496 or 1505, died 1561), who broke with the Catholic Church and associated himself with the Anabaptist movement. At once he repudiated the Münster excesses, which were also denounced in Moravia by Jacob Hutter, founder of the Hutterites. Menno Simons began his work in East Friesland but later moved into north Germany and then into the Netherlands. It is said that he was "a man of integrity, mild, accommodating, patient of injuries, and so ardent in his piety as to exemplify in his own life the precepts he gave to others."[13] Certainly his studied moderation stood in sharp contrast to the wild turbulence of the Münster fanatics and qualified him for the task of reuniting the scattered remnants left over after the debacle in that city. He purged Anabaptism of its more fanatical elements, renounced its apocalyptic ideas, introduced decency and order, and labored to establish communities of regenerated men and women based on the standards of the early church. To this end he stressed the need of personal conversion and commitment of which adult baptism was the outward sign and seal; he advocated the principle of nonresistance; and he demanded complete spiritual freedom without interference from the state. He himself died in 1561 after a life of hazards and incessant toils, but his followers, known as Mennonites, increased in influence and became a real religious force in the Netherlands where in later years they enjoyed the protection of William the Silent, Prince of Orange. From Holland they spread to other lands, and it is estimated that some 500,000 are still in existence, of whom 250,000 have their homes in the United States. The great Baptist Church of modern times derived many of its doctrines from the Mennonites, and to them too may be indirectly traced the early origins of the Quakers and the Independents who since the seventeenth century in England and America have played so vital a part in the life of their communities.

Before we consider the general tenets of Anabaptism, mention must be made of one name more, that of David Joris (c. 1501-56). He is remembered not so much for his teaching as for his checkered life which, though in some respects unique, was in others not dissimilar to the stormy experience of so many of the brethren. This man's father was a shopkeeper in Delft, who in his spare time took up amateur acting as a recreation. It is said that on one occasion he played the part of King David and for this insufficient reason, when his son was born about 1501, he gave him the name of David. David's first occupation seems to have been the painting of glass for church windows. After his marriage in 1524 he became a Lutheran, and for an outrage on the Sacred Host in 1528 a hole was bored in his tongue and he was banished from Delft for three years. In 1533 he joined the Anabaptists, was rebaptized, and later came under the influence, first of Melchior Hoffmann and then of Menno Simons. He claimed to see visions and to possess the gift of prophecy, and he identified faith with spiritual experience. "I do not bother my head," he said, "whether the Lord is above or here below . . . if I am of like disposition to Him in heart, mind and spirit, that must suffice me." Till 1544 his activities were confined to Holland, but in April of that year he migrated to Basel in Switzerland. Here he was known as Jan van Brugge and ostensibly lived as a country squire. Little did the city fathers realize that they were harboring a notorious Anabaptist! For twelve years more, till his death in 1556, he kept in touch with his followers in the Netherlands, pouring out for their benefit an unending stream of writings. When he died he was buried with full religious honors, but even this was not the end. In 1559 his identity was betrayed, he was posthumously convicted of heresy, and his body was exhumed and burned. The story of David Joris is surely one of the strangest in all the annals of the sixteenth century and its climax a not uncommon example of contemporary intolerance bordering on vindictiveness.

When we turn to examine the tenets of Anabaptism we are met with the insuperable difficulty that one group held certain beliefs, another group quite different beliefs, and it is impossible to make a comprehensive survey that will apply to all. In any case the Anabaptists as a whole emphasized the ethical and practical side of religion rather than the theological, and Christianity to them was not so much a system of doctrines as a way of life. This emphasis on right conduct has led Professor Bainton to write that "if the Catholic Church had improved its morals they [the Anabaptists] might not have found it too hard to return to her fold." [14] While it is difficult to reconcile this judgment with the Anabaptist views of the sacraments and their insistence on the freedom of the church from state control and support, they were nevertheless nearer Catholicism than Protestantism in their emphasis on man's free will and the necessity of good works, more especially holy living and brotherly love. They renounced the idea of predestination; even if a man is reborn, opportunities are present to be used, and if they are not used the man will perish. Christian ideals and Christian faith were in themselves not enough: the Anabaptists insisted that they must be carried out in practice.

Nevertheless all men must believe something: it is manifestly impossible to live without faith of some kind, and the Anabaptists did hold certain distinctive tenets. From time to time in the course of this chapter we have mentioned some of them in dealing with certain groups. Many Anabaptists, for instance, were pledged to the doctrine of nonresistance, though in the end this resolution yielded before the frightful persecutions they were compelled to suffer. Again, many would have no recourse to litigation or any truck with politics; they refused to take an oath, since Christ had categorically said, "Swear not at all." (Matthew 5:34.) Then again, in the manner of the first disciples, there were experiments in communism, at least to the extent of sharing goods in common and sometimes (as among the Hutterites) of common ownership of property.

Various documents were drawn up at different times to crystallize the faith. In 1527 appeared *Seven Articles* agreed on by the brethren in Switzerland and southwest Germany,[15] and in 1539 was published Menno Simons' *Book of Fundamentals* which sets out a number of commonly accepted Anabaptist doctrines. From these and other sources[16] it seems certain that the fundamental aim of all the brethren was a return to the pattern of early Christianity. This largely determined their views of the church and led them to assert the complete separation of church and state.

According to Anabaptism the church was not thought of as the invisible church but rather as the visible church composed only of believers ready to testify to their faith. Individual responsibility was emphasized, and the individual conscience, lit by the "inner word" and directly inspired by the Holy Spirit, was the sole judge of Christian truth. Each group or "church" was independent and free from outside influence: church and state were sharply separated. It was intolerable that the regenerate should be subject to the authority of the civil powers, since the state legislates for all within its bounds while the church is composed of the elect and has its own unimpugnable authority and its own organization.[17] The church also had power to excommunicate any unworthy member, but there the punishment ended and no further penalty was exacted. In this respect the practice of the Anabaptists compared favorably with that of the Catholic Church which delivered excommunicated heretics to the state for further punishment. As the brethren claimed for themselves, so they accorded to others complete liberty of thought and belief. In thus demanding the right to religious freedom they were far in advance of their times, and it was they who first blazed the trail to a more humane tolerance.

It might be said that the Anabaptists were in the world but not of it. They drew a sharp line of contrast between the world and the church, and as far as might be, they withdrew from the world and from contact with the ungodly.[18]

As regards the sacraments they held distinctive ideas. They entirely departed from the sacramental view both of baptism and of the Lord's Supper. Baptism was the outward sign of conversion and followed from it; it was not "a means of regeneration" but rather "a sign that it had been accomplished."[19] Thus everywhere the Anabaptists insisted on rebaptism, or as they termed it, baptism, since infant baptism was no true baptism but only an empty rite without efficacy.[20] The only true baptism was that which followed a definite act of personal commitment to Christ and was the solemn pledge to follow His way of love and service.

Similarly the Lord's Supper was without sacramental value. It was a memorial of the death of Christ with efficacy only according to the faith of the participant. It was also a common meal shared in by brothers and sisters in the faith, an *agape* or love feast to deepen the sense of fellowship and brotherhood.

It only remains to add that the Anabaptists were everywhere animated by an ardent missionary spirit: every member of the group regarded himself as an ambassador for Christ. Many of them became itinerant preachers: they heard God's call and immediately responded. There is the story of Hans Ber of Alten-Erlangen, a poor peasant. "He rose from his bed one night and suddenly began to put on his clothes. 'Whither goest thou?' asked his poor wife. 'I know not; God knoweth,' he answered. 'What evil have I done thee? Stay and help me to bring up my little children.' 'Dear wife,' he answered, 'trouble me not with the things of time. I must away, that I may learn the will of the Lord.' "[21] With such emissaries of the faith the survival of Anabaptism was assured.

Its influence on the modern world is clearly discernible. In direct succession are the Mennonites and Hutterites and derived from Anabaptism is the modern Baptist Church which forms so large a part of Protestantism in all the continents of the world.[22] The Englishman John Smyth (c. 1554-1612), in exile at Amsterdam, came under the influence of the Mennonites, baptized himself, established a church, and may be regarded as the founder of the modern Baptist Churches. In 1612 some of his followers returned to England and established a church in London, the first of its kind in Great Britain. From this modest beginning the Baptist movement in Britain has branched out in all directions, and today with its 3600 churches it numbers some 350,000 members with 2000 pastors. In the United States its growth has been even more remarkable. We have already observed that missionary zeal was one of the prominent features of sixteenth-century Anabaptism, and this sense of mission has been kept alive by the modern Baptist Church. As the frontiers were pushed westward, Baptist preachers were everywhere found among the pioneers, and it is not surprising that at the present time there are over 19,000,000 Baptists in America. Their influence on the community as a whole would seem to be even greater than their numbers might indicate. The visitor to the United States is impressed by two characteristics of the religious life, and sometimes wonders whether there may not be a connection between the two. First, he is impressed by the extent and vitality of the Baptist Church, the largest of all the Protestant sects; and second, by the spirit of mutual helpfulness that animates church members of every denomination. While no one would gainsay the soundness of the faith in the great churches of America, the emphasis among them seems to be laid not so much on creed and doctrine as on service and real *practical* Christianity. This may be due in part to the temperament of the American people themselves, but it may not be entirely fanciful to trace this tendency back, by way of the strong modern Baptist Churches, to the Anabaptists of the sixteenth century and their cherished ideal of mutual helpfulness and brotherly love.

4

JOHN CALVIN

✠

The story is told of a young American woman who was traveling in the Highlands of Scotland. Stopping one day at a little cottage she began to talk with the old woman who lived there. In the course of the conversation she remarked: "It may surprise you to know that I too have Scottish blood in my veins." "Well," replied the old woman, "that's always something. It'll not keep you from sinning, but it'll keep you from enjoying it." This story illustrates one aspect of Calvinism, the popular idea of an austere sect that suspects the world and all its works; that stresses the need of abstinence, not only from sin, but from pleasure and frivolity. Calvin himself seems to support the theory when he writes: "Either the earth must become vile in our estimation, or it must retain our immoderate love. Wherefore, if we have any concern about eternity, we must use our most diligent efforts to extricate ourselves from these fetters."[1] There is the authentic note of Calvinism.

The work of Calvin in Switzerland was not without its preparation. First, there was the land itself, a small country of pleasant upland valleys, girt round with majestic Alpine peaks. Here lived the sturdy Swiss animated with fervent patriotism and the ardent love of freedom. Though nominally a part of the Holy Roman Empire, the thirteen Swiss cantons were virtually autonomous. They were bound together by defensive treaties and held a kind of Diet from time to time to transact business common to them all. They had their own flag, a white cross on a red ground, bearing the famous motto, "Each for all, and all for each." Though the Swiss were rent by internal divisions, they could still be counted on to present a united front against external threats.

Of all the European nations Switzerland was the most strongly opposed to papal domination. Its people recalled the two great church councils that had been held on Swiss soil in the first half of the fifteenth century, at Constance in 1415 and at Basel in 1431. Both had been antipapal, both had insisted on the need of ecclesiastical reform; and now a century later the Swiss were in no mood to truckle to papal demands. In 1518, for example, when Pope Leo X asked the Swiss Diet to furnish 12,000 soldiers for a war against the Turks, the Diet promised 10,000, adding sardonically that the pope could have two thousand priests from Switzerland, if he wanted, to make up his numbers. Again a few years later the Diet took a strong stand against the sale of Indulgences.

Thus Switzerland afforded fruitful soil for the seed of the Reformation once it was sown. The first Swiss Reformer was Ulrich Zwingli, born on January 1, 1484, a few weeks after Luther. In 1519, as a parish priest at Zürich, Zwingli denounced ecclesiastical abuses, including the sale of Indulgences. Other Catholic practices fell under the lash, such as the celibacy of the clergy, monasticism, the Mass, the confessional. Presently he was preaching the typically Reformed doctrines of justification by faith, the priesthood of all believers, the authority of the Bible, and Christ the only Mediator between God and man. By 1524 reforms were effected in Zürich along the lines laid down by Zwingli, and other cities soon followed its lead.

Zwingli, then, was the first forerunner of Calvin, and the second was William Farel. But at this point we must break off for a little to glance at the condition of Geneva.

Here was a flourishing commercial city of some thirteen thousand inhabitants situated on the lovely shores of Lake Geneva. In pre-Reformation times there were three rival parties in the city; first, the Bishop of Geneva who was also the civil ruler; second, a council of citizens; and third, the Duke of Savoy who asserted his sovereignty over both bishop and people. In 1513, however, the duke's party and the bishop's were fused together, for in that year Pope Leo X appointed a bishop who belonged to the House of Savoy. Accordingly, from 1513 the struggle for power resolved itself into a straight fight between the ducal-episcopal faction and the people.[2] It is unnecessary to enter into the details of the strife. The upshot was that in 1526 the people, with the assistance of Protestant Bern, won the day and Geneva became an independent city.

To this recently liberated city came William Farel in 1532, an emissary from Bern and a Frenchman by birth. By August 1535 he had converted the city to Reformed ideas and the Genevan Council officially abolished Romanism and also began to impose Protestantism on all the citizens, not the best method of instilling a new faith. If Christianity is anything, it is a voluntary appeal. State decrees cannot make a man a Christian or legislation purify his morals. And it was the moral condition of Geneva that was most alarming. Farel manfully threw himself into the struggle but he had no gifts for this kind of task. Geneva at this time required a man of tougher fiber to organize and legislate, and that man arrived in July 1536. He came from France and his name was John Calvin.

Leaving Geneva for the present we turn to look at the life of this man who was destined to become a power, not only at Geneva, but in all the lands where Protestantism has gained a foothold.

In Calvin's life there were four distinct phases, and the easiest way to remember them is to relate them all to Geneva. Accordingly, the four periods might be described thus: *prior to* Geneva; *at* Geneva; *away from* Geneva; and *back to* Geneva. Calvin was twenty-seven years old when he first came to the city. He worked there for two years and was banished for three. Then he came back to Geneva, remained there for the rest of his life, and died at the comparatively early age of fifty-five.

The First Period: Prior to Geneva: 1509-36. John Calvin was born at Noyon, Picardy,[3] some sixty miles from Paris, on July 10, 1509, a few months after Henry VIII ascended the throne of England and not long after Luther had begun his work at Wittenberg. Calvin's father, Gérard, was a notary, while his mother, Jeanne le Franc, daughter of a well-to-do innkeeper, is said to have been beautiful as well as devout. There were six children, four sons (of whom John was the second) and two daughters.

In August 1523, when Calvin was fourteen, his father sent him to Paris to further his education. First he enrolled at the Collège de la Marche where he studied under Mathurin Cordier, an interesting person and one of the most learned men of his age. (Later when he was converted to Protestantism, he ingeniously spread Reformed doctrines among his pupils by means of the sentences he gave them to turn into Latin! When Calvin settled in Geneva, Cordier followed him and made his home there till he died at the ripe old age of eighty-seven.) From the Collège de la Marche, Calvin was transferred to the Collège de Montaigu, a famous seat of learning which numbered Rabelais and Erasmus among its former students and was soon to receive within its walls another man of destiny, Ignatius Loyola, founder of the Society of Jesus. Calvin from the beginning was an outstandingly brilliant student. His critical faculty was specially keen, and he gave the impression of a maturity far beyond his years.

It was originally intended that Calvin should enter the church; but in 1528 his father changed his mind and requested John to abandon theology in favor of the law. Like a dutiful son John acquiesced and proceeded to Orleans the same year to commence his legal studies. Here also he was the most distinguished student of his day. In the absence of the regular staff he was sometimes called to lecture, and it is said that he might have aspired to any eminence of the legal profession. But his interests lay elsewhere, and after he had taken his degree and following the death of his father in 1531 he returned to Paris to devote himself to the study of the ancient classics. The next year he published a commentary on the *De Clementia* of Seneca, a work of monumental learning remarkable in one so youthful.[4]

Calvin's conversion may have taken place in 1533 or in the following year. At any rate 1534 was a decisive year in his life. Having by that time renounced Romanism he decided to leave France, possibly to escape persecution but more probably because the unsettled conditions in France were not conducive to the life of study that Calvin had mapped out for himself. He arrived in

Basel, and there in the spring of 1536 he published the first edition of one of the world's famous books, the *Institutio Christianae Religionis* or *Instruction in the Christian Religion,* which gained for him the proud title of the "Aristotle of the Reformation" and which, according to Lindsay, was "the strongest weapon Protestantism had yet forged against the Papacy."[5] The book was prefaced by a letter to Francis I, King of France, described as "one of the great epistles of the world," throbbing "with a noble indignation against injustice, and with a noble enthusiasm for freedom and truth," not imploring "toleration as a concession," but claiming "freedom as a right."[6] It was the Reformation's Declaration of Independence. Later in this chapter we shall return to the *Institutes,* but meantime we must again note that it was a most remarkable book for a young man to write: Calvin was twenty-six when the first edition was published. In it are all the essentials of Calvinist theology which was destined to exert so profound an influence on both his own and succeeding generations.

Shortly after the publication of the *Institutes* Calvin arrived at Geneva. He had no intention of settling there and the worldling might say his coming was a pure accident. But "God moves in a mysterious way, His wonders to perform," and surely it was by the providence of God that Calvin was led to Geneva. His own purpose was to devote himself to a life of study at Strassburg. But because of a war then raging between the king of France and the emperor he was unable to proceed by the direct route and was forced in the interests of safety to go the long way round by Lyons and Geneva. The story is told of Isaac Watts that he went for a weekend to the house of Sir Thomas and Lady Abney and stayed on for thirty years. This was practically what Calvin did. He intended to stop at Geneva for one day, but as things turned out he was there, with a short break, for the best part of thirty years till his death in 1564. It was certainly not what he desired or planned. He had no wish to be embroiled in public affairs but wanted to live a quiet, studious life. It was Farel who appealed to him to remain and help in the difficult task of organizing the church. Like Moses, Calvin demurred as not being a fit person, but Farel was not to be gainsaid. To quote Calvin's own words, "finding that he [Farel] gained nothing by entreaties, he proceeded to utter an imprecation that God would curse my retirement, and the tranquillity of the studies which I sought, if I should withdraw and refuse to give assistance, when the necessity was so urgent. By this imprecation I was so stricken with terror, that I desisted from the journey which I had undertaken."[7] Calvin believed that he was divinely called and that (as he said) "God had stretched forth His hand upon me from on high to arrest me."

The Second Period: At Geneva: 1536-38. Thus began the second period of Calvin's life. And here we return to the point at which we broke off a short time ago—the state of the city at the time of Calvin's arrival, and the nature and magnitude of the task that confronted him.

"No period," writes Dr. J. S. Whale, "was more critical for the Reformation than those years 1530-40 which saw Calvin's appearance on the stage of world history."[8] While the Reformation had been legally established, much still remained to be done. There were many convinced Romanists, dormant for the time being but only waiting for an opportune moment to emerge. There were others, lukewarm Protestants, who nostalgically looked back to the old days, "Ere ever Luther came, or Rabelais." We must also remember that the break with Rome, which was even more a break with the Duke of Savoy, was inspired by political as well as religious motives. Everywhere in Geneva there was confusion and uncertainty. Among the people there was the crying need of instruction, discipline, authority; and these Calvin set himself to provide and *did* provide in several ways.

He began his work at Geneva as a professor in sacred learning, starting off with daily lectures on the Pauline Epistles. But the need of the times was not so much academic as simple, practical teaching. The citizens as a whole were uninstructed in the new faith, and to remedy this defect Calvin and Farel applied their energies. A brief compendium of the Christian faith was drawn up and a catechism prepared for the instruction of the young.

Worship too was organized: the preaching of the Word, a simple ritual, the encouragement of psalm-singing, monthly celebrations of Holy Communion for those judged morally worthy.

But in addition to instruction in the faith, moral reform was equally urgent. The vice and dissoluteness of the Roman clergy had poisoned the morals of the whole city, and now with the greater liberty of the Reformation there was the very real danger that freedom might degenerate into license. Consequently there was the need of discipline, which Calvin and Farel were not slow to administer. To deal with delinquents a panel of ministers and magistrates was appointed, and regulations were laid down for proper behavior and even for dress. We read that "a card-player was pilloried; a tire-woman, a mother, and two bridesmaids were arrested because they had adorned the bride too gaily; and adulterer was driven with the partner of his guilt through the streets by the common hangman, and then banished."[9] Almost at once arose the cry of "ecclesiastical tyranny." The simple truth is that the rulers of Geneva completely failed to understand the meaning of a Calvinist Reformation, which aimed at a return to the purity of the early church not only in faith but also in morals.

At this time Geneva was governed by two councils, the Little Council of twenty-five members and the Council of Two Hundred, both of which in January 1537 had adopted Calvin's twenty-one Articles concerning the government of the church. This was virtually to commit Geneva to Calvinism, which included a "discipline" as well as a code of beliefs. But the rulers of the city failed to realize the implications involved. It was one thing to authorize the Articles but quite another to see them enforced in practice and defaulters punished. A crisis arose, Calvin's supporters fell from power, others less friendly assumed control, and the ministers were curtly warned to leave politics alone and to confine themselves to preaching the Gospel. But Calvin regarded the enforcement of discipline as a spiritual and ecclesiastical office in which the civil power had no right to dictate or even to interfere. It was not that he demanded the subjection of state to church, but in moral and spiritual matters he would not permit the church to be dominated by the state, as was now happening in Geneva. Other reasons combined to make Calvin's position untenable, and the upshot was that in 1538 he and Farel were ordered to leave the city within three days. Before he left he was threatened and insulted in the streets; crowds gathered round his house, fired shots, and sang obscene songs. "If we had served men," he said, "we should think ourselves badly paid; but we serve a great Master and He will pay us." Calvin's first attempt to institute a true Reformation had failed, and the penalty of failure was exile.

The Third Period: Away from Geneva: 1538-41. And so we arrive at the third period of Calvin's life, the years 1538-41, which we have described as *"away from* Geneva." During this time he was domiciled at Strassburg where he lectured in theology, preached, and wrote. To this period belong a revised and enlarged edition of the *Institutes* in Latin and the first French edition, a *Commentary on the Epistle to the Romans,* and his *Tract on the Lord's Supper.* He ministered to a congregation of four hundred French exiles. He was also commissioned as a delegate to the German Reformed churches where he met Melanchthon and other Lutherans.

But his mind was not wholly occupied with theology: he suddenly bethought himself of taking a wife, not any kind of wife, but one who was "modest, decent, plain, thrifty, patient, and able to take care of my health." An approach was made to a young woman who seemed to combine all the advantages desired, but the marriage was called off because she refused to learn French. Undaunted, however, Calvin persevered in his aims, and in August 1540 at the age of thirty-one he married Idelette de Bures, a widow from Liége. The union was a happy one; she lived for only nine years after their marriage, and Calvin never ceased to mourn her death. Their one child, a boy born in July 1542, lived for only a few days.

Meantime, while Calvin was in Strassburg, affairs in Geneva were going from bad to worse. With no real leader at the helm, disorders broke out, irreligion was rampant, and morals had so far deteriorated that the ministers of Bern wrote in protest. Party political strife threatened the existence of Geneva as a free city. On top of this the Romanists, sensing an opportunity, emerged from their underground retreats and began to plot for a revival of the old faith. Clearly the time had come when a strong hand was required to restore order in the distracted city. Calvin's enemies fell from power, more moderate men were appointed in their place, and almost at once there was an agitation for his return. He had no wish to go back, for he still retained painful recollections of his previous harsh treatment. Writing to a friend he said: "There is no place I have such a terror of as Geneva," "that place of torment," as he called it; and to Farel he said he would rather die a hundred times than again take up that cross on which one must daily perish a thousand times (*in qua millies quotidie pereundum esset*). At last he yielded to the importunity of his friends both within and outside the city. He believed it was God's will that he should return. "Therefore," he said, "I submit my mind bound and fettered to obedience to God." As Professor A. J. Grant has remarked, "All Calvin is in that sentence."[10] On September 13, 1541, when he re-entered Geneva he received an uproarious welcome. As a postscript it might be added that he was promised a yearly stipend of five hundred florins, twelve measures of wheat, and two tubs of wine.

The Fourth Period: Back to Geneva: 1541-64. We have now arrived at the last period of Calvin's life, from 1541 to his death in 1564. He was not only the leading man in the Genevan church but probably the busiest person in the city. He taught theology three days a week, preached daily every second week, held a weekly meeting of his consistory, wrote books and commentaries, maintained a voluminous correspondence, and argued with opponents. In a letter to a friend he writes: "I have not time to look out of my house at the blessed sun, and if things continue thus I shall forget what sort of appearance it has." There was often no time to sleep! And through it all he was in weak health, suffering specially from severe headaches and asthma. As with many of the saints, his exertions were a triumph of the spirit over the flesh.

Calvin's dominant aim was to establish Geneva as a city of God on earth. His conception was a theocracy in the sense that it was the rule of God in church and state and the reverse of certain ideas commonly held at the present time. In recent years we have heard much of creating a brave new world, and always the suggested method is the same. Build up from men to God, we are told; improve men's material conditions, provide them with finer opportunities, civilize them, educate them, let the kindly light of science play upon them: thus shall God's kingdom come upon the earth. But Calvin, like the author of the Revelation, held the opposite view, the scriptural view, that the method of building is not from men up to God but from God down to men. "I John saw the holy city, new Jerusalem, *coming down* from God out of heaven." (Revelation 21:2, italics mine.) And Jesus said: "Seek ye first the kingdom of God, and His righteousness" (Matthew 6:33); seek it first, not second or third or tenth, but first. That is the true way to found the ideal commonwealth. Later we shall consider the methods Calvin employed, but his general idea was that the city is a church; and though the state might legislate in civil affairs, all must bow to the authority of the church in matters of faith and conduct.

But before that happened Calvin was obliged to fight many a stern battle. His measures were too stringent for the ordinary citizen, and the growing opposition came to a head in January 1546, when one Pierre Ameaux (a member of the Little Council), a manufacturer of playing cards, saw his business vanishing as a result of Calvin's reforms. He tried to discredit Calvin, but Calvin humiliated him by forcing him to march through the streets in disgrace. Another man, Jacques Gruet, a notorious free thinker, was arrested and beheaded. The most famous case concerned the Spaniard Servetus, an interesting person who deserved a better fate. He had advanced ideas on medicine and is said to have anticipated Harvey's discovery of the circulation of the blood; but in theology he had denied the doctrine of the Holy Trinity. This Calvin could not tolerate and already had refuted the opinions of Servetus as "the ravings of a heretic." In 1553 Servetus was on his way to Naples, and with greater bravado than common sense decided to stay in Geneva over the night of August 13. He was recognized, arrested, put on trial for heresy, and on October 25 was condemned (like so many heretics all over Europe) to be burned at the stake. Calvin and the civic authorities had acted throughout in complete harmony; Calvin prepared the charges against Servetus, the councils sustained them and pronounced the death penalty. The decision was generally approved by Reformed leaders both inside and outside Switzerland.

Even then Calvin was no dictator, but he was the acknowledged leader of the Genevan church and was consulted on all kinds of questions—legal, economic, commercial, industrial, even on questions of sanitation (the sanitation of Geneva was universally admired). From all over the continent visitors came to him, the undisputed champion of the Reformation in Europe.

But now incessant work began to take its toll. In the early part of 1564 it became evident that his life was drawing to a close, and on February 6 he preached his last sermon. Yet to the end the habits of a lifetime asserted themselves and he was continually occupied. When his friends pleaded with him to rest, he said, "Would you that the Lord should find me idle when He comes?" He died on May 27, 1564, not quite fifty-five years old. Prior to his death he had forbidden the chief magistrates and ministers to erect a monument over his grave, and to this day the place where he was laid to rest is unknown.

It has been said that Calvin is to be credited with two achievements, a book and a city. The book was his *Institutes* and the city was Geneva. Let us consider these, or in other words Calvin's theology and his legislation.

First, then, his theology. The story is told of an eighteen-year-old freshman at Harvard (or was it Oxford?) who handed to one of his professors a bulky manuscript with this note appended: "This is the first volume of a series of books that I'm going to write. In this volume I have explained the universe." Explaining the universe in one volume, however large, is rather like trying to summarize the theology of Calvin in a few pages.

That theology is found in his *Institutes*. As we have already seen, the first edition was published at Basel in the spring of 1536. It contained six chapters: on the Ten Commandments; on faith and the Apostles' Creed; on prayer, with an exposition of the Lord's Prayer; on the two sacraments, baptism and the Lord's Supper; on the false sacraments of Rome; and, sixth, a chapter on Christian freedom, ecclesiastical power, and civil administration. The *Institutes* passed through many editions, always growing and expanding, so that in the definitive edition of 1559 there are no less than four books and eighty chapters.

What John Richard Green wrote of the English people might equally be said of Calvin, that he was a man of a book, and that book the Bible. To him the Bible was the one source of divine truth, the only rule of faith, the clear revelation of God's will, and its writers were the "sure and authentic amanuenses of the Holy Spirit." From beginning to end it is the pure Word of God and contains everything that we need in order to know God and our duty to Him.

The center and foundation of Calvin's theology is his doctrine of God. God is a personal Being, transcendent in power and holiness and of infinite goodness. Everything has been ordained by Him and His sovereign will rules the universe. This conviction is fundamental to Calvinism, the absolute and unquestionable sovereignty of Almighty God.

Over against God stands man who is altogether guilty and depraved, how utterly depraved we realize only when we place him against the background of God's perfect holiness. Calvin speaks of "that horror and amazement with which the Scripture always represents the saints to have been impressed and disturbed, on every discovery of the presence of God. . . . Man is never sufficiently affected with a knowledge of his own meanness, till he has compared himself with the Divine Majesty."[11] Man at the beginning, in the days of his innocency, might have won blessedness by his own power, but the Fall completely ruled it out even as a remote possibility. In the Fall of Adam all men fell: even infants at birth bring their own condemnation, for shut up in them they have the seed of evil, which is abominable to God.[12] Such is human nature now that everything man wills and does is sin. To make matters worse, man is spiritually helpless and can do nothing to save himself. He needs the Son of God to redeem him from his guilt and corruption; and so Christ came and took upon Him human flesh, fusing in His own person divine and human nature. By His Incarnation, by His life of perfect obedience, by His sufferings and death on the Cross, by His Resurrection and Ascension, Christ fulfilled all the requirements of a Redeemer and so merited for men the grace of salvation.[13] But even so, man cannot receive the benefits of Christ until he enters into union with Him, and this is effected by the working of the Holy Spirit through human faith, so that we die unto sin and live unto righteousness as new men in Christ. By this faith man is justified, his sins are all forgiven, the righteousness of Christ is imputed to him, and he is reinstated as a child of God. By faith, too, and by the working of the Holy Spirit man is not only justified but regenerated and sanctified, so that his whole life is turned to God.

Nevertheless not all men are thus saved, but only those who are God's elect. Here we encounter the idea of predestination, which to Calvin operated in two ways: there was the predestination of the elect and of the reprobate. "Predestination, by which God adopts some to the hope of life, and adjudges others to eternal death, no one, desirous of the credit of piety, dares absolutely to deny. . . . For they are not all created with a similar destiny; but eternal life is foreordained for some, and eternal damnation for others."[14] No doubt Calvin would like to have been more pitiful. He hated the thought of millions of heathen and their infants eternally damned. He spoke of it as the *decretum horribile*, the horrible decree, but he was unable to avoid it; inexorable logic drove him to the conclusion that if some are predestined to be the elect, it inevitably follows that all the others are predestined to be reprobate.

But if, as Calvin asserts, this is an unchallengeable conclusion, there is no room for free will. "We believe in predestination," reads a printed card to be found in many American ministers' offices, "but drive carefully, you may hit a Presbyterian." Such advice may be well meant, but it is somewhat misleading. For if a person, even a Presbyterian, is predestined to be hit, it is also predestined that someone is going to drive carelessly. God not only predestines the end but also the means; He predestines not only salvation but the means of salvation which is holiness; and He predestines not only that some should be reprobate but that they shall also choose to follow the evil path that leads to perdition. In the first (1536) edition of the *Institutes* Calvin had referred briefly to the doctrine of predestination, but in the second (1539) edition he dealt with it in a special chapter, in which (as contrasted with the first edition) he asserts that God was instrumental in causing the Fall and everything that men do. That God is the cause of all things is the direct testimony of the Bible, and the Bible is the authentic Word of God. To those who object that predestination is unjust, either of the elect but more especially of the reprobate, Calvin would have replied that no man deserves anything—"if thou, Lord, shouldest mark iniquities, O Lord, who shall stand?" (Psalm 130:3.) If we had our deserts, we should all perish; and if some are saved to eternal life, it is only through God's infinite mercy. But in any case, who is man that he should presume to judge God's acts, "man, that is a worm? and the son of man, which is a worm?" (Job 25:6.) Whatever we may think, everything that God does is right and just, simply because He does it.

Calvin's claim to rest his doctrine on the Bible is one that has often been challenged. Though many isolated texts may be quoted in favor of it, as many more may be adduced against it, and (surely a vital consideration) the general tone of the Bible and more especially of the Gospels seems to lend little support for predestination and none for the predestination of the damned. And yet whether or not we agree with Calvin on this doctrine, we can at least understand his standpoint, which was not peculiar to him but was common to all the Reformers. Both he and they desired to make it crystal clear that salvation was the work of God and of no other, and that it could not be attained by good works but only as a free gift from God. "Calvin gave it [predestination] an essential place in a system whose controlling principle was the majesty and might of God. As a result to reject or even to minimize it seemed to limit God and throw contempt upon Him."[15] The idea as promulgated by Calvin was in essence the same as Luther believed, as Melanchthon, Bucer, Zwingli, and all the Reformers. What Calvin did was to give it a definite place in his *Institutes,* which more and more became the textbook of Protestantism.

It has been said that whereas Lutheranism spared "everything that Scripture did not expressly forbid," Calvinism sacrificed "everything which Scripture did not directly sanction and justify."[16] In the Christian life the first keynote was austerity. Not only must sin be abhorred but even frivolity must be avoided. If "man's chief end is to glorify God, and to enjoy Him forever," he must not allow his concentration to be broken or his energies dissipated by lesser things, but must be ever engaged in the King's business. The second keynote was otherworldliness. If our citizenship is in heaven, we are only strangers and pilgrims on the earth. And if death but opens the door to life, the body is only the prison-house of the soul. As Calvin puts it, "But till we escape out of the world, 'we are absent from the Lord.' Therefore, if the terrestrial life be compared with the celestial, it should undoubtedly be despised and accounted of no value."[17] Frugality to the point of asceticism, self-denial for Christ's sake, are the true marks of the Christian believer.

But even the believer is not sufficient to himself, and in order that his faith may be nourished and sustained God has supplied such external aids as the church and its sacraments. The church is both visible and invisible. The invisible church is the multitude of the elect who acknowledge one common faith. But there is also a visible church whose function is to preach the Word and administer the sacraments. Wherever on earth God's Word is truly preached and the sacraments rightly administered, according to Christ's institution, *there* is a church. Generally speaking, Calvin would have maintained that outside the church there is no salvation. "I shall begin with the Church, in whose bosom it is God's will that all his children should be collected. . . For it is not lawful to 'put asunder' those things 'which God hath joined together' . . . that the Church is the mother of all who have him for their Father."[18]

Calvin defines a sacrament as "a testimony of the grace of God towards us, confirmed by an outward sign, with a reciprocal attestation of our piety towards him."[19] He recognized only two true sacraments, baptism and the Lord's Supper. Baptism was more than the sign of initiation by which men are received into the church and more than a public confession of faith. Linked up with the idea of regeneration, it had true sacramental value, being a means of grace to the person who received it. Regarding the Lord's Supper, Calvin came nearer to Luther than to Zwingli. To Calvin the Lord's Supper is a spiritual feast in which Christ is virtually present. "Now, that holy participation of his flesh and blood, by which Christ communicates his life to us, just as if he actually penetrated every part of our frame, in the sacred supper he also testifies and seals."[20] Communicants feed upon Him, partaking of His body and blood "not after a corporal and carnal manner, but by faith . . . to their spiritual nourishment and growth in grace." (Westminster Shorter Catechism, Question 96.)

Around Calvin's theology a storm of controversy has raged, and yet there was nothing in it fundamentally original. We have to remember that he was a Reformer of the second generation, and his greatest service was to define and systematize what had been already formulated. Some part of Calvin's theology has been discarded with the passing of the centuries, but down the years it has been a wonderful astringent in human life, fortifying men's wills and steeling their souls in all the lands to which it has spread, and not least in Scotland, among the English Puritans, and in the United States.

But even more important than Calvin's theology was his work as a legislator. We have already observed that he is to be credited with two achievements, a book and a city, theology and legislation. They were not separate but interdependent. Calvin's polity was a result of his theology, and each was a buttress for the other. One of his basic convictions was that both man and society must live a moral life, and in Geneva he strove to put this into effect. There can be no doubt that he achieved his aim. We have the testimony of no less a person than John Knox, who lived in Geneva for a time and had a close-up view of Calvinism at work; and this is what he says: "Elsewhere . . . the Word of God is taught as purely, but never anywhere have I seen God obeyed as faithfully." [21] Calvin found the city a cesspool of licentiousness and immorality; he made it a "Protestant Sparta" which attracted men from all over Europe who loved truth and hated a lie.

How did he achieve it? Almost as soon as he returned to Geneva in 1541, he began to draft a constitution for the church in what are known as his *Ecclesiastical Ordinances,* which may be divided into two parts, the Ministry and the Consistory.

First, then, the Ministry. The Reformed clergy were rather a mixed lot. What they required above everything else was discipline.[22] Accordingly, Calvin began by laying down three tests for ministerial candidates: they must undergo an examination conducted by men already in the ministry, they must be duly elected by the people, and they must be regularly introduced. But this was only a beginning, and ministerial efficiency must be maintained. Thus was formed the "venerable company" of ministers which met every week to study doctrine and also to inquire into the conduct of the brethren. High standards were aimed at and high standards were achieved.

Next, Calvin set on foot an educational program: there must be an educated ministry and educated citizens. Though a liberal education was provided, it was based on religion, and it is said that Calvin so trained the boys of Geneva in the faith that each was able to give reasons for it "like a doctor of the Sorbonne." In 1559 he founded the Academy or University, a famous school to which men flocked from all over Europe, even from Russia: its first leader was Theodore Béza. The Venetian Suriano described Geneva as "the mine whence came the ore of heresy." Among those who came to Geneva was John Knox, who on his return to Scotland took back many of its ideas of education and reform.

Of immense importance in Calvin's system was the appointment of church officials. These were of four kinds: teachers to expound the Scriptures; pastors to preach the Word, administer the sacraments, and admonish and exhort the flock; elders to assist the pastors in the government of the church and in the maintenance of discipline; and deacons to care for the poor. The emphasis laid on the eldership gave laymen for the first time the right to speak in church affairs and prevented any possibility of ecclesiastical tyranny. Since the church is a divinely instituted society, the very body of Christ, any dishonor to it is a dishonor to Christ. Accordingly, church discipline must be rigorously enforced and offenders punished: impenitent and flagrant sinners are to be excommunicated. The maintenance of discipline is entrusted to the church's officials, whom all must obey as they strive to keep the church pure and unsullied both in doctrine and in conduct.

The second part of the *Ordinances* deals with the Consistory. We have already seen that Calvin was resolved to make the church a moral church and to make men moral beings. To this end was appointed a Consistory of six ministers and twelve elders elected annually. Invested with the dread power of excommunication, their duty was to enforce purity and punish moral offenses. Scandals were ferreted out, and every Thursday the Consistory met to consider cases and pass sentence. By modern standards the punishments were often excessive. One woman was banished for singing profane songs, another was scourged for singing them to psalm tunes; church attendance was enforced; dancing, theater going, and card playing were prohibited; adultery was punishable by death. According to Professor Grimm, between the years 1542 and 1546 "seventy-six persons were banished from Geneva and fifty-eight executed for heresy, adultery, blasphemy, and witchcraft, which were capital crimes in most of Europe."[23]

If those measures seem harsh by present-day standards, they were not by any means unusual in sixteenth-century Europe where the choice was one between rigid discipline and chaos. Not only in Geneva but all over Europe the state interfered with the private life of its citizens in ways that would seem to us downright tyranny. What happened in Geneva could be paralleled by restrictions and municipal despotism in almost every European city. If Calvin was severe, he was no more so than other leaders of his time. The Reformation, moreover, was still in its infancy. Implacable enemies threatened it on every side. Stern measures were imperative, and as Froude has said, "Intolerance of an enemy who is trying to kill you seems to me a pardonable state of mind."[24] One of Calvin's mistakes was his insistence that the state should punish those whom the church branded as culprits; as for his other measures, they were perhaps inevitable.

Taken all in all, it cannot be gainsaid that Calvin rendered conspicuous service to Geneva and to the world as a whole both in his own age and for all time. To Geneva he gave an educated ministry and people and "an heroic soul which enabled the little town to stand forth as the Citadel and City of Refuge for the oppressed Protestants of Europe."[25] Six thousand of them, or nearly half of the city's population, victims of religious persecution in their own lands, found asylum at Geneva. Moreover, it ought to be noted that, while Lutheranism was for Germany only, Calvin was the Reformer of a large portion of Christendom. Mark Pattison was right when he said, "Calvinism saved Europe." Left to itself, Lutheranism might well have foundered: it required Calvinism to keep the Reformed ship afloat. And in the world as a whole we may also remember Calvin as the greatest religious force in modern times. More particularly in his *Institutes*, and to a lesser extent in his other works, he provided a theology that ever since his own time has deeply imbued the thought of all the Reformed churches. He developed a system of church government, and the *only* system, that enabled the church to organize itself and to survive in states that were bitterly antagonistic, notably in France but also in Holland and Scotland, in all of which Calvinism proved itself the best suited of the Reformed systems for a "church under the Cross." His educational program was the pattern as it was the inspiration of similar programs in other lands. But above all Calvinism produced men of indomitable courage, of strong, robust character, of inflexible will power and determination to carry out their purposes; men animated with passionate faith in their cause and in themselves, the faith of those called of God to be laborers together with Him. With this new confidence emerged a new freedom. It may be, as the late A. C. McGiffert wrote, that "not liberty, but bondage was dear to Calvin,"[26] but nevertheless the Calvinist system has inspired men with an unceasing urge to liberty and is generally found among the freedom-loving peoples. This also is part of the rich heritage that Calvin has bequeathed to mankind, a gift which, after the Gospel itself, is among those most highly treasured in this modern world.

THE REFORMATION IN FRANCE

✠

The Reformation in France occupies a unique place in the annals of the time. All over Europe in the sixteenth century the nations implicitly accepted as reasonable the principle laid down both by the first Diet of Speyer and in the Peace of Augsburg, *cuius regio eius religio,* the religion of the state is that of its ruler. It was the doctrine of *une foi, un roi, une loi,* one faith, one king, one law. This truth was held to be so self-evident that it was acted on in every country in Europe, whether Catholic or Protestant; it was the practice observed in the German states, in Catholic Italy and Spain, in Protestant Geneva, in England, Scotland, and the Netherlands. Only in France at the end of the day was there, so to speak, a state within a state where the Protestant minority, never many more than one and a quarter million out of a population of fifteen to twenty millions, extorted from their Catholic adversaries by force of arms the right to worship God according to the dictates of their conscience. Before this end was achieved there was a bitter and protracted struggle. Even prior to the actual fighting, the years of so-called peace were not without their persecutions and tribulations. Then followed a thirty years' period of almost incessant warfare till at last under Henry IV the Edict of Nantes in 1598 brought peace to an exhausted nation.

The impulse to reform sprang out of the Renaissance, and as in other European lands Humanism played its part. The greatest exponent of French Humanism was Guillaume Budé (1467-1540), the friend and librarian of King Francis I. His chief interest lay in studying and teaching the ancient classics. The first Christian Humanist was that remarkable man Jacques Lefèvre d'Étaples (1455-1536). To begin with, he was not a theologian but a teacher of mathematics and physics, and it was not until he had passed the age of fifty that he began to learn Greek and Hebrew. In these erudite studies he made such progress as to be able to write commentaries and to translate portions of the Old and New Testaments. In 1509 he published an edition of the Psalms, in 1512 a commentary on the Pauline Epistles, and in 1522 another on the Gospels. It is interesting to recall that these commentaries were used by Luther in his early days as a lecturer at Wittenberg. In June 1523 the indefatigable Lefèvre issued a new French translation of the four Gospels, and of the entire New Testament before the end of the year. By 1525 he had also translated portions of the Old Testament, notably the Psalms. In his commentaries he anticipated Luther in his insistence on the uselessness of good works apart from God's grace, and he also denied, if guardedly, the doctrine of transubstantiation. In these ways Lefèvre, though himself no Reformer but an Erasmian Catholic to the end, prepared the way for the introduction of Protestantism into France.

The mantle of Lefèvre fell upon his younger disciple, Guillaume Briçonnet (1470-1533), from 1516 Bishop of Meaux. Briçonnet may be regarded as the first French Reformer, not in the sense that he desired to break with Rome, but that he applied himself to the task of reforming the church from within. Zealous for religious revival, he brought to Meaux his former teacher Lefèvre, along with Gérard Roussel and William Farel who figured so prominently in the reforming movement in Switzerland. Of equal importance was Briçonnet's influence on Marguerite d'Angoulême (1492-1549).

Marguerite was the sister of Francis I and a most intriguing personality. Influenced by the New Learning, she fluently spoke Latin, Italian, and Spanish, as well as French, her mother tongue. Later she took up Greek and Hebrew, in order, as she said, to study the Bible in the original. She was the authoress of the notorious *Heptameron*, a collection of licentious tales told with the purpose of pointing a moral, surely a strange method of edifying. But her literary efforts were not confined to writing scurrilous tales, for she also kept up a correspondence with Calvin. She sheltered and protected Protestant refugees, and, though a

Catholic to the end, she was attracted by Protestant ideas and was at one with the Reformers in their insistence on justification by faith and not by works. Marguerite's second husband was King Albret of Navarre. Her only child was Jeanne d' Albret, a convinced and ardent Protestant and the mother of Henry of Navarre who was later to reign as Henry IV of France. It may well be that Marguerite's religious enthusiasm and liberal outlook influenced her daughter and grandson—and consequently the whole course of the Reformation in France—to a far greater extent than is commonly realized.

Meanwhile in the early 1520's the ideas of Luther and Zwingli were percolating into France. Officialdom was immediately up in arms, and as early as 1521 the Sorbonne prevailed on the Paris Parlement to issue a decree banning the Reformers' writings. But legislation cannot stay the march of ideas, and Luther's teaching in particular, spreading ever more widely in spite of official prohibitions, greatly influenced many Frenchmen.

During the Reformation struggle in France the throne was occupied by six rulers: Francis I (1515-47), Henry II (1547-59), Francis II (1559-60), Charles IX (1560-74), Henry III (1574-89), and Henry of Navarre who reigned as Henry IV (1589-1610). The first was Francis I, that superficial and vainglorious monarch who loved to strut and fret upon the stage of history. At the outset of his reign he prided himself on his up-to-date Renaissance outlook and liked to think of himself as an enlightened patron of the New Learning. Possibly his attitude was not entirely a pose, for he seemed to be genuinely interested in French Humanism, while in religious matters he inclined to toleration. With such a broad-minded ruler at its head, the nation might well look forward to a more liberal and spacious age.

But all was changed after Francis' ill-starred incursion into Italy and after his defeat and capture by the Emperor Charles V at the Battle of Pavia (1525). While the king was immured at Madrid, the Queen Mother, Louise of Savoy, took matters into her own hands. Anxious to propitiate the pope, she considered the death of a few Lutherans a cheap price to pay for the good offices of the pope in the release of her son. Accordingly, she initiated repressive measures against the Protestants, and through the agency of the Sorbonne (the theological faculty in the University of Paris) and of the parlements, especially that of Paris, a number of burnings took place. In the ensuing persecution Lefèvre and Roussel fled for safety to Strassburg. Francis was liberated in March 1526, and on his return to France immediately relaxed the severities of the previous months, recalled Lefèvre, and even appointed him tutor to one of his sons and his librarian at Blois.

But with Francis one could never be sure. He blew hot and he blew cold; he persecuted and then ceased to persecute. If in the joy of his homecoming he inclined to toleration in 1526, two years later an event occurred that turned him the other way. An image of the Virgin Mary was desecrated in Paris, and the enraged populace, having marched in solemn processions to avert the Virgin's disfavor, clamored for vengeance to be exacted. Francis, who had himself taken part in the religious ceremonies, at once decided upon sterner measures. Heresy was attacked and martyrs died. But soon for political reasons Francis called a halt to the persecutions, and once again the Protestants breathed freely.

More serious was the affair of the *placards* on October 18, 1534, when the ashes of persecution were again fanned into flame. On the morning of that eventful day pamphlets appeared on the streets of Paris and elsewhere denouncing transubstantiation and "the horrible abuses of the Papal Mass." It was idolatrous to suppose that Christ's corporeal presence could be in the wafer, "a man of twenty or thirty years in a morsel of paste." The pamphlets were couched in the most violent and abusive terms. "The Pope and all his vermin of cardinals, of bishops, of priests, of monks and other hypocrites, sayers of the Mass"—they were blasphemers all, and all liars! The crowning indignity was the affixing of a copy to the king's bedroom door at Amboise. Both he and the people, incensed at the effrontery, vowed vengeance on the Protestants. Before the end of the year eight persons were put to death and thirty-five in January of the next year; hundreds were arrested and incarcerated. But once again politics intervened to mitigate the severities of religion and by the Edict of Coucy (July 1535) the persecutions came to a temporary conclusion.

Presently, however, the fickle monarch was piping a different tune, and the first few years of the forties were indeed grim for the Protestants. The culminating point was reached in the Massacre of the Waldensians. In the fourteenth century a colony of Waldenses from Switzerland had been invited to settle in a depopulated district between Dauphiné and Provence. Peace-loving and industrious, the immigrants lived blameless lives and proved themselves useful members of the community. In 1532 they had drawn up a confession of faith after having received from the Reformers Bucer and Oecolampadius a number of answers to questions they themselves had raised. They also contributed five hundred crowns to help finance a new French translation of the Bible. For those "crimes" they were compelled to pay a fearful price. They were persecuted first by the Inquisitor of Provence, Jean de Roma, and then by the Archbishop (1535). The helpless people appealed to the king, who gave them his support for the next ten years; but in 1545 they were falsely accused of rebellious intent, and Francis, deceived by a report that he took no trouble to verify, ordered the "guilty" Waldensians to be put to death. Soon the countryside became a shambles. Twenty-two out of thirty villages were burned to the ground and over three thousand innocent persons—men, women, and children—were put to the sword. This wholesale massacre ranks among the most wanton and frightful atrocities of history.

In the following year Francis perpetrated a second horrible crime, the death of the "Fourteen" at Meaux. After severe torture the Fourteen were burned alive and many others were cruelly treated. And the reason? They had celebrated the Lord's Supper in the Reformed way.

Francis I died on March 31, 1547, and it may be well to pause at this point and take stock of the strength of the new religion. We have seen that the first influence was Lutheranism, but with the emergence of Calvinism it swiftly receded, and certainly from the death of Francis I Calvinism was the dominant force in the French Reformation. After all, Luther was a foreigner, whereas Calvin was a Frenchman, one of themselves. But there were other reasons. The publication of Calvin's *Institutes* in 1536 provided a clear-cut, systematic theology to take the place of the inchoate teaching of Lefèvre and the mystical piety of Briçonnet. The *Institutes* were later translated into admirable French, like all Calvin's works. Calvinism, moreover, with its combination of cold logic and burning passion, immediately appealed to the logical and ardent French people. "It satisfied at one and the same time the intellects which demanded logical proof and the souls which had need of enthusiasm."[1] Then again, while Lutheranism was largely dependent on the support of the state, Calvinism had the power of self-government, a vital factor to a minority fighting for its very existence. Calvin's influence was further deepened by the unceasing flow of correspondence he maintained with his co-religionists in France, thus sustaining their courage and fortifying their faith in the dark days and forging a bond between them and their fellow believers in Geneva across the Swiss frontier. Long before the death of Francis, books had poured into France from Geneva, and Calvinists came to preach their master's doctrines. Gradually small groups were formed all over France and met in secret for Bible study and for worship in accordance with Reformed principles. Later these groups formed themselves into churches, adopting the model of Geneva.

When Francis I died in 1547, Protestantism was firmly rooted in French soil. The persecutions of his reign, though vigorous, were intermittent; and the Protestants were afforded sufficient respite to consolidate, to organize, and to spread. The persecutions only drove them underground, ready to emerge whenever a favorable opportunity presented itself. The work continued uninterrupted: secret meetings were held, doctrines disseminated from house to house, and treatises circulated by pedlars over the countryside. With the one exception of Brittany, Protestantism was entrenched in every district of France and was specially strong in the towns, along the great waterways and rivers, in those areas that lay at a distance from Paris or were accessible to foreign influence; and strongest of all in Dauphiné, northern Provence, and along the foothills of the Cevennes and the Pyrenees. Indeed, in Dauphiné and eastern Languedoc the Protestants were actually in the majority. It was their unequal *distribution* that strengthened them, for otherwise, with their comparatively small numbers, they could never have been a real threat to the Catholic majority.

Regarding the personnel of the rival parties, it may be said that generally speaking the two extremes of French society continued loyal to the Catholic Church, at one end of the scale the peasants and the great city masses, at the other the higher nobility; to these may be added government officials. The Catholic leaders were the Guises, of whom more will be said later. The Protestants, who about 1552 were given the name "Huguenots"[2]—and by this name we shall henceforth refer to them—were for the most part townsmen drawn largely from the commercial and lower professional classes. In their ranks were numbered a few of the nobility. The Queen of Navarre, Jeanne d' Albret, mother of Henry IV of France, was a valuable acquisition to the Huguenot cause. Her husband, Prince Anthony of Bourbon and King of Navarre, became a Protestant in 1548 but relapsed in 1560 into the Roman fold. His brother, the Prince of Condé, joined the Huguenots; but by far the most illustrious name was that of Gaspard de Coligny (1519-72), admiral of France, nephew of the Constable de Montmorency, and the most sincere of all the Huguenot leaders.

Meantime Henry II had ascended the French throne, and from the beginning was determined to jettison all half measures for the suppression of Protestantism. The method he chose was legislation, which may on rare occasions succeed but is far more likely to fail, as it failed eventually in this instance. Henry came to the throne on the last day of March 1547, and by October 8 of the same year had set up his infamous *Chambre Ardente* to deal with heretics, "the burning chamber," which fully lived up to its macabre name. Between December 1547 and January 1551 nearly five hundred persons were tried, and many lost their lives. So intolerant was this royal bigot that he would have established the Inquisition had not the Paris Parlement refused its consent. But opposition only made him more determined, and in 1551 was issued the savage Edict of Châteaubriand which decreed that heresy must be extirpated by every means at the disposal of the state. Protestant writings were forbidden entry into France, books banned by the Sorbonne were prohibited, heretics were to be excluded from teaching and from state posts and were to be relentlessly hunted down. Informers were promised as reward one-third of their victim's property. We might almost imagine that we were reading one of the more lurid pages of the history of the early Roman Empire, when the informer *(delator)* played so conspicuous a part and was awarded a similar prize.

But Henry in his last years defeated his own ends. By the Edict of Compiègne (1557) heresy cases were remitted to the civil courts where no punishment could be imposed less than death. But sympathy for the persecuted victims was gradually engendered. When the king visited the Parlement of Paris in 1559, one of the judges to try heretics, du Bourg, said to him that "it was a most serious matter to condemn those who, from the midst of the flames, called upon the name of Jesus Christ." Du Bourg paid dearly for his boldness, for he was immediately arrested and executed. But there were other magistrates who tried to protect the Protestants: many heretics were allowed to slip through the fingers of the law, and many sentences were passed but not executed. Nevertheless, the death of Henry on July 10, 1559, following a wound sustained in a tournament, was a fortunate break for the Protestants.

And yet, in spite of twelve years of bitter suffering, Calvinism during Henry's reign had steadily marched forward. Many converts were made, and in its organization, too, the church had made notable progress. The first outstanding date is 1555, when it may be said that the churches were really organized. Before this time the Protestant congregations had been more or less small, disunited companies of believers. In 1555 the first French Calvinist church was opened in Paris, modeled on the church at Strassburg which Calvin had founded in 1538, and having the three offices of minister, elder, and deacon. Thirteen similar churches were organized between 1555 and 1557, and thirty-six by 1560: it is estimated that prior to 1567 about one hundred and twenty ministers were sent from Geneva to France. The second notable date is May 25, 1559, when the first National Synod of the French Protestant Church met at Paris. Seventy-two churches are said to have been represented, and the delegates proceeded to draw up a confession of faith, the *Confessio Gallicana,* based on a similar one compiled by Calvin in 1538 and still for the most part accepted as the Confession of the French Protestant Church. The assembly also produced a scheme of church government or "discipline" which placed congregations under the rule of a consistory composed of minister, elders, and deacons. Groups of congregations met in colloquy; superior to the colloquies were the provincial synods; and highest of all was the General or National Synod. Thus was the French church brought into line with Calvinist churches in other lands.

Of the sons of Henry II and his queen, Catherine de' Medici, it has been said that "the eldest, Francis II, was an invalid; the second, Charles IX, a nervous wreck, if not a madman; the third, Henry III, a degenerate."[3] We begin with the "invalid" Francis II who ascended the throne in 1559. His short reign of seventeen months, however uneventful in other respects, was momentous for religion and the Huguenots. The new monarch was only fifteen at his accession but he was already married to the sixteen-year-old Mary Queen of Scots, that strong-minded young woman who was to prove her mettle—and her bigotry—when in the early summer of 1561 she returned to her own kingdom of Scotland. Right from the beginning of Francis' reign the Catholics assumed control. Though his mother Catherine de' Medici was nominally regent, the chief power devolved on the semiroyal family of the Guises. Duke Claude when he died in 1550 was survived by three sons, all men of eminence: Charles, who was Archbishop of Rheims and later Cardinal of Lorraine, one of the most forceful personalities in the Roman Church; Louis, who was also a cardinal; and the new Duke Francis who was commander of the armed forces and an able military leader with the laurels of Calais (captured 1558) not yet withered on his brow. The sister of those brothers, Mary of Lorraine, had married James V of Scotland in 1538 and was the mother of Mary Queen of Scots who became the wife of Francis II when he was dauphin and now sat at his side as Queen of France. Having, then, the support of the church and the backing of the armed forces, and with a niece occupying the throne, the Guises rapidly rose to power. According to the Florentine ambassador, "the Cardinal is Pope and King." From the first he made no attempt to disguise his aims. He had been the prime mover in the persecutions of Henry II's reign, and he was determined that in the present reign the severe measures would be intensified.

But now the temper of the Protestants had undergone a profound change. Into their aspirations had crept a political element. Before this time they had endured in silence, but now they had hardened their hearts and were ready to take up arms in defense of their faith. This belligerent spirit was deplored by Calvin, who was opposed to the use of force and frankly said, "If one drop of blood is shed in such a revolt, rivers will flow; it is better that we all perish than cause such a scandal to the cause of Christ and His evangel." Was Calvin mistaken? Or could the Protestants by the sole use of Christian weapons have survived and won the day? If we substitute Christianity for Protestantism and Communism for Catholicism, it is evident that our own age is posed with a not dissimilar question and men are still perplexed about the proper answer.

Calvin was not the only person to urge conciliation: it was eagerly sponsored by the Queen Mother Catherine. She saw how the parties had aligned themselves into two hostile camps, both demanding complete victory for their creed and both willing, if need be, to resort to arms. Catherine, realizing that peace was essential to her own self interests, strove hard to effect a reconciliation, calling to her aid the wise, humane Michel de l'Hôpital, whom she appointed chancellor. Unluckily Catherine's policy was compromised by the so-called "Tumult of Amboise," a senseless attempt by Huguenot hotheads to seize the king and the Guises and so control the government. The plot was disclosed and the guilty punished, but, surprisingly, by the ensuing Edict of Amboise (March 1560) it was declared that religious persecution should cease, though preaching was still forbidden.

In August an assembly of Notables (prominent men in church and state) was held at Fontainebleau to search out means of finding religious peace. It was decided that a meeting of the Estates-General be called at Orleans, whither the King of Navarre and his brother, the Prince of Condé, were summoned. The latter was arrested by the Guises and condemned to die on December 10, but this fate was providentially averted by the timely death of Francis II on December 5.

Francis was succeeded by his brother Charles IX, then a boy of ten and so a minor. The Guises fell from power and the regent, the Queen Mother Catherine de' Medici, grasped the reins of government. Catherine is one of history's most enigmatical personalities. Was she a monster or a woman full of the milk of human kindness—the ogress who planned the Massacre of St. Bartholomew's Day or the devoted mother who passionately loved her children? Her chancellor, l'Hôpital, said there was no gentler woman in all the world (*Femina . . . qua non mitior ulla est omnibus in terris*). In these opposite directions the pendulum of opinion has swung. Born in 1519, and so forty-one when she came to power in 1560, she was the daughter of an Italian banker to whom Machiavelli dedicated his *Prince,* and the niece of Pope Clement VII. In 1534 she married the future Henry II who shamefully neglected her. Catherine was a born diplomatist and an adept at playing off one party against the other. Said an English traveler of the time, "She had too much wit for a woman, and too little honesty for a Queen." With a craving for power and no fixed principles, she followed compromise as her policy and expediency as her guide. By inclination and necessity she took the side of Rome (like the majority of her subjects), but she was no fanatic.

In order to savor the sweetness of power she required peace, and this she hoped to gain by tolerating but not encouraging Protestantism.

In pursuance of this policy a meeting of the Estates-General was held at Orleans at the end of 1560. Of the three houses, the clergy not unnaturally advocated vigorous action against the Huguenots, the nobles were somewhat divided in opinion; but the commons urged that persecution should stop, "since it is unreasonable to compel men to do what in their hearts they consider wrong." As a consequence, on January 28, 1561, a royal edict was issued prohibiting further persecution and demanding the release of all religious prisoners.

Catherine's next step was to summon a conference or colloquy at Poissy on September 9. There the famous Reformer, Theodore Béza, was invited to state the Protestant case, while the Catholic speakers were first the Cardinal of Lorraine and then Lainez, the general of the Jesuit Order. The Chancellor l'Hôpital presided. Whatever hopes of reconciliation the regent may have cherished were wrecked by the intemperate and abusive language of Lainez, who referred to the Protestant ministers as "wolves," "foxes," "serpents," and "assassins." The general atmosphere was hardly one to stimulate good will; yet in the issue toleration was granted to the Protestants in theory if not in practice, and the way was prepared for the edict of January 1562. Sponsored by Catherine, it was a genuine attempt to reach religious toleration. The Huguenots were permitted the right of private worship everywhere and of public worship anywhere outside walled towns, and were also allowed the management of their religious affairs subject to a measure of supervision. For the first time Protestantism was legally recognized.

"A man may be a citizen without being a Christian," said l'Hôpital at the January conference. But the Guises would not have it so. They insisted that all citizens must be Christians and all Christians Catholics; to them toleration was a word without meaning. It is one of the ironies of history that Catherine's January Edict of Toleration was virtually the cause of the bitter wars that followed and continued intermittently for more than thirty years. The immediate cause was the Massacre of Vassy carried out by the orders of the Duke of Guise on Sunday, March 1, 1562. The Duke and his brother the cardinal had stopped at a church to hear Mass. In a nearby barn a Huguenot service was being held—where it had no right to be held, since Vassy was a walled town. The Duke ordered the Protestants to leave off, only to be greeted with loud insults and a shower of stones, one of which actually struck him. Immediately he commanded his armed retinue to open fire, and as a consequence sixty-three out of some six or seven hundred Huguenots were killed and more than a hundred wounded. Elsewhere other massacres took place. The Huguenots retaliated by tearing down images, destroying relics, and defacing altars. Catherine's policy of conciliation had broken down: all must now depend on the dread arbitrament of war.

The ensuing wars, though for the most part inconclusive, were so grievous as to bring France to the brink of ruin. The Huguenots, always inferior in numbers, had the advantage of an efficient secret service and of excellent commanders, the Prince of Condé, Admiral Coligny, and at a later date Henry of Navarre. Both sides shamelessly put party before country and invoked foreign help, the Catholics appealing to Philip II of Spain and the Protestants to Elizabeth of England.

The wars broke out in 1562, the very year in which the Counter Reformation was launched in Europe. A series of three wars was fought between 1562 and 1570, in the first of which Condé was defeated by Montmorency at the Battle of Dreux where both commanders were taken prisoner but later released. The Duke of Guise now became the acknowledged leader of the royal forces, Coligny of the Huguenots. In February 1563 the Catholics suffered a setback when Guise was shot in the back by Jean Poltrot de Méré. With or without sufficient reason the Guises charged Coligny of complicity in the crime, and Henry, the murdered duke's son, brooding on his wrongs, avenged himself at last by instigating Coligny's death on the eve of St. Bartholomew's Day, 1572. Meantime, the Peace of Amboise (1563) which concluded the first war permitted the great nobles to hold religious services in their homes for all who cared to attend; the lesser nobles were allowed to hold private services for their own families only; Huguenot worship was sanctioned in the suburbs of one town in each administrative district; persecution for religious opinions was halted. It would seem that the Huguenots had won considerable gains, but the peace conditions were ignored by both sides.

The second war was precipitated by what is known as the "Enterprise of Meaux" on September 26, 1567, when an abortive attempt was made by Condé to seize the person of the young king. It was during this war that La Rochelle came over to the Huguenots, a most valuable acquisition because of its excellent harbor and proximity to England. After some desultory fighting peace was concluded at Longjumeau (1568) where the terms of the Peace of Amboise were confirmed.

The third war, practically a continuation of the second, was a much more serious affair. At its outbreak l'Hôpital was deprived of office and banished from the court, but to counterbalance the loss of his moderating influence the Huguenots gained new allies in the Queen of Navarre and her son Henry. A further loss, however, was sustained by the death of Condé following the Battle of Jarnac (March 1569). There, with typical French dash and a force of four hundred horsemen, he recklessly charged against the whole Catholic army. After a determined stand he was compelled to surrender; and though his safety was promised, he was treacherously shot through the head by a Catholic officer, one Montesquiou. The Huguenots now looked to Coligny as their leader; but able commander though he was, he made an inauspicious beginning and was heavily defeated (largely because of the indiscipline of his troops) at the Battle of Moncontour, where the Huguenot casualties amounted to nearly ten thousand. But by an amazing march he succeeded in leading his army to the Huguenot strongholds of Gascony and Languedoc, and was even able to negotiate with Catherine the Peace of St. Germain (August 1570), by the terms of which freedom of worship was given to the

Huguenots in *two* towns of each administrative district and Protestantism was permitted to remain in those parts where it had been practiced. In addition the Huguenots were allowed to control four fortified towns as a guarantee that the treaty would be observed, the towns being La Rochelle, Montauban, Cognac, and La Charité—all of them from a military standpoint of the highest importance.

Thus far the Huguenots had held their own, but now the shadow of impending tragedy fell upon the scene. Events marched inexorably to their awful climax, the Massacre of St. Bartholomew's Day (August 24, 1572). The motive was there and soon the opportunity presented itself. The Regent Catherine felt herself beset with difficulties. Her son Charles had begun to take an active interest in politics, and to Catherine's chagrin was relying more and more on the guidance of Coligny. But Coligny, anxious to relieve the tension of the civil wars and to gain new allies for his co-religionists, was now advocating a national war against Spain in the Netherlands. Such a policy was abhorrent to Catherine. She resented Coligny's growing influence with her son, but even more she dreaded a war with Spain, the strongest military power in Europe. The safety of France, possibly even its very existence as a sovereign nation, was at stake and swift emergency action was imperative. Coligny must be liquidated and to attain this end Catherine resolved to join forces with the Guises.

Meantime, Paris was full of Protestants who had come to the capital for the wedding of Henry of Navarre to Charles' sister, Margaret of Valois. Henry himself had arrived at court with his mother's parting words still ringing in his ears "to speak up, to brush his hair from his forehead, and to hold fast to his faith." The marriage took place on August 18, 1572, and all Paris joined in the celebrations.

Four days later, with the connivance of Catherine, the Guises procured the services of an assassin to murder Coligny. As he was returning to his lodging he was shot at from a nearby window, but though wounded in the hand and arm he was able to make a dash for safety and to escape with his life. The attempted murder at once caused feelings on both sides to run high. The Huguenots then thronging Paris would naturally demand an inquiry into the affair. If Catherine's complicity was disclosed, her fall from power (to say the least) was certain. And so, as was commonly believed, in order to distract unwelcome attention from herself she planned a greater atrocity. The king's consent was gained following the false report of a Huguenot plot against him; the stage was set; and Catholic Paris waited expectantly for a government signal to commence the massacre.

That signal was dramatically given at midnight of the 23rd. By the instruction of Henry of Guise the wounded Coligny was murdered in cold blood and his body tossed through his bedroom window into the street, a second Hector for all to mutilate and outrage. Henry of Navarre and the young Prince of Condé were spared on renouncing their Protestant faith, but for three days all over the city the Huguenots were tracked down and slain, and similar massacres were carried out in many other French towns. As regards the number slain it is impossible to hazard even an approximate estimate. No exact records were kept, and especially in an atrocity of this kind contemporaries are notoriously prone to exaggerate. Ten thousand are said to have died in Paris alone, and, according to Sully, seventy thousand in the country as a whole. If we divide these figures by four or five, we shall probably be nearer the truth. Protestant Europe was stunned by news of the massacre but the Catholics were everywhere jubilant. Pope Gregory XIII had a medal struck and decreed an annual *Te Deum* to commemorate the occasion; he attended a special service of thanksgiving, and Rome was illuminated for three successive nights. The Spanish envoy wrote to his master, "not a child has been spared. Blessed be God." And Philip himself when he heard the news laughed for almost the only time in his life. The comment of the Duke of Alva was more restrained: "France has lost a great captain," he said, "and Spain a great foe."

As a direct result of the massacre a fourth war had broken out. La Rochelle was invested, but the Huguenot garrison held out and peace was restored in June 1573 by the Treaty of La Rochelle.

The higher nobility were permitted the privilege of private worship in their own homes, liberty of conscience if not of worship was accorded to all others, and *three* towns in each administrative district had now the right of Protestant worship.

Between the fourth and fifth wars there was a change of sovereign. Charles IX died in 1574, a prey (it is said) to remorse for his part in sanctioning the Massacre of St. Bartholomew's Day. He was succeeded by his brother Henry III, a degenerate prince who wore a pearl necklace and earrings and who, according to Sully, used to carry round with him "a basket full of little dogs hung to a broad riband about his neck." The fifth war broke out almost immediately, but now it was war with a difference. For the first decade of the wars the Huguenots had aimed at making Calvinism the religion of France, but the situation had now changed and their aspirations were more modest: now they fought not so much for victory as for survival. At the same time, their cause was strengthened by the emergence of a new party, the *politiques,* composed of both Catholics and Huguenots, who put country before party, who desired above all things the welfare of France and the restoration of its unity, and who to achieve this end were ready to grant complete freedom of faith and worship. In a real sense Catherine de' Medici was a *politique;* but the greatest of them all was l'Hôpital, who as early as December 1560 had expressed the enlightened view to a meeting of the Estates-General at Orleans, "A man does not cease to be a citizen for being excommunicated. . . . Let us get rid of these devilish words, these names of party, of faction, of sedition—Lutheran, Huguenot, Papist—let us keep unadulterated the name of Christian." The *politiques* saw the dreadful pass to which France was drifting and the ruination caused by the religious wars. After the Massacre of St. Bartholomew's especially they lent their support to the Huguenots and in May 1575, led by the Duke of Alençon, came over to the side of the Protestants. Their influence is probably reflected in the Peace of Monsieur (May 1576) which terminated the fifth war. It was one of the most liberal documents of the age and certainly more liberal than the Edict of Nantes which eventually brought peace to the warring parties. It allowed by-gones to be bygones: it declared Catholicism to be the official religion of France but permitted complete freedom everywhere (except in Paris and at the court) to the Huguenots whatever their rank or station in life. To guarantee the observance of the treaty special law courts were to be set up in which both Catholics and Huguenots would have representation, and in addition eight fortified cities were to be held by the Huguenots.

But the age was not yet ripe for such broad-minded measures, and one of the results of the Peace was the formation of a Catholic League under the leadership of Henry of Guise. At a meeting of the Estates-General at Blois in December it was re-solved that Catholicism should be the only religion in France. The Assembly also requested Henry of Navarre to return to the Catholic fold. (Ten months earlier, in February 1576, Henry had escaped from Paris and renounced the Catholicism he had pro-fessed to save his life at the time of the Massacre.) Henry de-clined to abjure his Protestant faith, and shortly afterwards desultory fighting broke out—the sixth war—which ended with the Peace of Bergerac (September 17, 1577). Its terms were less favorable to the Huguenots than those of Monsieur, but it pro-vided the basis of an uneasy peace that endured for the next seven years. The seventh war, of 1580, hardly deserves the name of war. Fighting was ended by the Peace of Felix (November 1580), the terms of which were similar to those of Bergerac.

We come now to the years 1585-88, the period occupied by the eighth war. The year before the outbreak was crucial. In 1584 had occurred the death of the Duke of Anjou, the only surviving brother of the childless Henry III. The next heir to the throne was the king's cousin, Henry of Navarre, but he was a heretic (in fact since the assassination of William of Orange in July 1584 the leading champion of Protestantism in Europe), and so according to the Catholics ineligible. "Better a Republic," they said, "than a Huguenot king." Henry VIII of England might impose his religion on his people, but in France they did things differently: there the Catholics were determined to impose *their* religion on the king. Suddenly the Catholic League became active. Under the supervision of the Duke of Mayence, Henry Guise's younger brother, the notorious "Council of Sixteen," representing the sixteen districts of the city, was set up to govern Paris. Its methods were arbitrary and its rule tyrannical. In July 1585 Henry III was forced to capitulate to the League and by the Treaty of Nemours to depart from the policy of toleration. Also in 1585 Pope Sixtus V excommunicated Navarre and Condé and forbade their succession to the throne. This was the setting at the outbreak of the eighth war, commonly known as the War of the Three Henries—the three being Henry III, Henry of Guise, and Henry of Navarre.

Henry of Navarre rapidly proved himself a most capable military leader, and on October 20, 1587, routed the Duke of Joyeuse at the Battle of Coutras, the first Huguenot victory in the field since the outbreak of hostilities in 1562. In contrast to his cousin Navarre, the king played a most inglorious part. Still smarting under the indignity of his surrender to the Guises, he returned to Paris in December 1587, and in self-protection established in the suburbs a force of four thousand Swiss guards: he also forbade entry to the Duke of Guise. In defiance of the king the duke entered Paris on May 9, 1588, and on the eleventh the Swiss guards were ordered into the city. On the following day, however, the "day of the Barricades," the citizens erected barriers across the streets, isolated the guards, and virtually made the king a prisoner in his own capital. The Duke of Guise proposed terms that were quite unacceptable and Henry's only recourse was to flee from the city (May 13). But on July 11 he was again obliged to defer to Guise's wishes—the suppression of heresy, the nomination of Guise as Lieutenant-General of France, and the calling of the Estates-General, which met at Blois on October 16 and sat for two months. The remaining part of the story reads like the denouement of a Greek tragedy. Sullen with resentment, Henry III vowed vengeance on the Guises, and on December 23, after inviting the duke to his room, had him murdered by assassins lurking in the antechamber. Next day by the king's orders the duke's cardinal brother was also murdered. A third death, from natural causes, occurred on January 5, 1589, when the king's mother Catherine de' Medici breathed her last.

As a result of his crimes Henry III was denounced by Paris and the Sorbonne, and almost all the towns sided with the League against him. Thus isolated, he was compelled to seek sanctuary with Henry of Navarre and the two cousins joined forces outside Tours (April 30, 1589). Together they marched on Paris and invested the city (July 29), but on August 1 a fanatic friar insinuated himself into the camp and stabbed the king, who died the following day.

Thus did Navarre become King of France as Henry IV.[4] He was one of the most colorful figures of the age, a great lover, a great soldier, and a great statesman. Sully tells us "his hair is a little red, yet the ladies think him not less agreeable on that account." He was the type of hero who appealed to the popular imagination—gallant, courageous, and humane, but prudent as well as bold; and for all his glamorous reputation as a prince of romance he had a firm grasp of practical affairs. His mother, Jeanne d' Albret, was a staunch Calvinist with a lively sense of humor, but somewhat haphazard as a parent. It is said that her first two children died because of her carelessness, and Henry might well have shared their fate but for the timely intervention of a determined grandfather, who later taught him Latin and tennis. As a youth of twelve he had a Jesuit tutor, but he adhered to Protestantism, though never a convinced Calvinist, and refused to hear Mass at his wedding. His first marriage with Margaret of Valois was both unhappy and childless. His second wife, Mary de' Medici, presented him with the future Louis XIII. Henry always expressed his interest in the common man and his sympathy with the poor, and looked forward, as he said, to the time "when every peasant would have a chicken in his stew-pot." He was a *politique* in the sense that he considered his first duty to be not so much to any one religious sect as to France. He would have abolished all religious distinctions: he wanted as his subjects not Catholics or Huguenots, but Frenchmen.

Henry, then, was king of France, but he was still obliged to fight for his throne in what may be alternatively regarded as a ninth war or merely as a prolongation of the eighth. It is unnecessary to describe his exploits in detail. He won great battles— at Arques on September 21, 1589, and at Ivry on March 4, 1590— he invested Paris and almost forced its surrender when it was relieved by the arrival of Parma and his army of Spaniards from the Netherlands. Convinced at last that victories alone would not win the throne, Henry bowed to the inevitable. On May 18, 1593, he intimated to the Catholic archbishops his willingness to be "instructed" and on July 25 he was received into the Roman Church. The ceremony took place a dozen miles from Paris at the Church of St. Denis where generations of French kings lay buried and where Joan of Arc had hung up her arms. Paris, he is said to have declared, was well worth a Mass. Henry was crowned at Chartres on February 27, 1594, entered Paris on March 22, was officially recognized as lawful king, and the following year was released by Pope Clement VIII from his excommunication.

Henry's problem was how to remain friendly with the Catholics and at the same time to satisfy the Huguenots. During the next few years negotiations were carried on between the two parties till at last, on April 13, 1598, was signed the Edict of Nantes which officially terminated the religious wars. This document of ninety-two articles and fifty-six additional articles was, as already observed, less liberal than the Peace of Monsieur which ended the fifth war in 1576. By it Catholicism was acknowledged to be the official religion of France and to "be restored and reestablished" in all places "in which its exercise had been interrupted," but a number of concessions were made to the million and a quarter Huguenots. They were permitted freedom of conscience and of private worship, and accorded the right of holding religious services in the houses of the nobles, in all places where the Reformed religion "had been established and publicly observed" in 1596 and 1597, and also in two towns in each administrative district. The practice of this religion was

expressly forbidden at court, in Paris, and within five leagues of
the city. The Huguenots were to be represented on courts of
justice, were free to occupy any office or position in the realm,
and were not to be excluded "for education in universities, col-
leges and schools, nor in the reception of the sick and needy into
hospitals, almshouses or public charities." They were allowed
the right of holding assemblies, both religious and political, after
receiving the king's permission. As a guarantee for the proper
observance of the edict the Huguenots gained control of two
hundred fortified towns, "places of surety," which included such
important centers as La Rochelle, Montaubon, and Montpellier.
Finally, the edict was to be "perpetual and irrevocable."

The Edict of Nantes has been described as "the Charter of
French Protestantism,"[5] but the description is more rhetorical
than real. For one thing it contained no original ideas but
merely echoed the terms of previous edicts. Again, in its aims it
was as much political as religious, being designed to avoid
"trouble or tumult" and to restore the "State to its original
splendour." Though it terminated the protracted series of wars,
it was a compromise rather than a final settlement, an armistice
rather than a lasting peace. While granting a large measure of
tolerance, it withheld complete religious freedom and failed to
satisfy the zealots of both parties. As long as Henry lived, its terms
were rigorously enforced, but when in 1610 his strong arm was
removed, the instability of the peace gradually became more apparent. The Catholics especially were determined to withdraw
its concessions, as in fact they were withdrawn in 1685 by Louis
XIV when he felt strong enough, if need arose, to subdue rebellion by force.

Nevertheless, by ending the fighting and ensuring safety for a
minority, the Edict of Nantes gave France a much-needed respite
and saved her from those disastrous wars of religion that ravaged
Europe in the seventeenth century. While other nations were
squandering their resources, France was able to lay the foundations of that future greatness which burst into flower in the
spacious days of Louis XIV. These were not small results and in

their achievement the Huguenots played a not unworthy part. Out of all proportion to their number they contributed to the steady development of French commerce and industry, while on the political side they cemented the alliances between Louis XIV and the Protestant states, thus enabling France to gain primacy in the chancellories of Europe. In the history of religion, too, the Edict of Nantes was an important milestone. It enunciated the principle that more than one form of religion could exist in the same nation and admitted the possibility of a "free church in a free state." After the revocation of the Edict in 1685 Protestantism became illegal and "heretics" were visited with the most rigorous penalties. Many Huguenots were compelled to recant, while others—some 300,000—fled to nearby Switzerland and Holland, to England, and to America, there to seek asylum. If the revocation was a catastrophe to France, it was an immense boon to those countries in which the refugees made their new homes and in which they proved themselves more than useful citizens. Thus in the last resort the Huguenots not only contributed to the greatness of France but to the development of Protestantism both in Europe and in America.

6

THE REVOLT
IN THE NETHERLANDS

✝

Human nature is so constituted that the sympathies of the average man go out to the underdog. Strength may be respected, but weakness has an appeal all its own. One of the stories that have enthralled generation after generation and captured the imagination of men is that of David and Goliath, of the immature youth who defied the Philistine giant so strong and mighty in his clanking armor. Not dissimilar, to outward appearances at least, was the epic struggle between the Netherlands and Spain in the sixteenth century.

The triumph of Protestantism in the Netherlands is a supreme illustration of the unlikely instruments God uses to further His eternal purposes. The struggle was dominated by the two great antagonists, Philip II of Spain and William the Silent. At first sight it would seem that there could be only one outcome, for Philip held in his hands every apparent advantage. Not only was he the absolute ruler of Spain, the foremost power in Europe, but he also wielded authority over widespread domains—in the kingdoms of Naples and Sicily, in the Duchy of Milan, in the Rhine valley, in the Netherlands, and in Central and South America. In addition, under his command was the finest army in the world led by a succession of illustrious captains: by the able (if ruthless) Alva, by Don John of Austria, and by the even more brilliant Parma. Against this powerful combination William was the leader of a small country divided into seventeen autonomous provinces, ten of which detached themselves from his rule before the end. He was himself a second-rate military leader and was never able to win a battle in the field. His troops were badly trained, his resources scanty. From the common-sense point of view the struggle was hopeless from the beginning. But William and his compatriots brought to it an ardent love of freedom and presently a burning religious faith, spiritual assets both of them that ultimately triumphed over all material advantages.

And yet the patriots were not without other strong assets. All their lives they had waged a ceaseless struggle against powerful natural enemies and chiefly against the ocean to prevent its salt water from inundating their land. As a consequence there grew up a hardy, robust breed of men with the love of freedom pulsating in their hearts. Then their proximity to the ocean caused them to be sea minded and to realize the vast importance of sea power, which in the end proved to be a decisive factor in the revolt against Spain. Again, situated at the mouth of the Rhine, one of the great waterways of Europe, the Netherlands were strategically placed for the expansion of trade and commerce, a natural asset of which the Dutch took full advantage. Industrious and enterprising, they had become the richest and most progressive nation in Europe. In this respect they compared favorably with Spain, credited as she was with the fabulous wealth of the Americas, a wealth that was more legendary than real, so that long before the end the Spaniards were beset with financial difficulties. If wars are not won by money alone, it is certain that the lack of adequate financial resources is a crippling handicap, and this was amply proved as the struggle in the Netherlands deepened.

The revolt was initially a fight for freedom; but since it later developed into a war of religion, it is necessary to consider the religious situation. Soon after Luther's break with Rome, Reformed ideas were introduced into the Netherlands, and they took root in a ground that was well prepared to receive them. First, there was the work of the "Brethren of the Common Life" and the educational centers they had established. They aimed at spreading an enlightened Christianity among laymen with special emphasis on the teaching of the Gospel. Thomas à Kempis, author of the famous classic, *Of the Imitation of Christ,* lived the greater part of his life in a convent near Utrecht. Pupper of Goch and John Wessel, two "Reformers before the Reformation," were sons of the Netherlands. Prominent among the aims of the Brethren was the desire to see the Bible translated into the language of the people, and such a translation was published at Delft in 1477. By about 1530 there were some twenty-five Bible translations in the common tongues, French, Dutch, and Flemish. It is also well to remember that Holland was the home of Erasmus, most illustrious of all the Christian humanists, and of Cornelius Hoen, whose views on the sacraments were not without influence on Zwingli. Then came Luther's break with Rome, and presently both his ideas and his writings came flooding into a country ready to imbibe them.

At this point there strode upon the scene the sinister figure of that slow-witted but bigoted youth, the Emperor Charles V. Born on February 24, 1500, he was elected emperor of Germany in 1519 following the death of the Emperor Maximilian. In addition to wearing the imperial crown Charles by birth had inherited the Netherlands on his father's side and Spain on his mother's. He came of age in 1515; and, urged by the tendency of the times, he aimed to bring into unity the various principalities over which he ruled. He was the supreme exponent of the doctrine of one faith, one king, one law. Thus when "heresy" appeared in his Netherlands domains, he set himself at once to extirpate it, and the better to achieve his end he decided to follow a practice that had yielded eminently satisfactory results in his other kingdom, Spain. There the greatness of the nation was identified with the supremacy of the Catholic Church, and to ensure this supremacy there lay to hand a convenient weapon, the Inquisition. This so-called Holy Office was founded, with papal approval, by Ferdinand and Isabella in 1480, and its purpose was the conversion or, failing that, the suppression of Moors and Jews. Later it was used to extirpate heresy, with such success that in an incredibly short time anti-Catholic ideas were completely stamped out. If the Inquisition was successful in Spain, why should it not be equally effective in the Netherlands? It was well worth a trial. And this, or something like this, was the method introduced by Charles V.

In 1521 the Emperor presided over the Diet of Worms where

Luther was condemned. On his return to the Netherlands he immediately forbade the reading of Luther's works and demanded their surrender on pain of death. The first victim was the Humanist Cornelius Graphaeus, a friend of Erasmus and town clerk of Antwerp. He was deprived of his office, imprisoned for two years, and finally banished. Henry Voes and John Esch, Augustinian monks and the protomartyrs of the Dutch Reformation, were burned at the stake at Antwerp (July 31, 1523). Thereafter decree followed harsh decree, forbidding the publication of any book unless passed by the official censors and banning all meetings for Bible study or for discussion of articles of the faith. But in spite of the stern edicts or *placards,* it was officially admitted that heretics were increasing in number. The first preachers in the Netherlands were ex-priests and monks, but these were later replaced by agents from South Germany and more especially from Geneva. Calvinism was early introduced, which, resting on principles of self-government, strongly appealed to the sturdy, freedom-loving Dutch and did much to harden their hearts to resist. Such was the state of affairs between 1521 and 1550. It was in 1550 (September 25) that Charles issued his last edict against heresy, its aim being "to exterminate the root and ground of this pest." It was the most severe of all his decrees, but it ought to be added that the regents appointed by Charles—his aunt Margaret of Austria till 1530, and from 1530 till 1555 his sister Mary of Hungary—were reluctant to persecute and under their rule the severity of his edicts was considerably mitigated. Public officials too were often slack in enforcing punishment. Nevertheless many Protestants, both men and women, suffered for their faith; and Charles might have gone to even greater extremes had he continued in office; but in 1555 he abdicated in favor of his son Philip II.

With all due pomp and splendor the abdication took place at Brussels on October 25, 1555. As the emperor moved forward to the throne he was upheld on the arm of the young Prince of Orange, later to be known as William the Silent and the champion of Dutch liberation. As Charles made his abdication

speech it is said that there were tears in his eyes, for the Netherlands had been his first kingdom before ever he had acceded to
the Spanish crown or the imperial throne. He spoke with fluent
ease the languages of the people. Unlike his son Philip, he was
one of themselves, and this is the radical difference between the
two rulers. In many ways they resembled each other: both were
conscientious and industrious in a plodding kind of way; both
were suspicious and reluctant to trust men; both believed in their
divinely ordained destiny, and they were at one in their bigoted
loyalty to the Catholic Church. But Philip was a stranger to the
Netherlands, and lacking his father's attractiveness he failed to
win the affections of the people as his father had done in spite
of all his harsh measures. Even at his accession Philip could
hardly have made a worse impression. Unable to address his
audience in Flemish, he began to speak in halting French, but
after the first few words could not continue and was forced to
call on the Bishop of Arras to speak to the gathering. The new
ruler was twenty-eight.

Philip lived in the Netherlands for four years after his coronation. During that time he continued the policy of his father, no
more and no less. At the first meeting of the States-General
(March 2, 1556) he requested, as his father had often done, a vast
sum of money. Again like his father he demanded a rearrange-
ment of episcopal dioceses and an enlargement of their number.
He issued decrees against heretics but none more harsh than his
father's which were said to have been "written not in ink but in
blood." In the four years of his personal rule his methods differed
in no essential from those of his father, and yet even then the
seeds of resentment were sown, resentment that presently hardened into opposition and finally broke out in open revolt.

In August 1559 Philip left for Spain and never again set foot
in the Netherlands. He appointed as his regent his half sister
Margaret, Duchess of Parma, a spurious daughter of Charles V.
This woman, aged thirty-seven at her appointment, was a native
of the country, and unlike Philip spoke its language and understood the ways of its people. Left to herself, she might have ruled

with tact and moderation, but her hands were tied. Back in 1531 Charles V had established three councils: a Council of State (the most important of the three), a Privy Council, and a Financial Council, all of which were composed of members nominated by the crown. Philip appointed the heads of these councils as a *consulta* to supervise the regent, and under their surveillance she had no option but to enforce the decrees against heresy. It is true that two of the Netherlands nobility, Count Egmont and William of Orange, were also members of the *consulta,* but they were excluded from all share in the management of affairs and were overshadowed by the Bishop of Arras (1517-1586), who was from 1561 Archbishop of Malines and the Cardinal de Granvelle, and by the other two presidents of Council. Granvelle, the leader, was a remarkable man who was "said to be able to tire out five secretaries while dictating to them in five different languages at the same time."[1]

But the real master was Philip himself, immured in his Palace of the Escurial in Madrid, brooding on affairs, and kept abreast of events by the confidential reports of secret agents. Completely intolerant and brushing aside all opposition, he determined to carry out his repressive policy whatever sufferings it might entail. Relentlessly he issued missives to Granvelle, who, whatever his own views may have been, had no choice but to carry out his master's orders.

The two great antagonists in the impending struggle were Philip and William the Silent, and at this point we may well pause to contrast their character and aims. Philip (1527-98) was the complete despot, holding in his own hands the reins of authority and disallowing any of his ministers to share that authority. (As compared with other countries it is remarkable that Spain produced no statesman of outstanding ability or note.) Philip was incapable of delegating duties to subordinates or of distinguishing between the vital and the trivial. All things were to him of equal importance, and as a consequence he was habitually submerged in routine tasks and blind to the most momentous issues. Autocratic and fanatical, he regarded the very idea of freedom as unthinkable: the function of a ruler was to command, of a subject to obey. His paramount aims were the supremacy of Spain and the extirpation of heresy. He stood for a rigid Catholic uniformity which he was prepared to promote with every weapon at his command, whether of force, fraud, or duplicity: of conciliation he knew nothing. As a devout son of Mother Church he conceived it his sacred duty to uproot heresy wherever it appeared in his domains. In 1566 he wrote to his ambassador at Rome: "Assure his Holiness that, rather than suffer the least thing in prejudice of religion, I will lose all my states and a hundred lives if I had them; for I will not live to be a King of heretics." Such was the first of the two protagonists.

The aims of William of Orange were poles apart from those of Philip, his twin ideals being love of freedom and hatred of oppression. Paradoxically William was a German and not a Dutchman. He was born at Dillenburg on April 25, 1533, and was one of twelve children. Though his parents were both Lutherans, William was brought up a Catholic in order to qualify him for taking over the family property of Orange situated in the south of France. During his teens he was one of the Emperor Charles' pages and then fought in the imperial army against Henry II of France. He won the emperor's favor, and, as we have seen, it was on William's arm that Charles leaned at his abdication. William was an excellent linguist, fluently speaking Flemish, German, Spanish, French, and Latin, and soon made his mark as a diplomatist. Following the Treaty of Cateau-Cambrésis in 1559, Philip II sent him to Paris as a state hostage for the implementing of the treaty. It was at that time that he gained the sobriquet of "the Silent." Philip and Henry II of France were secretly plotting to massacre all the heretics in their domains. The French king, thinking that the Prince of Orange was privy to the plot, openly discussed it in his presence. William was horror-stricken at the disclosure, but he swallowed down his anger, kept his countenance, and spoke not a word.[2] Whether or not the story is true, it is at least a pleasant legend, and certainly ever afterwards he was known as "the Silent," though it could hardly be said that taciturnity was one of his more noticeable qualities. William's purpose was now fixed. Though still a Catholic, he was determined, to quote his own words, to expel from the Netherlands "this vermin of Spaniards." His guiding motive both then and throughout his life was hatred of oppression and compassion for the victims who suffered so cruelly under the tyranny of Spain. "It was not patriotism, but pity, not love of what he was defending, but hatred of what he was attacking, that made him a liberator."[3] In agreeable contrast to the bitterness of the age, tolerance was his outstanding quality, as bigotry was Philip's. In religion, too, his love of freedom asserted itself. Though at heart a deeply religious man, he had little regard for the forms of religion. He allowed liberty of conscience to every man, and was himself in turn Catholic, Lutheran, and Calvinist. Such, then, was the leader who proved himself not only the inspiration but ultimately the savior of his people. By his faith, resolution, and unbending tenacity of purpose he gave them heart in their struggle against oppression and set their feet on the path of freedom.

Meantime, the situation in the Netherlands was rapidly deteriorating. Philip at his coronation had pledged himself to maintain inviolate the ancient rights and privileges of the provinces, but almost immediately he broke his word. He alienated the nobles by slighting them and estranged the common people by depriving them of their rights. Presently the whole country was in a ferment. Egmont and Orange especially smarted under their indignities. First, they resigned their commission in the Spanish army because Spanish troops were still quartered in the Netherlands; and then, excluded as they were from all direction of affairs, though nominally members of the regent's *consulta,* they stopped attending its meetings, and in July 1561 wrote to Philip complaining of the unfair treatment they had received and resigning their membership. As for the Netherlands people, they had chiefly three grounds of discontent: they bitterly resented the continued presence of Spanish troops on Dutch soil; they were strongly opposed to the suggested formation of new bishoprics; and they were appalled at the barbarous decrees against heretics and the savage treatment of the victims.

As regards the first, Philip had promised to recall his soldiery at the end of three or four months, but after more than a year he had done nothing to implement his promise. The behavior of the troops themselves was no better than that of other armies billeted in foreign lands, and was a perpetual source of irritation to the people. William of Orange merely incurred Philip's anger when he voiced the popular demand to have them withdrawn, and nothing might have been done in the matter had not the authorities on the spot, the Regent Margaret and Granvelle, taken the law into their own hands and sent the troops packing.

Philip was on firmer ground when he proposed increasing the number of bishoprics from six to fourteen. Clearly some kind of change was indicated: the existing dioceses in no way corresponded with the political structure of the country; and moreover their bishops were subject to the German Archbishop of Cologne and to the French Archbishop of Rheims. It was an intolerable situation that clamored for reform. But the Dutch people suspected the king's intentions; in his hands lay the appointment of the new bishops, who would be creatures of the government and possibly agents of the Inquisition. In any case the creation of new bishoprics was regarded as an infringement of ancient rights, and the same applied in the third cause of resentment; the decrees against heresy violated the privileges of the people.

In these three ways, then, Philip aroused the antagonism of the Netherlanders. When they pressed for the dismissal of Granvelle and gained their point (March 13, 1564), Philip's next move was to write a letter demanding the enforcement of the decrees of the Council of Trent. The Dutch nobles demurred on the grounds that some of those decrees outraged certain of their ancient privileges and charters, and they appointed Count Egmont to plead their cause with Philip at Madrid. Strong support was given by William of Orange, who denounced the government's repressive measures and added "that though he himself had resolved to adhere to the Catholic religion, yet he could not approve that

Princes should aim at dominion over the souls of men, or deprive them of the freedom of their faith and religion."[4]

In March 1565 Egmont duly arrived at Madrid and was courteously received by Philip, but his mission was entirely fruitless. The Spanish king was adamant in his decision to enforce the Tridentine decrees, and was ready (as he wrote) to sacrifice a hundred thousand lives rather than relent. The issue was now simple and clear-cut, and the choice one of obedience or revolt. When Philip's letter was read, the prince of Orange is said to have whispered to his neighbor, "Now we shall see the beginning of a fine tragedy."

The truth of those words was amply proved in the sequel. At once the country was aflame and the soul of the nation stirred. Pamphlets were circulated and kept the temperature of the people at fever heat. One of these documents sent to the king contained this memorable apologia of Protestantism: "We thank God that even our enemies are constrained to bear witness to our piety and innocence, for it is a common saying: 'He does not swear, for he is a Protestant. He is not an immoral man, nor a drunkard, for he belongs to the new sect'; yet we are subjected to every kind of punishment that can be invented to torment us."[5] The words ring with the simple eloquence of the Christian church in its early days of persecution and martyrdom.

The next milestone on the way to revolt was the "compromise" of 1566, an *un*compromising document drawn up by William's younger brother Louis of Nassau (a Lutheran), Philip Marnix (a Calvinist), and Viscount Brederode (a Roman Catholic). It requested the withdrawal of the Inquisition and the lifting of the *placards* or decrees against heretics. Some two thousand signatures were rapidly obtained, of Catholics as well as Protestants, drawn chiefly from the lesser nobility, merchants, and burghers. At a meeting of the new group it was decided to make an approach to the regent, and shortly afterwards two hundred members set out with their manifesto for the regent's palace at Brussels. She was somewhat dismayed at the sight of the large deputation, but one of her advisers, Barlaymont, thus reassured her: "What, Madam!

is your Highness afraid of these beggars *(ces gueux)* . . . by the living God, if my advice were taken, their request should be annotated by a sound cudgelling, and they would be made to descend the steps of the court more quickly than they came up." Thus lightly are nicknames given. The sobriquet "beggars" was used to good purpose by the confederates and rapidly became a watchword among them. Said Brederode: "They call us beggars; we accept the name. We pledge ourselves to resist the Inquisition, and keep true to the King and the beggar's wallet." As in later times the men of General Montgomery's North African armies prided themselves on the name "desert rats," so the Dutch confederates delighted in the name of "beggars." The beggar's wallet became a symbol, and all over the country men of every class and station appeared with a beggar's leather sack tied on their shoulders.

The burning question was: How would Philip react? At first it seemed as if he would relent, and in a letter to the regent (July 1566) he gave a tentative promise to withdraw the Inquisition and to mitigate the harsh antiheresy decrees. But within the velvet glove was clenched the mailed fist. Philip had no intentions of capitulating to the confederates' demands. His fair words deceived many, but one man he failed to deceive, William of Orange, who knew full well that the king was only biding his time to deliver his counterstroke.

The occasion was provided by a reckless outbreak of iconoclasm carried out by irresponsible mobs. All over the country images were defaced, shrines desecrated, and priceless works of art destroyed. The climax was reached at Antwerp in August 1566 when the famous cathedral was pillaged. On hearing the news of the outbreak Philip declared in a fury: "It shall cost them dear, I swear it by the soul of my father." Thus wantonly was cast away a golden opportunity which a wise and prudent ruler would have turned to his advantage. But Philip was not sufficiently intelligent or humane to profit by circumstances. The irresponsible outbreaks had a disastrous effect on the course of the Reformation in the Netherlands. It drove a wedge between Catholic and Protestant and alienated the moderates whose staunch adherence to the national cause not even the fiercest persecutions had been able to weaken. Everywhere Catholicism seemed to be on the crest of the wave, and now if ever was the hour for conciliation and gentle persuasion. To attain his ends Philip need only have murmured the word "moderation." Instead, he pronounced the word ALVA.

The Duke of Alva, a man of blood and iron and without mercy, was a well chosen instrument to terrorize a nation and bring its people into subjection. At the age of sixty, the victor of Mühlberg and in Tunis, he entered upon his new task with relish. Writing to Philip he boasted, "I have tamed men of iron, and shall I not be able to tame these men of butter?" He arrived in the Netherlands on August 8, 1567, after an epic march of nearly four months' duration over the Alps by way of the Mont Cenis Pass, and thence through Burgundy, Lorraine, and Luxembourg. With him marched an army of 20,000 troops, the finest fighting men in Europe. Now began one of the darkest episodes in all Dutch history, a period that lasted for six years, from 1567 to 1573. Margaret was still nominally regent, but the reins of authority were held by Alva. One of his first acts was to make a number of arrests: as early as September 9 Counts Egmont and Hoorn were treacherously taken. To implement his will Alva set up the *Council of Tumults* or *Council of Troubles,* popularly known as the *Bloody Tribunal.* Its rule was arbitrary and its authority final, and suddenly a reign of terror spread over the land. Heresy was identified with treason, and the penalty of treason was death. Heretics were remorselessly tracked down, informers were set to work to rout out delinquents, mock trials were held, and wholesale condemnations followed, in some instances running into hundreds at a time. "The gallows, the wheel, stakes, trees along the highways, were laden with carcasses or limbs of those who had been hanged, beheaded, or roasted; so that the air which God made for the respiration of the living was now become the common grave or habitation of the dead." [6] Thousands fled to other lands and the economic life of the country was paralyzed. In October 1567 Margaret of Parma resigned from the regency. Alva was appointed regent in her stead and also governor-general, and now with none to restrain him he became even more violent. On June 5, 1568, Counts Egmont and Hoorn after a mock trial were beheaded in the public square of Brussels. Doubtless their death was intended to act as a warning to all malcontents, but it only inspired deeper hatred of the Spanish tyranny and raised up two martyrs for the cause of freedom. The deed was not only a crime but also an act of insensate folly that could never be rectified.

At this point we may ask how William of Orange was employed. And first we may note that he was not in the Netherlands at all. He had always distrusted the veiled promises of Philip, and early in 1567 before Alva arrived he had tried to prevail on Egmont and Hoorn to take up arms as a last resort; but having failed in the attempt, he and his family set out for their ancestral home in Germany (April 1567). Up to this time William was not ostensibly in opposition to the king, and his banners bore the legend, *Pro Rege, Grege, Lege,* "For King, People, and Law." And even now he was only taking up arms against the "sanguinary and tyrannical government of the Duke of Alva." Even when he was denounced at Brussels as a rebel, a traitor, and an outlaw (January 24, 1568), he was careful to avoid casting blame on the king; and in his famous *Justification Against His Calumniators,* a document published in April 1568 and translated into several European languages, his accusations were rather directed against Philip's evil advisers. It was not until October 1573, when he became a Calvinist, that he came out into the open, renounced his loyalty to the king, and threw all his energies into the fight for independence against the power of Spain. Meantime he twice gathered an army and entered the Netherlands; but his mercenary troops, discontented and on the point of mutiny, were no match for the Spaniards in the field. The year 1569 was one of the darkest periods in William's career. Defeated in battle, he was forced to withdraw from the Netherlands, and Alva was able to write to Philip, "We may consider the Prince of Orange as a dead man; he is without influence or credit."

But Alva had his own difficulties which progressively increased and soon were insuperable. First, there was the geographical factor. The Netherlands were an intricate network of rivers and canals, which in days before the invention of the Bailey bridge and other modern facilities frequently interrupted the fluency of military operations and sometimes brought them to a complete standstill. Moreover, the land was below sea level at high tide; and consequently, by cutting the sea walls, the cities near the coast could repel the invader, who was forced to retreat before the onrush of salt water while they themselves, situated on rising ground, were safe.

But there were other factors which were even more vital and which in the end were decisive. As already observed, Spain suffered from two fatal lacks, money and sea power. While it would be idle to claim that William of Orange was a military leader of the first rank, his ceaseless activities caused Alva to incur enormous expenses which he was unable to meet. The Spanish troops clamored for pay and he had no money to pay them. To escape from this dilemma he was forced to adopt an expedient that nullified all his previous successes. In March 1569 he proposed a scheme of taxation which, if it had been carried out, would have meant commercial and economic ruin. One per cent was to be levied on property (commonly known as the "100th penny"), five per cent on every sale of property (the "20th penny"), and ten per cent on all sales of goods (the "10th penny"). The last tax meant stark ruination. No measure could have been more disastrous or more unpopular, and as soon as it was mooted the whole country was up in arms, including the Romanists, who resented being touched in their pockets even more than they resented heretics. Pressure was applied for the payment of the 100th penny, but as regards the other two impositions Alva was compelled to desist and to accept instead a payment of 2,000,000 florins to be spread over the next two years. Nevertheless, he had committed a gross blunder from which he never recovered.

The lack of money, then, was one of the decisive factors in Alva's discomfiture; and the second, no less decisive, was the lack of sea power. The vital importance of naval power has been proved too often in modern times to require comment. But in sixteenth-century Europe it was generally disregarded among the nations, and in this respect Spain was notably remiss. The glory of Spain was her army crowned with a century's laurels, unsurpassed in Europe, and led by a succession of brilliant commanders. If Spain had been comparably strong at sea, if she could have patrolled the coasts and closed the harbors, resistance in the Netherlands would have collapsed almost immediately. But the naval methods of Spain were antiquated, effective enough in a landlocked sea like the Mediterranean (as witness Don John's victory over the Turks at Lepanto in 1571) but completely inadequate in ocean waters. The Spaniards made no effort to repair their deficiencies, and consequently the initiative passed to their enemies. The ships of the seafaring Dutch sailed out from the Netherlands, harried and plundered the Spaniards, cut their communications, and thus deprived them of essential supplies. Presently these "Sea Beggars" (*Gueux de Mer*) became more adventurous. Hitherto their greatest handicap had been the lack of a suitable port in which to shelter and to store their booty. Queen Elizabeth of England had permitted them the use of English harbors, but on a protest from Spain this facility was withdrawn. It was essential that the Sea Beggars should secure an anchorage in order to continue their activities; and being driven to take refuge off Brill and finding the town undefended by the Spanish, they promptly took possession (April 1, 1572). If one town could be seized and used as a base, why not others? Accordingly Flushing was taken and then other towns: soon nearly the whole island of Walcheren was in their hands, and still the revolt spread. It was about this time that the patriotic song was composed which is still the rousing national anthem of the Netherlands. Holland, Zeeland, Gelderland, and Friesland declared for William, and in July he was proclaimed stadtholder of Holland. Now was the time to strike; but even as William stood poised for the blow, his arm was stayed by the alarming news from France of the Massacre of St. Bartholomew's Day. William was dependent on French help, and when this was no longer available, he was obliged to postpone his operations.

It was then that Alva wreaked a fearful vengeance on all the

cities that had declared for William. Town after town he reduced
and plundered. Starting with Malines, he maltreated Protestants
and Catholics alike and for three hideous days gave the city over
to pillage. Zutphen and Naarden suffered even more cruelly; Haarlem was besieged, starved into surrender, and its survivors massacred. Among a dispirited people only the resolution of William
shone undimmed. "When I took in hand to defend these oppressed Christians," he said about this time, "I made an alliance
with the mightiest of all Potentates—the God of Hosts, who is
able to save us if He choose."

The hardy seamen, too, at this nadir of their country's fortunes,
played a notable part. They completely routed the Spanish fleet
and by this and other heroic exploits they inspired their com-
rades on land to further resistance. Alva had failed to break the
spirit of the people; and now again without money to pay his
troops, he knew he had reached the end of his tether. There was
nothing more that he could do, and at his own request he was
recalled from his post on December 18, 1573. It is typical, both of
the man's intransigence and of his complete inability to learn,
that his parting advice to his successor was to "drop all gentleness, mercy, and negotiation, and to look only to arms."

The new regent, Don Luis Requesens-y-Zuniga, a Spanish
nobleman, was a man of quite a different stamp. Left to himself
he would have aimed at a reconciliation, for he was under no
delusions concerning the fierce resistance he would meet from
men who were fighting for home and fatherland. He began by
removing Alva's iniquitous taxes and in other ways made a show
of moderation. But it was now too late: the iron had entered into
the soul of the people: the time for conciliation was past. Now,
indeed, the Netherlanders demanded not only the removal of
Spanish officials and troops and the restoration of their own
ancient rights, but also full liberty of faith and worship. Religious
fervor thus fortified patriotic zeal. On the religious issue William
and Philip were equally uncompromising, the one in demanding,
the other in denying, freedom of conscience. A complete deadlock
was reached and the repressive measures continued.

But now a colorful episode lit up the scene. Nowhere could the Netherlanders defeat the Spaniards in pitched battle, but they were more successful in holding fortified towns, while at sea they were unquestionably supreme. Gradually they became bolder and with every new success more confident. In 1574 they captured Middleburg and occupied Leyden. The sequel reads almost like a dime novel. The city was invested by Spanish troops, a relieving force under Louis of Nassau was routed near Nymegen, and capitulation seemed certain. On William's suggestion the dykes were cut to allow the sea to flood the land, but the waters rose so slowly as almost to extinguish the hopes of the besieged, while contrary winds kept off the food ships. The citizens were faced with starvation; some complained and spoke of capitulating, but the burgomaster fortified the spirits of the wavering with the dauntless words: "Here is my sword; plunge it, if you will, into my heart, and divide my flesh among you to appease your hunger; but expect no surrender as long as I am alive." On October 1 the wind miraculously changed, the water streamed over the land, the Spanish troops fell back; on October 3 the food ships brought supplies to the beleaguered garrison, the retreating Spaniards were routed, and the city was saved. As a thank offering for its deliverance William proposed the founding of Leyden University which was destined to be a famous seat of learning in succeeding centuries. The epic defense of Leyden was the turning of the tide, and from then onwards the Netherlanders never looked back in their fight for freedom. The war dragged on, the Spaniards won battles, but they could not subjugate their hardy opponents.

The Regent Requesens died of typhus in March 1576. On April 25 at Delft a meeting was convened of the states of Holland and Zeeland which not only appointed William commander-in-chief of the armed forces but also invested him with supreme political authority. The next event, in November 1576, was what has been called the "Spanish Fury." Once again the cause of the disturbance was arrears of pay. Some of the troops had been unpaid for three years, none of them for less than twenty-one months. Not unnaturally they demanded their money, and when for lack of funds this was denied, they broke out in open mutiny. First they outraged Alost, but the climax was reached when they systematically plundered Antwerp, the richest town in the Netherlands and among the most famous of European cities. The civil population was subjected to unbelievable atrocities; everywhere were scenes of arson and rapine, and some seven thousand citizens were massacred. As never before the country blazed with white hot anger and insistently clamored for united action.

Meantime, since October 19, a congress had been sitting at Ghent, where delegates both Catholic and Protestant had come together from the northern and southern provinces to adopt concerted action to rid the country of foreign troops. In the midst of their deliberations came the startling news of the outrages at Antwerp which so accelerated proceedings that almost immediately a treaty was signed, the famous *Pacification of Ghent*. By its terms the ten southern and seven northern provinces, roughly the modern Belgium and Holland, pledged themselves to expel the Spaniards from their territories, to abolish the edicts against heresy, and later to address themselves to a solution of the religious problem. It was also resolved to appoint William of Orange as governor of the seventeen provinces.

Such was the state of affairs when Requesens' successor arrived in February 1577. The new regent, aged thirty-two, was Don John of Austria, an illegitimate son of Charles V and thus half brother to Philip. He had won fame as a military leader against the Moors and as recently as 1571 had routed the Turks at Lepanto. His banner bore the defiant words that as he had conquered the Turks, so would he conquer heretics. But the heretics were not so easily quelled, and the regent was forced to accept the terms laid down in the *Pacification*. By this agreement, known as the Perpetual Edict (February 12, 1577), Don John consented to the immediate withdrawal of all foreign troops and to the maintenance of the charters and liberties of the provinces. In a letter to Philip he wrote: "The Prince of Orange has bewitched the minds of all men. They love him, and fear him, and wish to have him as their Lord." On September 23 of the same year William entered Brussels in triumph. It was the zenith of his adventurous career. He was acclaimed on every side and was received, as an English witness testified, "as though he were an angel from heaven"; and women knelt before him "as though it were some god who passed through the city."

But presently the flowing tide receded. Philip made yet another attempt to subdue the obstinate Dutch, and in January of the following year (1578) he dispatched an army of 20,000 veterans led by the redoubtable Duke of Parma. Parma was not only the most illustrious captain of the age, but as a diplomatist he was as astute as William himself; and in both capacities he immediately made his presence felt. He routed the Netherlanders at Gemblours (January 31), and when Don John died of a fever on October 1, Parma assumed full control. Subtle diplomatist as he was, he exploited the divisions and jealousies of north and south and succeeded in detaching from William the southern Catholic provinces. Unfortunately the Calvinists in an excess of fanatical zeal played into his hands. At Ghent especially there was a fresh outbreak of iconoclasm: churches were desecrated, monasteries pillaged, and monks put to death. The resistance of the Catholic south began to harden. There the Reformation had never taken firm root and now the Jesuits were active with their preaching and propaganda. The upshot was that a defensive league was formed among the Catholics, and by the Union of Arras (January 5, 1579) it was declared that there be "a general reconciliation with the Catholic King, our natural Lord and Prince." The Protestant reply was the formation of a counter league among the northern provinces, the Union of Utrecht (January 29). These provinces became the United Provinces of the Netherlands, a new Protestant state. From now on the war was definitely one of religion, a war that must be fought out to the bitter end without thought of compromise.

The year 1581 was one of the most memorable in all the history of the Netherlands. On March 25 of that year Philip aimed yet another shaft at his dauntless opponent by declaring him a traitor and placing him under a ban. In this declaration William is described as "an enemy of the human race" and the document continues: "We promise to anyone who has the heart to free us of this pest, and who will deliver him dead or alive, or take his life, the sum of 25,000 crowns in gold or in estate for himself and his heirs; we will pardon him any crime, if he have been guilty, and give him a patent of nobility, if he be not noble; and we will do the same for all his agents and accomplices." William's reply was his famous *Apology,* a justification of his opposition to Philip and a rich mine of biographical detail. The *Apology* was translated into French, Dutch, and Latin, and a copy sent to the heads of all European courts. More important was the reaction of the northern provinces, which repudiated their allegiance to Spain and declared their independence as a sovereign nation. This Act of Abjuration was signed at The Hague on July 26, 1581, and includes the famous words: "All men know that God appoints a king to cherish his people as a shepherd his flock. When he fails in this duty he is no prince but a tyrant. Then may the Estates of the land legally remove him and put another in his place." Thus came into being the United Provinces, the seven small sovereign republics of Holland, Zeeland, Utrecht, Friesland, Gelderland, Overyssel, and Groningen; with Holland numbering two-thirds of the population and possessing three-fourths of the wealth it naturally assumed the leadership. The Dutch Declaration of Independence was a notable milestone in the march of history and the human race. "It was the first great example of a whole people officially renouncing allegiance to their hereditary and consecrated monarch; and it was by two generations in advance of the English Commonwealth, by two centuries in advance of the American and French Republics. It was destined to have a crucial influence over the course of modern civilization."[7]

But now the sands were running out for William. Philip, by his ban of March 25, 1581, had sanctioned murder as a legitimate means to silence him, and scarcely a year had elapsed when an abortive attempt on William's life was made by Juan Jaureguy (March 18, 1582). Gaining access to William's presence, the assassin shot at point-blank range, but by a miracle the wound was not mortal though the ball passed under William's right ear and out by his left jaw. But where one had failed others were ready to try, and the end came at Delft on July 9, 1584, when a fanatic Balthasar Gerard shot William dead. He was only fifty-one when he died: his last words were, "My God, have mercy on my soul and on these poor people."

William of Orange has been justly named the "father of his country." It may be that he failed in his main purpose of welding the seventeen Netherlands provinces into one nation, but he had the satisfaction of knowing that he had created the United Provinces and he had also the reasonable expectation that his life's work would endure. Like other great figures in history he looked on himself as an instrument of God and a man of destiny, and that may explain his unwavering tenacity of purpose in face of seemingly overwhelming odds. Though beaten on many occasions, he refused to acknowledge defeat, and in the hour of misfortune he stood a tower of strength to those who were less resolute. The lodestar of all his hopes was the liberation of his people from the tyranny of Spain, and for that ideal he sacrificed wealth and ease, position, and ultimately life itself. But such was his heroic ardor that doubtless he counted as adequate reward the good success that crowned his efforts. To him as founder may be attributed not only the independence but the future greatness of the Dutch people, and patriot as he was his name is also inscribed on the roll of those who in all the lands have championed the cause of freedom.

William's death was a crippling blow to the Dutch resistance movement. But though the struggle was to drag on for a further period of twenty-five years, the patriots were now launched on a rising tide. Two factors especially contributed to the final victory. First, there was the fatal dispersion of Spanish military effort. Instead of concentrating his forces for a last onslaught on the Netherlands, Philip allowed himself to be drawn into futile adventures, first against England and then in France. Again and again was Parma thwarted. While the Dutch were gathering their strength, he was ordered to stand by with an army for the conquest of England. The defeat of the ill-fated Armada was almost as much a relief to Holland as to England. But Philip was incapable of learning from hard experience, and he must needs further dissipate his efforts by interfering in the French civil wars. Parma was unable to apply himself to his task of subjugating the Netherlands, and when he died in 1592, there was removed the last real threat to Dutch independence. Though the war dragged on, Parma's successors—the Archduke Ernest of Austria and later the Archduke Albert—were only half-hearted in its prosecution.

The first decisive factor, then, was the Spaniards' failure to concentrate their forces in the Netherlands, and the second was the great good fortune of the Dutch in their new leaders. In succession to William the Silent arose his seventeen-year-old son, Maurice of Nassau, who in the succeeding years proved himself a consummate military leader. Passing over to the offensive, he fought four remarkable campaigns and drove the last Spanish soldier from Dutch soil. Working in close conjunction with Maurice was the able diplomatist, John van Oldenbarneveldt; and he, by his wise statesmanship, as Maurice by his brilliant victories in the field, enabled the Netherlands not only to resist but to overcome the Spanish threat. At last, on April 9, 1609, not a peace treaty but a twelve years' truce was signed at Antwerp. The Dutch, content with the reality of success and not snatching at its shadow, tactfully omitted all reference to religion! The long, obstinate struggle was ended, though it was not until the end of the Thirty Years' War in 1648 that Europe as a whole recognized the United Provinces as an independent state.

The revolt in the Netherlands ushered in a golden age for the Dutch people, an age that numbered among its great names those of Grotius, of Descartes and Spinoza, of Van Dyck, Frans Hals, Hobbema, and Rembrandt. Politically it proved what could be achieved by a people inspired by the love of freedom, and on the religious side it demonstrated yet once again the astringent quality of the Calvinist form of Protestantism to fortify a nation's soul.[8]

7

THE REFORMATION IN ENGLAND

✠

THE ANGLICAN CHURCH

It is universally admitted that the English people* possess in the highest degree the twin gifts of compromise and muddling through, and these were never more evident than at the time of the Reformation. The Reformation in England passed through four phases, corresponding to the four reigns it covered, those of Henry VIII, Edward VI, Mary, and Elizabeth. Edward and Mary tried to hustle the people, one to Protestantism, the other back to Romanism, and the people resented being hustled: it was un-English; it went against the grain. Far better was the comfortable middle way by which Henry and Elizabeth steered, and which admirably suited the compromising English temperament. And what a compromise this Reformation was! Froude tells how Chevalier Bunsen once said, "that, for his part, he could not conceive how we had managed to come by such a thing."[1] It is what many people have wondered. Henry VIII, especially in his last years, with careless abandon now beheaded a Roman Catholic, now burned a Protestant. People never knew where they stood. As Sir Maurice Powicke has remarked, "nobody with the exception of Cranmer was sure what the Church of England was."[2] It defies definition. It cannot be described as Lutheran, Zwinglian, or Calvinist. It stands alone, a fantastic compromise, a wierd and wonderful product, a church, as H. A. L. Fisher aptly put it, that is "Erastian in government, Roman in ritual, Calvinist in theology."[3] Once again the English ran true to form: even in their religion they were content to muddle through, and not unsuccessfully.

The common idea of the English Reformation is that it be-

* Throughout this chapter "English" means English and does not include Scottish.

gan because Henry VIII wanted a new wife, and to gain this end was forced to break with Rome. But while it is true that reformation might have been delayed for many years and would certainly have followed a different course, it is an oversimplification to say that it was caused by Henry's matrimonial dealings. His divorce may have been the occasion but was not the cause, since not even an autocrat like Henry could have forced so complete a revolution upon a reluctant people. Before the change was possible there must have been the desire for change, and the England of that age was ripe for reform.

First, we may note that the teaching of John Wycliffe was still remembered, and even before Luther's revolt in Germany there was a considerable leaven of heresy in England. In 1511 Andreas Ammonius, the Latin secretary of Henry VIII, wrote in a letter to Erasmus that there was a scarcity of wood because so much had been used to burn heretics.[4] Ten years later, in 1521, five hundred Lollards were arrested by the Bishop of London. Lollardy, with its emphasis on the Bible and its claims of individual judgment, was the first cause of the English Reformation.

The second was the Renaissance learning. Henry VIII attracted to his court a group of scholars, Humanists like Sir Thomas More, Dean Colet, and the Dutchman, Erasmus. These men denounced ecclesiastical abuses and the evil practices of the age; and though averse to any change of system, they were eager to see a reformation of the church from within.

Third, there was widespread anticlericalism. It was said that "if Abel had been a priest, Cain would have been acquitted" by any jury of London citizens.[5] It is true that anticlericalism will never bring about a reformation if, as so often happens, it is divorced from genuine religion. But there was nothing like that in Tudor England. The people were loyal to the church, desiring only the removal of certain glaring abuses.

The fourth factor was the percolation and diffusion of Lutheran doctrines. Coming early to England, they infected first the universities of Oxford and Cambridge and then spread through the whole nation. These four factors—dissent, the New Learning, anticlericalism, the infiltration of Lutheran ideas—all prepared the ground for the Reformation and assured Henry of solid support when he came to defy the power of Rome.

Henry VIII came to the throne on April 22, 1509, aged nearly eighteen. Two months later, in deference to his father's dying wish, he married Catherine of Aragon, the twenty-four-year-old daughter of Ferdinand and Isabella of Spain. This was the first of his matrimonial experiments: other five lay before him. In those early days Henry "had all the qualities of a prince of romance"; he was strong and handsome, a skillful rider and archer, a competent performer on lute and harpsichord.[6] He was also quite a scholar. As his father's second son, he had been destined not for the throne but for the church. If his elder brother Arthur had survived, Henry might have climbed the ladder of ecclesiastical preferment and become, incredibly, an archbishop and primate of all England! It is an intriguing thought. Even after he became king he maintained his interest in theology, and in 1521 wrote a polemic entitled *The Defence of the Seven Sacraments Against Martin Luther*. He dedicated the pamphlet to Pope Leo X who rewarded him with the title of *fidei defensor,* a title used to this day on British coins. Tradition dies hard.

During the first part of Henry's reign the dominating personality was Thomas Wolsey, the son of an unscrupulous butcher whose name appears on the town records of Ipswich for selling meat unfit for human consumption.[7] Wolsey's rise to power was meteoric. Educated at Magdalen College, Oxford, he was appointed a king's chaplain in 1507, aged thirty-four or thirty-five. Further promotion came in 1513 when he was consecrated Bishop of Lincoln and then Archbishop of York: two years later he became a cardinal. On several occasions he aspired, but without success, to the papal throne itself. As chancellor from 1515 to 1529 he was, under the king, the most powerful man in England, unrestrained in his conduct of affairs by Parliament or Convocation. England had never seen his like.

Accordingly, in 1527 when the "king's great matter" arose,

Henry looked to Wolsey to steer it to a happy issue. The "great matter" was the king's divorce, though strictly speaking it was not a divorce that Henry wanted but only the simple declaration that he had never really been married at all.

To understand his viewpoint we must go back to the year 1501. In that year, in order to cement an alliance between England and Spain a marriage had been arranged between Arthur, Prince of Wales, and Catherine, the younger daughter of Ferdinand and Isabella of Spain. The wedding took place in St. Paul's Cathedral on November 14, but five months later, on April 2, 1502, Prince Arthur died. When a decent interval had elapsed, the widow was betrothed to Henry, the new Prince of Wales, and Pope Julius II was requested to grant a dispensation. But marriage with a brother's widow is forbidden by canon law, and the pope was uncertain whether it lay in his power to grant a dispensation. At last in 1504 he reluctantly consented, and Catherine was free to marry Henry when the time came.

From the beginning it was an unfortunate union. Only one of their seven children survived infancy, the Princess Mary, born in 1516 and destined thirty-seven years later (1553) to reign as Queen of England. By 1525 it was evident that Catherine would have no more children, and the thoughts of Henry, pathetically eager to secure a male heir to the throne, began to turn more and more to the possibility of a separation.

He was influenced by several motives. First, there was the burning question of the succession, momentous not only for himself but for the nation. England had suffered cruelly in the past from disputed successions; the upheavals in the previous century from this cause and their attendant miseries were still fresh in men's memories. For reasons of state Henry was gravely concerned.

Second, he may have been genuinely perturbed by conscientious scruples. Henry read his Bible, and in Leviticus (20:21) he found this: "If a man shall take his brother's wife, it is an unclean thing . . . they shall be childless." It fitted perfectly with his own case. Was not the death of his children God's punishment for entering into a marriage that was no true marriage? The obvious way out was to induce the pope to declare it illegal. To reasons of state were added scruples of conscience.

But about this time Henry fell violently in love with Anne Boleyn, a vivacious young woman of twenty-four with lovely black eyes and hair so long that she could sit on it. Henry was probably influenced by all three motives—politics, conscience, passion. In fact, the more he thought about the matter, the more convinced he became that he had never really been married at all but that he was a poor, ill-used bachelor.

It would seem that neither Henry nor Wolsey anticipated any difficulties. The cardinal would fight the case on the not unreasonable grounds that the papal dispensation of 1504 was beyond the power of any pope to grant. The present pope, like a sensible man, had only to nullify what from the beginning was invalid, and the whole affair would be settled to everybody's satisfaction.

And so it might have fallen out at any other time: but 1527 was an unlucky year to choose. It was the year when the imperial troops sacked Rome and the pope was virtually a prisoner of the Emperor Charles V. Now Charles was a nephew of Queen Catherine, and he had no intention of allowing his aunt to be humiliated, especially when he had the pope in his power. If Pope Clement had been a free agent he might have acted differently, but his hands were tied and all he could do was to play for time. And so followed a series of sorry expedients—hedging, temporizing, procrastinating. The pope even suggested bigamy, anything in fact so long as he was absolved from responsibility.

But Henry and Wolsey insisted on legal correctness as the one essential; if Anne had a son, he must be recognized as the legitimate heir. The pope must assume full responsibility and the divorce must be decreed by papal authority. A complete deadlock was reached because from first to last the pope's actions were dictated by political necessity.

It is unnecessary to follow the details of the case. After the semblance of a trial in England it was referred to Rome. Henry realized that this was the death of his hopes, and now his anger fell on the hapless Wolsey. On November 4, 1530, Wolsey was arrested on a charge of treason, but he obligingly died of an illness at Leicester on his way to London. Near the end he was heard to murmur, "If I had served God as diligently as I have done the king, He would not have given me over in my grey hairs."

Wolsey's successor in power was Thomas Cromwell, the famous ancestor of a more illustrious descendant. Born about 1485, the son, it is said, of a blacksmith, he was in turn soldier, banker, and man of business. In 1520 he entered the service of Wolsey, and now in 1531, aged forty-five or forty-six, he supplanted him in the king's service. Ruthless, cynical, completely unscrupulous, he never wavered in his loyalty to his master, and during the next nine years he was the chief instrument in giving effect to the king's wishes.

Henry realized by this time that he could hope for nothing from Rome, and that since persuasion had failed, force must be applied. First, it was necessary to secure his home base, and accordingly Parliament was called (November 1529), the famous "Seven Years'" or "Reformation Parliament" which was gratifyingly anticlerical and even antipapal, so that Henry was fully assured of lay support. The next step was to bring the clergy to heel. Suddenly and without warning he trumped up a charge accusing them of infringing certain old statutes[8] which forbade subjects to take outside England plaints that might be heard in the king's own courts at home. This was in 1531. At the same convocation the bishops were forced to acknowledge him as "their singular protector and only supreme lord, and, as far as that is permitted by the law of Christ, the supreme head of the Church and of the clergy." It was all that Henry required to make himself master in his own house.

His hands were now free to turn against Rome, and in the next twelve months he played three trump cards against which there was no defense. First, in 1532 he took up the question of the annates or first year's income paid over to the pope when a new incumbent received a benefice. Parliament enacted that the annates should be paid directly to the king and that he at his discretion might or might not hand them over to the pope. It all depended on whether the pope behaved properly, that is, on whether he nullified the king's marriage; and Henry made this brutally clear in a letter he sent to the pope and cardinals. "I do not mean to deceive them," he wrote, "but to tell them the fact that this statute will be to their advantage, if they show themselves deserving of it; if not, otherwise." There was no mistaking the implied threat.

Second, Parliament passed the Act in Restraint of Appeals (February 1533) which virtually repudiated allegiance to the pope. From now on it was illegal to take appeals from the archbishop's court to Rome. In other words, if the pope was unobliging, the king's case would be decided in England.

Third, Henry had Thomas Cranmer appointed to the vacant see of Canterbury (March 1533). If the pope had been wise he would have prevented his consecration, for Cranmer had already proved himself a king's man in trying to enlist for Henry the support of the European universities. He could be relied on to expedite the king's business to the king's satisfaction, which is precisely what he did two months after his appointment.

Meantime Henry had secretly married Anne Boleyn in January 1533; and since a child, the future Queen Elizabeth, was due to be born in September, there was no time to be lost in declaring the marriage valid and thus assuring a legitimate heir to the throne. It is here that we see the astuteness of the second and third measures noted above, the Act in Restraint of Appeals and Cranmer's appointment. The case could now be tried on English soil and Cranmer would try it. The result was a foregone conclusion. Before the end of May, Cranmer declared Henry's marriage with Catherine void from the beginning and the marriage with Anne valid. The pope commanded Henry to put away Anne within ten days on pain of excommunication. Henry replied by having Anne crowned queen, by forbidding the payment of annates, and by proclaiming himself head of the church in England. Ratification came the next year when Parliament passed the Act of Supremacy which declared that henceforth the king and not the pope was head of the church, and that it was treason to deny his supremacy.[9] The break with Rome was complete and irrevocable: the English Reformation was an accomplished fact.

Henry, then, was supreme in England both politically and ecclesiastically, but he was as far away as ever from having a male heir. Much to his relief the ill-starred Catherine died in January 1536, to be followed after a few months by her supplanter Anne Boleyn, who was accused of misconduct and executed. Some ten days later (one historian[10] says the day after Anne's death) Henry married Jane Seymour, who realized Henry's hopes by presenting him with a baby boy, the future Edward VI who was born in October 1537. The queen herself died a few weeks later.

The next important step in Henry's reign was the dissolution of the monasteries, carried out in two stages, in 1536 and 1538. The monastic lands were sold to nobles, public servants, and merchants; not only was Henry enriched by the transaction, but there came into being a new landed class, loyal to the crown and devoted in their own interests to the Reformed cause. "It was," as Fisher writes, "designedly or undesignedly, the master stroke of Henry's antipapal campaign."[11]

Henry also applied himself to doctrinal changes, embodied in the *Ten Articles,* the first doctrinal statement of the Church of England. The original title was *Articles devised by the King's Highnes Majestie to stablysh Christen quietnes.* Five of the ten articles dealt with doctrine and five with ceremonies, but they adhered for the most part to orthodox Catholic dogma. In 1537 a brief manual of instruction was issued under the title of the *Bishops' Book,* which was revised by Henry and published in 1543 as the *King's Book.* These too were medieval in their theology, their chief aim being to secure peace and unity.

By far the greatest blessing that accompanied the *Ten Articles* was the injunction that a Bible in English be placed and read in every parish church. The translation of Miles Coverdale, authorized by the king in 1536, was used until 1538-39 when it was supplanted by what is known as the *Great Bible* or *Cranmer's Bible* (because Cranmer wrote the preface). Based on the fine translation of William Tindale, it was used till the publication of the King James Version of 1604-11. The importance of an open Bible cannot be overestimated: it was the very keystone of the Reformation.

Thomas Cromwell fell from power in 1540 when he unwisely exaggerated the charms of the homely Anne of Cleves as a possible fourth wife for Henry. The marriage took place but almost immediately was dissolved on a technicality, and Cromwell was beheaded. The real truth is that he believed that England could not stand alone in isolation from the Protestants on the continent, and that an alliance must be formed with a German royal house. He failed to appreciate that Henry's idea of a Reformation was vastly different from the Lutheran conception. But even apart from seeking this impossible alliance, Cromwell of late had been moving too fast for the king. His term of usefulness was over and he died under the executioner's axe.

In the last years of Henry's life the Reformation was not advanced but retarded. In 1539 he induced Parliament to pass the notorious Six Articles Act, which was entirely Catholic in tone. In this Act, known as "the bloody whip with six strings," transubstantiation was reaffirmed; the cup was withheld from the laity; the clergy were not permitted to marry; monastic vows were binding; Masses might be heard in private; and, sixth, oral confession was encouraged. It must be remembered that Henry had always favored the middle way, aiming to take his people with him, averse to moving too swiftly for them; and the people, if antipapal, were still Catholic in their sympathies.

Henry died on January 28, 1547. The Reformation he inaugurated was not so much a religious movement as the subordination of church to state. His purpose was to appropriate to himself ecclesiastical as well as political supremacy. If this entailed religious reform, it was little more than an incidental; there was no "uproar for religion" among the people as there was in Scotland a few years later. It required the flames of persecution which Mary kindled at Smithfield and the fears of Spanish domination to stir the English people to a true reformation of the spirit.

Meantime in 1547 the throne was occupied by a nine-year-old boy, Edward VI, and the government was carried on by a protector and a council. So far as the Reformation was concerned, the central theme of Edward's reign was liturgical reform which amounted to a "revolution in practical religion." [12] The English Reformers had in mind two aims: first, to turn "the Mass into a Communion," and, second, to render into English and to simplify the other services of the church. Accordingly, a *Book of Communion* was prepared and then a more general service book, *The First Prayer-Book of King Edward VI,* which appeared in 1549. It was introduced by an Act of Uniformity which ordained that this form of service should be universally used in England, and enacted penalties on any who refused to conform. The chief compiler of the prayer book was Archbishop Cranmer, the outstanding figure of the reign, and his book is a landmark in liturgical history. With its sonorous phrases and lovely cadences it has exercised an enduring influence on the public worship of the English-speaking race. And yet it was a compromise which Protestants and Romanists alike might use without offense to their conscience. [13] Its real novelty was that, being all in English, it could be understood by every worshiper. [14]

The liturgy was revised in the *Second Prayer-Book of King Edward the Sixth* (1552) which in all essentials is the book still used in the Church of England. Like the first, it was enforced by an Act of Uniformity which made its use compulsory in every church. In the second prayer book the structure of the communion service was changed, "minister" was substituted for "priest" and "table" for "altar," and the idea of transubstantiation was discarded. John Knox, who was then in England, preached a sermon against the practice of kneeling to receive communion; and it is said that as a result of his fulminations the famous "Black Rubric" was hurriedly inserted to explain that a kneeling posture expressed reverence and thankfulness only and not adoration.

After the liturgical question was settled, attention was turned (in a strange inversion of the natural order) to dogma, which was embodied in the *Forty-Two Articles*. Both Lutheran and Calvinist traces are found in them, together with a declaration of distinctively Reformed doctrines—justification by faith, the supreme authority of the Bible, a reduction in the number of the sacraments from seven to two, and a complete repudiation of the Roman doctrine of transubstantiation. The Forty-Two Articles were reduced to thirty-nine in the reign of Queen Elizabeth and remain to this day the Thirty-Nine Articles of the Church of England.

The young king's life was now drawing to a close, and on July 6 of the following year (1553) he died at the age of fifteen. His half sister, Mary Tudor, was crowned queen in Westminster Abbey on October 1, 1553.

It seems certain that in the last years of Edward's reign under the Protector Northumberland the Reformation had been pushed forward too rapidly for the liking of the majority of the people, and now the inevitable reaction set in.[15] One cannot avoid speculating on the course of events if Mary had been gifted with tact, understanding, and even a measure of tolerance. Endowed with those qualities she might have steered England back to the Roman orbit, for the Reformation was not yet built on stable foundations. But Mary in her eagerness to restore England to the Roman obedience eventually flung caution to the winds and indulged in an orgy of persecution that revolted the English sense of decency and fair play.

The turning point of the reign was Mary's marriage in 1554 to Philip of Spain, which from the first was unpopular with the English people. When a Spanish embassy came to arrange it, the boys of London pelted them with snowballs, and Mary publicly appealed for courtesy to be shown to her future husband on his arrival in England.[16] More serious in its effects was the revolt led by Sir Thomas Wyatt as a protest against the marriage and its threat of Spanish domination. The revolt itself was easily suppressed, but it served to harden Mary's heart: if leniency had failed, there was still persecution to be tried.

The last years of the reign are a sorry tale of martyrdom. From 1555 to 1558 nearly three hundred men and women suffered for their faith, but the climax was reached with the burning of Ridley, Latimer, and Cranmer at Oxford. Their deaths were not in vain. "Be of good comfort, Master Ridley," cried Latimer to his friend as the flames billowed around them. "Play the man. We shall this day light such a candle, by God's grace, in England as I trust shall never be put out." But it was Archbishop Cranmer's martyrdom that had perhaps the greatest effect. Several times this weak old man had been forced to recant his so-called heresies, but at the last he redeemed himself. Led to the burning stake, he thrust his right hand into the flames and said: "This which hath sinned, having signed the writing, must be the first to suffer punishment"; and there with superhuman endurance he held it till it was scorched and charred.

Of all the expedients that Mary could have adopted, persecution was the most disastrous to her own ends. It was regarded as part and parcel of the Romanism she was trying to instill, and it disgusted the average humane Englishman. More than any other cause the severities of "Bloody" Mary made England a Protestant nation and inspired the people with real enthusiasm such as they had never known in the more placid days of Edward.

Mary's last years were inexpressibly bitter. She was painfully aware that she had undermined her own cause, she was slighted by her husband and hated by her people. Everything she attempted turned to failure and sorrow. It would be hard to imagine a life more tragic than that of Mary Tudor. She died on November 17, 1558, and it is perhaps symbolic that she was buried in a nun's habit.

Her successor was Anne Boleyn's daughter Elizabeth, an astute young woman of twenty-five with a mind of her own and no little determination. When she came to the throne (1558), England was at a low ebb, an easy prey for a resolute invader, and only the political rivalry of two Catholic powers, France and Spain, saved her when she was weak and thus gave her time to gather strength so that she could no longer be subdued. As so often since, time was on England's side. But Elizabeth also played her part, staving off danger with a hint of marriage here and a suggestion of matrimony there. At length when Philip of Spain, abetted by the pope, decided to strike, it was too late: England was strong enough to repel his Armada.

In England itself it was debated whether Elizabeth would favor Protestantism or retain the still official Romanism, but she did not keep her people long in doubt. It is true that she went to Mass; but when the Abbot of Westminster and his clergy met her with spluttering candles in their hands, Elizabeth imperiously waved them aside and cried, "Away with these torches, we have light enough without them." Her first Parliament also clearly indicated the shape of things to come. It revoked the Catholic legislation of the previous reign, recognized by an Act of Supremacy Elizabeth's headship of the English church, and added an Act of Uniformity enjoining all ministers to use the Second Prayer Book of Edward VI. Bishops and other clerics who refused to recognize the queen as head of the church were deprived, and there was a time when England was almost without bishops. But gradually the sees were filled with men approved by Elizabeth; Matthew Parker was appointed Archbishop of Canterbury; and the change to a moderate Reformation was effected smoothly and peaceably. By 1563 the Elizabethan Settlement was complete and the Church of England established in the form that has lasted to the present time.

What Elizabeth's own religious standpoint was no one can say with any degree of certainty. That shrewd judge of people, John Knox, once said of her that she was "neither good Protestant nor yet resolute Papist."[17] "She agreed with the Pope," as the Cambridge historian puts it, "except about some details; she cherished the Augsburg confession, or something very like it; she was at one, or nearly one, with the Huguenots."[18] In other words, she was Romanist, Lutheran, and Calvinist rolled into one.

The Elizabethan Settlement was a compromise, a *via media,* if not between Rome and Geneva, at least between Luther and Calvin. It rested on a political basis and aimed at cementing national unity. If conscientious scruples could be allayed by terminological vagueness, the end justified the means. Elizabeth further showed her tactfulness by disclaiming the title of "supreme head" of the church and assuming the less offensive "supreme governor."

And yet if the Elizabethan Settlement was agreeable to the vast majority of Englishmen, there were two dissentient parties, the Puritans (with whom we shall deal in the second part of this chapter) and the Catholics. As we have seen, political necessity restrained Elizabeth in her dealings with the Catholics: England was perilously weak, the queen's throne was insecure, and she could not risk offending either the pope or Philip of Spain. After 1570, however, harsher methods were adopted. These were not of Elizabeth's choosing but were made inevitable by a series of Catholic provocations. First, in 1570, Pope Pius V on his own initiative published a bull excommunicating and deposing the queen. It astounded Europe and not least that good Catholic, Philip II of Spain, who had not been consulted beforehand and was said to be most annoyed when the startling news reached him. The pope's precipitate action was a political blunder of the first order, but more was to follow. A Catholic refugee, William Allen (1532-94) had founded an English college at Douai in 1568. At first a rallying ground for English refugees, it became an educational center run on Jesuit lines to train young Catholics as missionaries for the re-establishment of Romanism in England. The movement spread to other centers and by 1580 there were thought to be about a hundred seminary priests from Douai and elsewhere in Europe operating in England and disseminating Catholic propaganda. The third step taken by the pope, now Gregory XIII, who had succeeded Pius V, was to send to England a Jesuit mission led by Edmund Campion and Robert Parsons (1580). Lastly, Pope Gregory, whom no qualms of conscience disturbed where heretics were concerned, implicitly sanctioned the assassination of Elizabeth, and two attempts on her life were actually made (in 1581 and 1584). To the average patriotic English-man who loved his queen, the Catholic menace appeared in the light of a political offense and a national betrayal. As for the government, it intensified the penal laws against Catholics. Heavy fines were imposed for recusancy and for the hearing of Mass, imprisonment was threatened, and all Jesuits and seminary priests were ordered on pain of death to leave the country within forty days. In the remaining twenty years of Elizabeth's reign Roman-ism was a lost cause and Protestantism had come to stay. The only question was: What form of Protestantism would commend itself to the people? Anglicanism or Puritanism or both existing side by side?

THE PURITANS

We pass now to the Puritan revolution, which is so important as to merit separate treatment. First, who *were* the Puritans, and what did they stand for? There never was a "Puritan party" as such: there were diverse groups who stood on the common ground of opposition to the Elizabethan Settlement. Puritanism was an attitude, an outlook, a temper of mind. It was the generic name given to all Protestants who aimed at purifying Anglicanism from the dregs of Roman superstition, hence the nickname "Puritan." To use Milton's phrase, Puritanism was a movement "for the re-form of reformation." It was felt that the Church of England as settled in 1563 was an incongruous mixture of Catholic ceremonial and Protestant doctrine, that Reformation must be carried to its logical conclusion, and that the break with Rome must be clear-cut and complete. It might also be said that the Puritan took life more seriously than the average churchman. If he was austere it was because he saw life as an unceasing struggle between good and evil, a lifelong battle that absorbed all a man's strength and energies. His guiding principle was his responsibility before God. As Milton wrote (somewhat precociously) on attaining the age of twenty-three,

> "All is, if I have grace to use it so,
> As ever in my great Task-Master's eye."

Rectitude rather than love was the inspiration of Puritanism, simplicity of worship and moral integrity its ideals.

The name "Puritan" came into general use about 1564. The groups traced their origins to those returning exiles who had fled from the Marian persecutions and who, though still a small minority of the population, rapidly increased in number. At the beginning of Elizabeth's reign the Puritans were for the most part inside the church, striving within its framework to change its ritual and government to a more definitely Reformed pattern. It was only later that a movement was set on foot that aimed at the separation of church and state.

The first quarrel between Anglicans and Puritans was over vestments and is known as the "Vestiarian Controversy" (1563). Certain vestments had been prescribed by the queen in her religious settlement, but the Puritans held that there ought to be no compulsion in the matter of dress. They "scrupled" about the clergy's wearing of cap and gown on weekdays and the surplice on Sundays. The whole dispute was trivial in the extreme. "We confess one faith of Jesus Christ," said one, "we preach one doctrine, we acknowledge one ruler over all things; shall we be so used for a surplus (sic); shall brethren persecute brethren for a forkèd cap?" But presently the Puritans were objecting to other things such as the sign of the cross in baptism, kneeling at communion, the use of organs in churches, even of a ring in the marriage ceremony, and the observance of too many holy days. A petition was presented to Convocation requesting the abolition of these and, concerning vestments, the sanction only of the surplice. It is significant that the petition was defeated by only one vote, and the Puritans or "Precisians" felt encouraged to set themselves more and more against Romish habits and practices.

The second stage was reached in 1572. In that year a Puritan conference in London published a document known as the "First Admonition" which expressed the view that ministers, freely elected by congregations, should take the place of bishops. The Puritan leader at this time was Thomas Cartwright, who in a "Second Admonition" outlined a scheme of church government that was Calvinist and Presbyterian and included such ideas as the popular election of ministers, the provision of a directory of public worship, and the erection of presbyteries to administer discipline. Such a church he founded at Wandsworth in 1572. Here obviously was a much more serious development than the question of vestments. The whole structure of the established order was undermined and in the queen's eyes the stability of the state itself was threatened. Both she and her bishops were at one in suppressing the movement with the result that Cartwright was forced to flee abroad (1574). He was no secessionist but aimed rather at introducing the Presbyterian form of government into the Anglican Church. His chief contribution to Puritanism was that by his efforts it had become largely Presbyterian in outlook.

The first Separatist was Robert Browne of Cambridge who founded a congregational church at Norwich in 1580 or 1581. It can hardly be said that he was of heroic mold or, if the story is true, of a gallant disposition. "Old father Browne," we read, "being reproved for beating his old wife, distinguished that he did not beat her as his wife but as a curst old woman." In later life he recanted (admittedly under pressure) and was received back into office in the Church of England. And yet he left an indelible mark on the history of the English church, and the movement he initiated became the chief instrument of Puritanism in Elizabeth's reign. He enunciated the principle of "voluntaryism," or congregationalism, as the only proper form of the church, which was a company of believers and should be democratically governed. In a volume entitled *A Book which showeth the Life and Manners of all true Christians* he lays down the principle of a "gathered" church. Each church should be independent, free from state control and equally free from the jurisdiction of bishops and presbyteries: it should have the power of self-government in which all members would participate; and its officials—pastors, teachers, and elders—should be elected by the people. Discarding ritual, the Separatists used the simplest form of service; they relied on inspiration and were willing to dispense with an educated ministry. It is evident that Browne borrowed much from the Anabaptists, though unlike them he retained the practice of infant baptism.

The rise of Separatism clearly denied the possibility of a national church and immediately spurred the authorities to action. Elizabeth found a willing agent in the new Archbishop of Canterbury, John Whitgift, whom she skittishly called "her little black husband." The queen's first two archbishops, Parker and Grindal, had been moderate men, but Whitgift (1583-1604) was of a different stamp. Though himself a Calvinist he aimed at the suppression of Puritanism. His first sermon after his appointment, preached at St. Paul's Cross on November 17, 1583, clearly declared his determination to bring the Puritans to heel.[19] The repressive measures began with his Six Articles of 1583, which demanded assent to the supremacy of the queen in church and state and to the scriptural nature of the Book of Common Prayer and the Thirty-Nine Articles. Heavy penalties for noncompliance were threatened and heavy penalties were relentlessly exacted. Defaulters were dealt with by the Court of High Commission which dispensed with the necessity of a trial in the civil courts and was inquisitorial in its methods. More than two hundred ministers were suspended. Many others, however, observed the letter but not the spirit of the Articles, and though adhering to the forms of the established church used Presbyterian ideas and methods.

Whitgift's next step (1586) was to prohibit the publication of all manuscripts unless approved either by himself or by the Bishop of London, hoping in this way to prevent the spread of Puritan ideas. But the only result was to harden the Puritans' determination, and in 1588 or 1589 there came the publication of the scurrilous "Martin Marprelate" Tracts, anonymous writings that ridiculed the bishops as "petty antichrists, proud prelates, intolerable withstanders of reformation, enemies of the gospel and covetous wretched priests." It was a vain gesture and impelled Whitgift to still harsher measures. Already in 1587 he had arrested Cartwright on his return to England and with him the two early Separatist leaders Barrow and Greenwood, who were imprisoned at the Fleet and detained there till their execution at Tyburn in 1593. A month later another Separatist leader, John Penry, shared their fate, and, all told, some seventy Separatists were imprisoned in the last years of Elizabeth's reign. The climax was reached with the Conventicle Act of 1593 which threatened with exile—and with death if they returned—all those who absented themselves from the established church and attended conventicles. Many Separatists were thus driven to seek refuge in Holland where they founded churches of their own with far-reaching consequences for the future. The Puritan martyrs suffered because they challenged the established religious order. Henry and Mary had persecuted people for having wrong ideas, that is, for heresy; Elizabeth and her agents persecuted people for refusing to conform to her religious settlement. At the time it seemed as if the queen had won all along the line. The Puritan ringleaders were deprived of their livings or imprisoned or exiled; ordinary men and women suffered; many more went in daily fear of their lives. But then as always the blood of the martyrs was the seed of the church, and though Puritanism seemed to have fallen on evil days, it was still a virile force. One notable feature of the reign of Elizabeth was the growing alliance between the Puritans and Parliament. In view of the relentless opposition of the queen it was natural that they should look to Parliament for support, and more and more Parliament came to side with them. It was a significant indication of things to come.

Toward the end of Elizabeth's reign Richard Hooker in his classic, *Of the Laws of Ecclesiastical Polity,* tried "to satisfy all tender consciences" and to reconcile the two opposing religious parties. But the time for composing differences had passed; by Whitgift's intransigence a deep wedge had been driven between Anglicanism and Puritanism and the stage was set for the internecine struggle that was to ravage England in the 1640's. Meantime, the queen's reign was drawing to a close, and men were anxiously gazing across the Scottish border with eyes fixed on the new king who should rule in London.

James VI of Scotland held a good opinion of James VI, and

when he became James I of England the change of title did nothing to lower him in his own esteem. At thirty-seven he considered
himself the repository of all wisdom. Was he not an expert in
theology and a past master in statecraft? Was he not already a
distinguished scholar and author? In one of his publications, *The
Trew Law of Free Monarchies* (1598), he had shown the world
where he stood and set out his claim to be God's vicegerent on
earth. The "free monarchy" was God's special creation; the monarch was responsible to none but God and must not be curbed
by governments or subjects. Rather was he "an image of God on
earth, a god sitting upon God's throne, and called a god by God
Himself." He must be the sole judge of all things in church and
state and all men must render him unquestioning obedience.
Thus was born the theory of the divine right of kings. James
labored under three disadvantages: he was a poor judge of men
and allowed himself to be influenced by favorites of the wrong
kind; he was obstinate without a sense of humor; and he made
the mistake of confusing book learning with wisdom and clever-
ness with common sense. In 1603 this garrulous pedant, "the wisest
fool in Christendom," ascended the English throne.

All three religious parties in the state—Catholics, Presbyterians,
and Episcopalians—expected much from the new monarch. The
Catholics looked on James as the son of Mary Queen of Scots,
that martyr for the true faith: the son of such a mother must
surely support their cause. (James indeed made them promises
but was unable to fulfill them; the disappointed Catholics there-
upon plotted against both him and Parliament, but with the
unmasking of the Gunpowder Plot in 1605 they were entirely
discredited.) The second party, the Presbyterians, argued that
James had been trained and educated in a Presbyterian land, and
that it was natural that he should want to encourage Presbyterianism in his new kingdom. They failed to understand that
though James was a Calvinist in theology, he abominated the
idea of democratic church government, and that he still remembered the indignities he had suffered at the hands of rugged
Scotch Presbyterians who would unceremoniously pluck his sleeve

and call him "God's silly vassal." The third party, the Episcopalians, guessed rightly. They knew how the Scottish ministers
had humiliated the king and that his high ideas of authority
could best be realized in their own church. They had not long
to wait to have their guess confirmed.

It is unnecessary for our purpose to study all the various acts
of James' reign. Right at the beginning he took up a position
from which he never retreated. He began as he meant to end and
continued as he began. This was obvious at the Hampton Court
Conference in 1604, when the Puritans submitted the "Millenary
Petition," so called because it was said to express the views of a
thousand ministers. Before James had become king many Puritans in their services had omitted parts of the Prayer Book ritual
which they disliked, and now they appealed for certain relaxa-
tions from ceremonies they found objectionable. The petitioners,
all members of the Anglican Church, proffered their request in
the most moderate terms, urging the abolition of the ring in marriage, kneeling to receive communion, and giving the sign of the
cross at baptism. James, who presided, was sternly uncompromising. They must conform, he said, or he would "harry them out of
the land." He insisted on the necessity of "one doctrine and one
discipline, one religion in substance and in ceremony." He told
them "a Scottish Presbytery agreeth as well with a monarchy as
God with the devil," and he added, quite irrelevantly, the famous
words, "no bishop, no king." Nobody had even suggested the
abolition of bishops: the question of episcopacy had never arisen.
All that the petitioners asked for was some modification of the
Prayer Book. Without sacrificing anything vital, a wise and tactful
ruler might well have granted their requests and so laid the
foundations of ecclesiastical unity. But James was neither tactful
nor wise; he wanted to grasp the shadow as well as hold the substance of power; and so was cast away a golden opportunity. The
only good thing that came of the conference was the appointment
of a committee which in the course of the next seven years produced that most famous of all English versions of the Bible, the
Authorized Version of King James. As for the rest, a wider chasm

was opened up between Anglicans and Puritans, and the seeds of a more bitter antagonism were sown. Already as a result of the Hampton Court Conference some three hundred Puritan ministers were deprived of their livings, conformity continued to be rigorously enforced and nonconformity to be punished. Puritanism was denied official recognition; the Puritans were expelled from the state church and thrown into the arms of the Separatists. But it was impossible that such a movement, increasing alike in numbers and influence, could live in perpetual outlawry. If freedom of worship were not conceded, it must be won; and if peaceful means were ineffectual, the sword must be drawn. Coming events were casting their shadows before them.

Meantime, before James died, an event took place the repercussions of which were destined to be felt all over the world. On September 6, 1620, there sailed from Plymouth the Pilgrim Fathers, with the words of John Robinson, their minister, still ringing in their ears, "I am very confident that the Lord hath more truth and light yet to break out of His Holy Word."

We have already seen how Whitgift's repressive measures forced many Separatists to seek refuge abroad, especially in Holland, and those refugees were joined by many more as a result of James' unreasonable severities. Separatist congregations were founded at Leyden, Middelburg and Amsterdam. The church at Leyden was set up by John Robinson in 1607-08, and it was from that congregation that the Pilgrim Fathers sailed in the *Mayflower*, a small ship of a hundred and eighty tons carrying about a hundred persons. They set sail for Virginia where they had received a grant of land, but arrived in Massachusetts at Plymouth Rock and immediately established a church. New England owes much to the heroic, if stern, virtues of those hardy settlers. Democratic in spirit and aggressive in zeal, they regarded difficulties as handicaps to be overcome, and even in the pioneering days maintained a high standard of education and culture. The churches they founded were congregational in form and eventually exercised a strong influence in promoting political democracy in America.

During the following twenty years there was a constant stream of emigrants across the Atlantic, some 20,000 of them during the eleven years of Charles I's personal rule without Parliament (1629-40). The New England church was composed of men who desired to worship God as their conscience dictated, and yet they were strangely intolerant. In 1631 the young Roger Williams became minister at Salem, Massachusetts, but four years later was banished for his alleged revolutionary ideas. Moving to the neighboring Rhode Island he founded a new religious colony where every man was granted the right of religious freedom. Though eventually the New England settlers largely shaped the political future of America, the emigrations from first to last were inspired by religious motives, as is proved by the fact that they ceased in 1640 when persecution in England came to an end. As one of the colonists wrote, "We now enjoy God and Jesus Christ, and is that not enough?"

While those settlements were taking root in America, affairs in England were moving from bad to worse. When James I died in 1625, resentment was running high, and his earnest, devout, but singularly tactless son, Charles I, far from allaying, only exacerbated the uneasiness felt by so many. With typical Stuart obstinacy Charles bent his energies to crushing nonconformity, and was loyally supported by that High Church bigot William Laud (1573-1645), who became Archbishop of Canterbury in 1633. The slightest irregularity was punished, Puritanism was suppressed, and at least outward uniformity was secured. But as Selbie, quoting from Tacitus, aptly puts it, "he made a wilderness and called it peace."[20]

If Laud's severities provoked the Puritans beyond endurance, Parliament was completely antagonized by the unconstitutional methods of Charles. Religious and political grievances combined to make war inevitable, and civil war broke out in 1642. It is unnecessary here to follow its course, but from the religious point of view mention must be made of the Westminster Assembly of Divines which met in London in 1643 and continued its sittings till 1647. It was composed of a hundred and twenty members—five Separatists, or Independents as they were now called, a few

Episcopalians, and the others Presbyterians or Calvinists. A Confession of Faith was drawn up together with a Larger and Shorter Catechism and a Directory of Public Worship, which are still used as subordinate standards by the majority of Presbyterian churches.

The war dragged on till 1646, Charles I was executed in 1649, and from then till 1658 Oliver Cromwell ruled as Lord Protector. The leading party were the Independents, Cromwell's party; but they were a small minority in the state, and with Cromwell's death their influence suddenly waned. It might be said of them that they won their war but lost the peace; and yet their ideas survived to color the religious thought of England. With the restoration of the monarchy in 1660 Anglicanism was reinstated, but the Independents' fight for liberty of conscience was not in vain, and indeed the very number of Protestant sects made toleration inevitable. Nevertheless nearly thirty years were still to elapse and a revolution was required before persecution came to an end and religious liberty was granted. At last in 1689 by the Act of Toleration, while the Church of England became the established church, religious freedom was extended to all Protestant dissenters, including Quakers, provided they were Trinitarians.

So ended what might be called the Puritan Reformation, the effects of which on present-day church life can scarcely be exaggerated. The modern Congregational and Baptist Churches are the lineal descendants of the Separatists, while both, along with Quakers and Methodists, owe much to the Puritan spirit of revolt. Indeed, it may be fairly claimed that the emergence of the Protestant *sects* was England's distinctive contribution to the Reformation.

A second point ought to be noted. From the time of Elizabeth onward, the persecutions were political rather than religious, and this fact is made clear by the emigrations that England, and only England, permitted. England was the only nation (with Scotland) that allowed the emigration of "heretics." Spain banned Protestants from South America, France denied the Huguenots the right of entry into Canada, and Holland placed similar restrictions on its Catholics. But any Englishman (or Scotsman), whatever his creed, was free at any time to collect his belongings and emigrate to America. Conservative and even reactionary in many ways, the Stuart kings were liberal at least in their colonial policy. It may be that they were acting in what they considered to be their own self-interests, but whatever the reason may have been, they encouraged a movement, big with promise for the future, that has greatly enriched the life of the church today in North America.

8

THE REFORMATION IN SCOTLAND
TO THE DEATH OF KNOX

✠

If the average citizen of the United States were asked the question: "What was the finest hour in your country's history?" his thoughts would probably stray back to the 1770's, to the stirring days of the Declaration of Independence and the determined fight for freedom. Similarly, if the average Scotsman were asked the same question, he too would speak of the epic struggle for freedom, waged four and a half centuries earlier, against the same enemy, England. He would think of his national heroes, of William Wallace and Robert Bruce, and say that their achievements overshadowed all else in his country's story.

But while one would be right, the other would be entirely wrong. Our American would be right because his War of Independence had a real impact on world history. If there had been no such war and therefore no United States as a sovereign nation, it is evident that world history would have run a vastly different course.

But this cannot be said of the Scottish War of Independence. Scotsmen look back to it with justifiable pride; but the fact remains that if Scotland had failed, if in the early fourteenth century it had been absorbed by England as a vassal state, the course of world history would not have been diverted. The Scottish people have a long, enthralling, and not dishonorable history, but only once in all the centuries did they as a nation decisively affect world affairs. That impact is not to be found in their wars of independence, but two and a half centuries later in the Reformation of John Knox and others. Then indeed Scotland exercised an influence that was world-wide, the repercussions of which are felt to this day. But for the stand taken by ordinary men and women in a small impoverished land on the fringes of civilization, life and thought would be radically different at the present time not only in Scotland and England, but also in Europe and not least in the United States of America. For one brief hour Scotland held in her hands the destinies of the world.

It happened in this way. The Scottish Reformation was a deeply spiritual movement: there can be no shadow of doubt about that; there was a veritable "uproar for religion." But at the same time there flowed a strong political undercurrent. Religion and politics marched together. A Protestant Scotland meant friendship with the old enemy, England; a Roman Catholic Scotland meant a continuation of the Franco-Scottish alliance and open hostility to England. Could England have withstood the shock, encircled as she was by hostile forces, ill-prepared for war, and disunited in religious convictions? Could England have remained a Protestant nation, an oasis, as it were, in a Roman Catholic desert? And if the two kingdoms of Britain had abandoned the Reformation, how long could the isolated Protestant communities in Europe have survived the onslaught of a united Romanism? And with the Reformation stifled in Europe, could the United States have become the predominantly Protestant nation it is today? All depended on the course of events in far-off Scotland, with its population at the time not greatly exceeding half a million souls. The fate of the Reformation hung in suspense, the destinies of the world were balanced on a razor's edge. These were the stupendous issues at stake when Knox returned to Scotland in May 1559.

But this is to anticipate, and we must start at the beginning. In the first half of the sixteenth century, Scotland was a poor, unenlightened country four hundred years behind the times, emerging but slowly from the Middle Ages. For centuries it had lacked a strong central government to restrain its turbulent nobles; its institutions were rudimentary; and progress was retarded by a succession of infant kings and regencies. At times there was complete anarchy.

On the spiritual side the picture was no less somber. It is true that the medieval church had faithfully served its day and generation. In the darkest hours it had kept the fire of devotion burning and the torch of learning alight; it had encouraged the practice of the gentler, more humane virtues; in a lawless age it had stood for an ordered authority. But the days of its usefulness were past and it was now rotten to the core. Alone among the countries in western Europe that adhered to Romanism, the Scottish church had made no attempt to reform itself. Living in the past, it had lost its hold on man's mind and conscience, while the abuses of its clergy brought upon it unmitigated and universal contempt.

Even Roman Catholic historians themselves admit the decay in the pre-Reformation church. There were all the usual ecclesiastical abuses, such as the scandalous practice of conferring benefices, clerical ignorance, and above all clerical depravity. Archibald Hay, writing to David Beaton on the latter's appointment in 1538 as Archbishop of St. Andrews and Primate of Scotland, bitterly complains of priests coming to the "heavenly table who have not slept off yesterday's debauch." Drunkenness and immorality were among the more heinous evils. It would be tedious to enter into details and one instance may suffice. "On the 27th of November 1549," writes Hay Fleming, "a provincial council of the prelates and clergy of Scotland met in the church of the Black Friars at Edinburgh" to extirpate heresy and institute reform. Of the seven constituent members, "the archbishop [of St. Andrews] and three out of the six bishops were shamelessly depraved men, and another of the bishops had an unsavoury reputation—a startling preponderance on the side of the devil."[1] It was a preponderance of five to two. And those were the men who would purify a church! The whole matter is summed up in Patrick's *Statutes of the Scottish Church:* "By far the most lamentable and irrepressible infirmity of the Scottish clergy [was] the corruption of morals and profane lewdness of life in churchmen of all ranks."

In these circumstances it is evident that sooner or later reformation of some kind was bound to come, but there were several factors that accelerated the process. First may be mentioned the influence of John Wycliffe's doctrines (Lollardism) which were probably circulated by some of the numerous Scotsmen who studied at Oxford when Wycliffe occupied the chair of theology at that university. In 1494, a hundred and ten years after his death, it would seem that his movement was still alive, and we have the remarkable episode of the so-called Lollards of Kyle, thirty-four in number, whose doctrines were identical with Wycliffe's and at complete variance with those of the Catholic Church. The Lollards of Kyle, though refusing to recant, seem to have escaped without punishment, but their movement mysteriously faded out. Lollardism as a whole was never of vital importance in Scottish affairs, and yet its name at least was not entirely forgotten as we may gather from the lines of a sixteenth-century metrical version of the Lord's Prayer:

> "Saif us from schame, and from dispair,
>   From enbeleve, and Lollard's lair" [teaching].

A second contributory factor was the importation of Lutheran books which were widely read and discussed. The danger from this source was early recognized and an Act of Parliament was passed in 1525 forbidding the practice as illegal. But religious forces cannot be stayed by legislation, and the flow of heretical books was unretarded.

Besides the importation of religious books from abroad, there were pamphlets written within the country itself, ballads and plays by which the eyes of the people were opened to the enormities of the Roman Church and clergy and by which the truth was spread. There was a collection of homely poems and songs entitled the *Gude and Godlie Ballatis,* published about 1542, bitingly satirical in tone but pervaded by an earnest evangelical piety, though often crude and hardly to be ranked as literature.

> "God send everie priest ane wyfe,
>   And everie nunne ane man,
>   That they mycht leve that haly lyfe,
>   As first the kirk began."

These ballads were widely circulated and enjoyed immense popularity, and through them the new doctrines were brought home to ordinary people in a simple and striking form that all could understand.

Brief reference must also be made to Sir David Lyndsay's poems, especially his *Satire of the Three Estates* which was performed before King James V and his court at Linlithgow on Ascension Day 1540. In this, too, were brought to light the abuses of the church, the widespread contempt of the clergy, the discontent among the people and their desire for the true preaching of the Word. Though not himself a Reformer, Lyndsay did much to promote the work of reform, and is thus described by Sir Walter Scott:

> The flash of that satiric rage,
> Which, bursting on the early stage,
> Branded the vices of the age
> And broke the keys of Rome.[2]

But when every allowance is made, the causes mentioned were only subsidiary, and there were two prime factors in bringing about the Scottish Reformation—a book and an example. The book was a volume from which the Scottish Reformers drew their strength and inspiration, and that book was the Bible. Realizing well that this book was the root cause of heresy, the Scottish bishops had prohibited the reading of it in the vernacular; but in 1542 Parliament was induced to permit the use of an English translation, so that, according to Knox, it was soon to be found on every gentleman's table, and those who could not read it for themselves had it read to them. As Professor Croft Dickinson has written, "With the reading and the knowledge of the Word of God there arises a desire for a new Church, a Church pure and undefiled, a Church free from man-made ceremony and invention."[3] An open Bible was the first prime cause of the Scottish Reformation.

The second was an example, the moving example of the Scottish martyrs, of men like Patrick Hamilton and George Wishart. There had been martyrdoms before their time, of such as the English Lollard James Resby in 1407 and the Bohemian emissary

Paul Craw or Crawar in 1433. But those were not comparable in their influence with the death of the young Patrick Hamilton, the "Proto-Martyr of the Scottish Reformation," who was burned at St. Andrews in 1528, and to whose pathetic story we now turn.

The name of Patrick Hamilton is one of three or four names that must be remembered in connection with the early Scottish Reformation. There is an aura of romance and glamor about this young man, the descendant of a family with royal connections,[4] who died so piteously at the age of twenty-five. Born in 1503 or 1504, he traveled extensively in his early youth—to Paris (where he took his master's degree), to Louvain, and later to Marburg— and it was during this time that he embraced Reformed ideas. In 1527 he returned to Scotland and began to preach. His piety and true evangelistic spirit are clearly shown in a treatise he wrote known as *Patrick's Places,* in which we encounter such sentiments as these: faith makes "God and man friends," it brings "God and man together"; or again, "O how ready would we be to help others, if we knew His goodness and gentleness toward us. He is a good and gentle Lord and He does all things for nought. Let us, I beseech you, follow His footsteps, whom all the world ought to praise and worship."

These surely are most admirable sentiments, and yet it was for such a blameless faith that he suffered. The truth is that he was becoming a menace to the Roman Church, and Archbishop James Beaton, of evil memory, sensed the danger. On false pretenses he lured the young man to St. Andrews, where eventually he was arrested and condemned, and on February 29, 1528, was burned as a heretic.[5] His death was slow and agonizing. Through some carelessness the fire was started before there was enough dry wood, so that, as one eyewitness (Alesius) put it, "he was rather roasted than burned." Near the end he cried with a loud voice, "Lord Jesus, receive my spirit! How long shall darkness overwhelm this realm? And how long wilt Thou suffer this tyranny of men?"[6]

Patrick Hamilton's martyrdom was not in vain. Knox tells us how one John Lindsay thus counseled his friend Archbishop

Beaton: "My Lord, if ye burn any more . . . let them be burnt in deep cellars; for the reek [smoke] of Master Patrick Hamilton has infected as many as it blew upon."[7] To Knox himself the death of this young man was the first decisive blow struck for the Reformation in Scotland. His "reek" indeed infected all, and men angrily began to question the justice of the condemnation of one so transparently blameless and good. Many followed his teaching and the Scottish Reformation spread. With us all, what we are and do speaks more loudly than what we say; so it was with Patrick Hamilton. His real influence lay neither in his theology nor in his teaching but in his martyrdom.

In the decade following Hamilton's death the Reformation had taken hold in many parts of Europe—in Germany and Switzerland, in France and the Netherlands, in England. Seated on his throne at Rome, Pope Paul III had ample cause for disquiet, and now he focused his gaze on far-off Scotland. Would she too abandon her ancient faith? Could nothing be done to buttress her allegiance? Was there in that northern kingdom a man to be found who would stem the rising tide of heresy—a loyal, ruthless man, unrestrained by scruples? There was indeed such a man, ambitious and devoted to Rome. He was the nephew of James Beaton, the late Archbishop of St. Andrews, and his name was David Beaton whom the Scottish Reformers denounced as the "bloody butcher of the saints of God." This was the man who in December 1538 was created Cardinal and Primate of all Scotland. From now on there were no half measures, and heresy was stamped out with unabating ferocity.

The climax was reached in 1546 with the martyrdom of George Wishart—and his is the second great name to be remembered. Born about 1512 or 1513, Wishart was educated at King's College, Aberdeen, and from there proceeded to the coastal town of Montrose where he became a schoolmaster. Sometime between 1535 and 1538 he was accused of heresy, his crime being that he taught children to read the New Testament in Greek! In order to escape persecution he fled first to England and later to Switzerland, where he imbibed deeply the teaching of Calvin. But his real work began in 1544 when he returned to his native land and was launched on his career as a preacher. It was a courageous step, for he was a marked man and an excommunicated outlaw. His chief center was Dundee, where he rendered conspicuous service —especially during a plague that ravaged the city, when he ministered to the stricken people, alike to their souls and bodies. It was only when the plague abated that he consented to leave the city.

After a time we find him preaching in and around Haddington, less than twenty miles east of Edinburgh, and it was there that a greater than he, John Knox, first came under his influence. When Wishart preached, Knox bore a two-handed sword for his protection, and Knox was present when Wishart was arrested at a neighboring village. In vain did he plead to accompany him: Wishart would not permit him. "Nay," he said, "return to your bairns [children—Knox was tutor to three boys who lived nearby], and God bless you. One is sufficient for a sacrifice."[8] He was under no illusions concerning the doom that awaited him. He fell into the clutches of Cardinal Beaton who immediately condemned him to death: he was burned at St. Andrews on the first day of March 1546, only eleven days after the death of Martin Luther.

But the days of the tyrant himself were numbered. Many of the bystanders at Wishart's burning ground their teeth and swore to wreak vengeance on this evil man who for eight long years had breathed out threatenings and slaughter against the disciples of the Lord. And they kept their word. Barely three months had elapsed when he was waylaid and then murdered in his own castle of St. Andrews, a deed to be deplored but an end devoutly to be wished, or as an anonymous contemporary verse puts it:

> "As for the Cardinal, I grant
> He was a man we well could want,
>   And we'll forget him sune;
> But yet I think, the sooth to say,
> Although the loon (rogue) is well away,
>   The deed was foully done."

We pass now to the most famous of all the Scottish Reformers whose name is a household word throughout the whole Protestant world, John Knox. The Reformation in Scotland has sometimes been termed, not without reason, Knox's Reformation, since without his energy, determination, and dauntless spirit the cause of reform might have been irretrievably lost. John Knox was a great man: let there be no question about that. Nor must we allow ourselves to be biased by our sympathy with a young, fascinating, clever queen who could dissolve into tears if she thought they might serve a useful purpose. Mary Queen of Scots was a lovely, attractive woman; but she was a bigoted Romanist who abhorred Protestantism and was prepared to go to any lengths to extirpate it. It was inevitable that she and Knox should disagree, as they actually did at a number of stormy interviews. But that comes later in the story.

Of Knox's early life we know practically nothing. It is now generally believed that he was born about 1515 and that he was ordained as a priest at the canonical age of twenty-five. He first enters on the stage of history in 1546 as the man who bore the two-handed sword at George Wishart's preachings. On Wishart's death he proceeded to St. Andrews where he joined the Protestant garrison defending the castle against the French. There his preaching abilities were quickly recognized and he accepted, most reluctantly (he tells us), the call to be a preacher. After his first sermon "Some said, 'Others sned [lop] the branches of the Papistry, but he strikes at the root, to destroy the whole.' . . . Others said, 'Master George Wishart spake never so plainly, and yet he was burnt: even so will he be.' "[9] It was fortunate for the Scottish Reformation that this gloomy prognostication was unfulfilled.

Nevertheless, the position of the besieged was hopeless. Lacking help from England and invested by a French fleet anchored off the city, they were forced to capitulate. A month later, in August 1547, Knox and the other defenders were made galley slaves. A vivid description of this ordeal is given by Lindsay in the second volume of his history. "For nineteen months he had to endure this living death . . . He had to sit chained with four or six others to the rowing benches . . . without change of posture by day, and compelled to sleep, still chained, under the benches by night; exposed to the elements day and night alike; enduring the lash of the overseer . . . feeding on the insufficient meals of coarse biscuit [cookies] and porridge of oil and beans; chained along with the vilest malefactors. The French papists had invented this method of treating all who differed from them in religious matters. It could scarcely make Knox the more tolerant of French policy or of the French religion." [10]

At last after nineteen harrowing months he was released and reached England by early April 1549, England then being a Protestant nation under Edward VI. It was during this time that Knox almost became a bishop. He was offered the bishopric of Rochester but declined. After a fruitful ministry at Berwick, he drifted south to London where he was appointed one of King Edward's six chaplains and where, too, he met his future wife, Marjorie Bowes, one of a family of fifteen children.

Knox's promising career was cut short in 1553 by Edward's death and the accession of Queen Mary Tudor (not to be confused with Mary Queen of Scots). Once again he was obliged to flee from persecution, and this time he went straight to Calvin at Geneva, where he studied at close range what he describes as the government of a "perfect city" in obedience to "the word of God." During his stay at Geneva he accepted an invitation to become one of the preachers to the English congregation at Frankfurt, Germany, but he remained there for only six months. His quarrel was with what he termed "unprofitable ceremonies" and so he left "that superstitious and contentious company."

In 1555 he paid a fleeting visit to Scotland, preaching and encouraging the faithful. If he was distressed to observe the temporizing of the Scottish barons, he was agreeably surprised to find that the Reformation had taken so tenacious a hold and that there was such "fervent thirst" and "groaning for the bread of life." All that was required was a strong leader, Knox himself, to harness the rising tide of discontent and revolt. But he con-

sidered the time not yet ripe, and after nine months of pre-
paratory work he left Scotland and returned to Geneva.

It was three years later, in 1559, that the great hour struck.
The Protestant leaders, convinced that he was the only man who
could save his country, sent a deputation to invite him to return.
Calvin and others warned him that he dare not refuse "unless he
would declare himself rebellious unto his God, and unmerciful to
his country."[11] Accordingly, he set out for Scotland and arrived
in Edinburgh on May 2, 1559.

During Knox's absence, especially from 1552 to 1558, the
Romanists had adopted a policy of conciliation. Mary of Guise,
mother of Mary Queen of Scots, was appointed Regent in April
1554. Knox made no attempt to conceal his unfavorable opinion
of this woman, describing her in pithy if unflattering terms as
"an unruly cow saddled by mistake." Being a Frenchwoman as
well as a bigoted Romanist, she naturally strove to buttress the
tottering French alliance. If for a time she spared the Protestants
it was not through any tender feelings for them; it was only that
leniency seemed to be the better policy. But in 1558, conciliation
having failed, she reverted to persecution which culminated in
the martyrdom of the eighty-year-old Walter Myln or Mill, the
last Scotsman to suffer for the Protestant cause. Bound to the
stake, he addressed those who stood by: "I am four score years
past and by nature have not long to live; but if I be burned,
there shall a hundred rise from my ashes better than I." His
death was the climax and culminating point: the Scottish people
were determined to tolerate no longer such acts of inhuman
barbarity.

The year 1559 was a fateful year in the annals of the Scottish
church and nation, and events rushed swiftly to a climax. The
queen regent died that year, and Knox on his return found the
country virtually in a state of civil war. At once he began ener-
getically to stir the people, and to the task he brought exceptional gifts. His voice, his appearance, his every look and gesture
testified to his burning conviction in the rightness of his cause;
his force of character, commanding personality, and uncompro-

mising spirit dominated all who came into contact with him; and he had the power of speech to move men, to appeal to them, and to stir them to resolute and determined action. His vehement preaching carried people off their feet. It was said that "the voice of that one man is able to put more life in us in one hour than five hundred trumpets blustering in our ears." Only a spark was required to set the magazine ablaze, and that spark was struck at Perth just nine days after Knox returned. On May 11, following a sermon against "idolatry," a priest was tactless enough to attempt to celebrate Mass and stupidly struck a boy who shouted in protest. The boy retaliated by throwing a stone which missed the priest but broke an image. Suddenly pandemonium was let loose and other monuments were destroyed. Similar demolitions were carried out in other cities, for Knox was resolved to obliterate every trace of corrupt worship and throw out the last poisonous dregs of papistry.

With exciting rapidity event followed spirited event. Edinburgh was occupied by the Reformers on June 29; civil war continued, but early in the following year, on February 27, 1560, by the Treaty of Berwick, Scotland and England promised mutual aid against France. An English army was dispatched to help the Scottish Protestants; on the night of June 10/11 the French garrison of Leith capitulated; and by the Treaty of Edinburgh on July 6 the revolution was an accomplished fact and Scotland was won for the Reformation. (It was said that for the first time in history a conquering English army departed from Scotland followed by blessings and not curses.)

Now, indeed, was Knox's opportunity. Daily in St. Giles' Cathedral he lectured on the book of Haggai and the building of the temple. On August 24 by a decree of Parliament, Romanism was abolished. A confession of faith was approved, a book of common order issued, and the First Book of Discipline prepared. Before considering these, let us pause for a moment to note the incredible speed with which the Scottish Reformation was accomplished. Only one year had elapsed between Knox's return and the establishment of the Reformed faith. Well might

Calvin write: "As we wonder at success incredible in so short a time, so also we give great thanks to God, whose special blessing here shines forth."

The three documents referred to in the previous paragraph, the Scots' Confession of Faith, the Book of Common Order, and the First Book of Discipline, were drawn up by the six Johns— John Knox himself, John Winram, John Spottiswoode, John Willock, John Douglas, and John Row—but they were basically the work of Knox. All three documents have been of vast importance in the history of the Scottish church.

The Confession of Faith was hurriedly prepared—actually in the space of four days*—and was adopted by Parliament in 1560. It makes no pretense of being a complete system of theology, but it held the field till 1647 when it was replaced by the Westminster Confession of Faith. Of its twenty-five chapters, the first fifteen are occupied with a statement of the New Testament doctrines of God, Christ, the Holy Spirit, redemption, and the Christian life. Chapters xvi and xviii deal with the church, which is discerned by three marks, the true preaching of the Word, the right administration of the sacraments, and discipline uprightly ministered. Two sacraments only are recognized, baptism and the Lord's Supper. A distinctive mark of the Confession is the absolute authority ascribed to the Bible, or to quote its own words, "the Books of the Old and New Testaments . . . sufficiently express all things necessary to be believed for the salvation of mankind." The Confession holds an honorable place among the documents of the Reformed churches. In its preface there is an interesting sentence, breathing tolerance and sweet reasonableness: "If any man will note in this our Confession any article or sentence repugnant to God's Holy Word, that it would please him of his gentleness and for Christian charity's sake to admonish us of the same in writing; and we upon our honours and fidelity by God's grace do promise unto him satisfaction from the mouth of God, that is from His Holy Scriptures, or else reformation of that which he shall prove to be amiss."

* Probably from a first draft written earlier in the summer.

The Scottish Reformers may have held strong opinions but they laid no claim to infallibility.

The Book of Common Order, known also as Knox's Liturgy and based on the Genevan liturgy of Calvin, was approved by the General Assembly in 1564. Though it was intended to be used, especially by readers when they read the common prayers in church, it was not in the strict sense a liturgy to be slavishly followed, but rather a guide for the conduct of ordinary services and of the sacraments, of marriages and burials, of the visitation of the sick; and it also provided forms for the election of superintendents, ministers, elders and deacons, and for the administration of discipline and other ordinances. Like the Confession it held its place for the best part of a century before it was superseded.

The third document of the Scottish Reformation is known as the First Book of Discipline, its aim being to lay the foundations of a truly Christian community. It was never officially approved by Parliament, but with amendments it served as a practical manual of church policy for more than a century. The object of the book, as stated in the preface, was that a "common order and uniformity be observed in this Realm, concerning Doctrine, administration of Sacraments, Ecclesiastical Discipline, and Policy of the Kirk."

The book opens with an exposition of doctrine, and then guidance is given for the administration of the sacraments and other services. Baptism is to be administered in public, the Lord's Supper to be celebrated four times a year, no one to be "admitted to that mystery who cannot repeat the Lord's Prayer, the Apostles' Creed and the sum of the law." The book recognizes five offices, those of minister, lay reader, superintendent, elder, and deacon. The people themselves have the right to elect their own ministers, the minister-elect to be publicly examined and proved. In the early days there was naturally a scarcity of ministers, which explains the book's sanctioning the nonpermanent offices of lay reader and superintendent. The reader's function was to read common prayers and the Scriptures to congregations without a minister. The superintendents were in charge of districts, to organize new congregations and appoint ministers. They were in no sense bishops, being subject in life and doctrine to the censure and correction of ministers and elders. The elders, that their power might be limited, were elected annually and acted as "assistants to the minister in all public affairs." Deacons, also elected annually by the congregation, dealt with matters of finance.

In the Church of Scotland today there are four ecclesiastical courts—kirk session, presbytery, synod, and General Assembly. Of these the kirk session and General Assembly came into being immediately. Presently the synod was instituted as an annual meeting of the ministers in a superintendent's district. Presbyteries are not mentioned in the First Book of Discipline and came into existence twenty-one years later, in 1581. But from the beginning they were foreshadowed in the "exercise" or weekly meeting of ministers and elders for the study of Scripture and its interpretation. No doubt presbyteries were originally intended, but in the early days there were not enough ministers to form them.

The president of a famous American theological seminary once said in an address to his students, "Scotland is the best educated and worst housed country in the world." If the first part about education is true, much of the credit must be given to John Knox and the Scottish Reformers. In the Book of Discipline a large section is devoted to a comprehensive scheme of education, ranging from the endowment of schools in every parish to increasing the influence of the universities. Though the scheme was never realized, it was an ideal that fired the people's imagination and inspired them through the centuries with a genuine love of learning.

The scheme was never realized because there were no available funds. Knox hoped that the revenues of the old church might be placed at the disposal of the new, but he reckoned without the avariciousness of the nobles who had already seized a large portion of the church's property and were strongly averse to disgorging it. The Reformers were handicapped at every turn for lack of funds—in the maintenance of their ministers, in their enlightened schemes of education, and in the relief of the poor. And yet in some ways the poverty of the church was a blessing in disguise. It forced its ministers to live with their people, the poor among the poor; in this way they came to understand their congregations' problems and needs, and to be one with them as they never could have been if they had lived as a class apart.

We noted above that one of the true marks of the church is discipline uprightly ministered as God's Word prescribes, whereby vice is repressed and virtue nourished. There was need of such discipline in a country where social disorder and moral uncleanness had been condoned if not encouraged by the medieval church. If the discipline was sometimes stern, it was always impartial, without respect of persons high or low. It may be that occasionally the punishments inflicted were excessive, but we must remember the laxity of the age and the need of a moral as well as a purely religious reformation. It is surely not to the discredit of the Scottish Reformers that they aimed at and toiled for the establishment of God's kingdom on earth.

We return now to the point of our story at which we left off. In 1560 Scotland became a Protestant nation, but the Reformers had still many difficulties to face. During the revolution the queen had been absent in France, where as a young child in 1548 she had been sent for safety. Ten years later she married the heir to the French throne, who became king but died in December 1560. The following August, Queen Mary, now eighteen, returned to Scotland. From the beginning Knox clearly realized the dangers that lay ahead, and thus he wrote of her arrival: "the very face of heaven . . . did manifestly speak what comfort was brought unto this country with her, to wit, sorrow, dolour, darkness, and all impiety. For, in the memory of man, that day of the year was never seen a more dolorous face of the heaven than was at her arrival . . . The sun was not seen to shine two days before, nor two days after. That fore-warning gave God unto us; but alas, the most part were blind."[12]

We need not concern ourselves with the many details and sordid intrigues of the next few years. Mary was pledged to restore Romanism at any cost, and to that end she employed all her considerable powers of charm and fascination. She won over nearly all the nobles, and but for Knox might well have succeeded in re-establishing popery within her realm. But Knox would not be cajoled: in interview after interview he stood firm and refused to surrender in any essential. At last by her intrigues and crimes Mary brought upon herself the wrath of her people, and in 1567 she fled for refuge to England. It was only then that the decrees of the 1560 Parliament were entered in the statute book.

Thus the end of the initial stage was reached and thenceforth Scotland was numbered among the Protestant nations. Its Reformation had still a long and stormy passage to weather, and many dark days lay ahead. The Scottish Presbyterians had need of all their determination and fortitude in the hard, grim struggle with the Stuart kings. They resisted attempts to introduce episcopacy and a liturgy; they entered into alliance with the English Parliament in the Civil War; their Covenanters suffered cruel tribulations in the days of Charles II and James II. It was not till the Revolution Settlement of 1690 that persecution ceased and Presbyterianism was recognized as the official religion of Scotland. In all its essentials it was the religious system established by Knox in 1560. Though often threatened and endangered in the century following his death, it could neither be suppressed nor superseded, for of all forms of Protestantism the Presbyterian most admirably harmonizes with the Scottish temperament and character.

The death of John Knox took place in 1572. In May of the previous year he left Edinburgh for St. Andrews, that old gray town by the sea in which he had preached his first sermon and which he loved so well. James Melville, then a student, relates that he attended Knox's expositions of the prophet Daniel with a view to taking notes, and he proceeds: "In the opening up of his text he was moderate the space of an half-hour; but when he entered to application, he made me so to grew [shudder] and tremble, that I could not hold a pen to write." Again he tells us that Knox was lifted up to the pulpit "where he behoved to lean at his first entry; but ere he had done with his sermon, he was so active and vigorous that he was like to ding that pulpit in blads [break it in pieces] and fly out of it."

In 1572 Knox was back in Edinburgh where he preached for the last time on August 31. On November 11 he fell ill, and the same day scrupulously paid his debts, remarking with grim humor to one of his servants as he handed over his wages, "Thou wilt never get no more of me in this life," but he gave him twenty shillings more than his due. On November 24 he breathed his last and was buried near St. Giles' Cathedral. His epitaph was pronounced by the Regent Morton: "Here lieth a man who in his life never feared the face of man."

Professor Dickinson writes that "Knox, like St. Paul, had the power to shape men's minds."[13] He did so chiefly by his preaching,[14] which fortified the spirit of the people and upheld the whole reforming movement when it was perilously near collapse. In a very real sense the Scottish Reformation is Knox's Reformation: what Knox did, only Knox could have done. He was impelled by one consuming purpose—to rid Scotland of Romanism and its errors—and by the burning desire to bring men to the light. His transparent sincerity and disinterestedness were among his strongest assets. While others would have intermingled politics with religion, he diverted the Reformation from all other channels and made it a distinctively religious movement. Some of the Scottish nobles gave their support from the sordid motive of gaining for themselves the patrimony of the old church; many ordinary men, disgusted with the immorality of the Roman clergy or groaning under their oppressive measures, simply desired to set themselves free from the toils. It was Knox in his single-mindedness who pointed out the way to better things and inspired men with new spiritual ideals. In a confused and uncertain age he was sure of himself and of the course on which he had embarked. His own unwavering conviction not only instilled in his countrymen faith and courage in the darkest hours, but enabled him to stand uncompromisingly, however grim and relentless the struggle might be, until his goal was attained. His ideas and the principles for which he fought have profoundly influenced Scotsmen ever since his own time and are reflected today in their lives and thinking. For he gave the church a Confession of Faith, a Prayer Book, and a form of church government that is still the basis of the Church of Scotland. Carlyle's tribute is one that all might endorse: "He is the one Scotchman to whom . . . his country and the world owe a debt."[15]

It is certain that Scotland, and in a sense the whole Protestant world, owes much to the events, the struggles, and the personalities of sixteenth-century Scotland. What, then, were some of the characteristics of the Scottish Reformation?

"If," writes Hay Fleming, "the Reformation in Scotland had to be characterised in one word, that word would be *thorough*."[16] John Knox himself, writing in 1566 (and could there be a more reliable witness?) said that, while other countries retained "some footsteppis of Antichrist, and some dreggis of Papistrie, we (all praise to God alone) have nothing in our churches that ever flowed from that man of synne."[17] On August 24, 1560, the Scottish Parliament adopted no half measures but expelled popery root and branch. It was a complete and thorough break with the past.

And yet (and this is the second characteristic) the Reformation in Scotland was effected with a minimum of bloodshed. The persecution there was not to be compared with the pogroms in France, Spain, Italy, Germany, the Netherlands, and England. There was no St. Bartholomew's Day Massacre as in France in 1572; there were no Smithfield burnings as in England during "Bloody" Mary's reign. Moreover, after the Reformation in Scotland was an accomplished fact, there was an immediate cessation of persecution: thenceforth not one person was put to death for his religion. As Macewen has written: "Altars and crucifixes were destroyed, but not human lives."[18]

The third characteristic of the Scottish Reformation was its democracy. It was a movement up from the people, and not as in England and elsewhere a movement down from the top. Democracy was further promoted by introducing elders and deacons into the government of the church, since no congregation could be dominated by one man. The layman had come into his own. In the first General Assembly held in December 1560 only six out of forty-two members were ministers, and even today there is one elder for every minister. Well might Archbishop Parker write to Cecil, Queen Elizabeth's secretary, as he did in November 1559: God "keep us from such visitations as Knockes hath attempted in Scotland; the people to be orderers of things." What Knox did for the nation has been called by Carlyle "a resurrection as from death. . . . The people began to *live*." [19] All through the First Book of Discipline runs the idea of Christian equality in the sight of God. On the one hand, discipline should be administered without fear or favor, whatever a man's station in life; on the other, every man should have a voice in church appointments and freedom of speech in the courts of the church. The General Assembly of the Church of Scotland today is the most truly democratic body in the world, where every member may speak and vote as the spirit moves him. And it was always thus. Said Knox on one occasion, "Take from us the freedom of Assemblies, and take from us the evangel." But the most eloquent testimony to Knox's principle was his own example. In his interviews with the queen he conducted himself in such a way as monarchs had never known before: it was unheard of that royalty should brook contradiction from ordinary mortals. There is the famous occasion when Mary's marriage was being discussed, and the Queen cried in exasperation: "What have ye to do . . . with my marriage? Or what are ye within this Commonwealth?" And this was Knox's reply: *"A subject born within the same,* Madam. And albeit I neither be Earl, Lord, nor Baron within it, yet has God made me (how abject that ever I be in your eyes) a profitable member within the same." Of this it has been said: "Modern democracy came into being in that answer." [20] It was not perhaps the kind of democracy that we know today, but it foreshadowed modern democracy by emphasizing the dignity of human personality whatever a man's rank or station. It was the sentiment expressed by Burns two centuries later:

> "The rank is but the guinea stamp,
> The man's the gowd [gold] for a' that."

In the Scottish Reformation are to be found the germs of modern democracy, the first awakening in men's minds of a conception that was later to be crystallized in unforgettable words, "that government of the people, by the people, and for the people, shall not perish from the earth."

9

OUR REFORMATION HERITAGE

✠

The Protestant Reformation of the sixteenth century is the most vital and far-reaching event in all Christian history since the Gospel was first preached by Christ Himself and by His Apostles. It was the second great schism to rend the church. The first occurred in the fourth century when East and West, differing on points of doctrine and precedence, were riven apart and elected to develop along their own lines. But in the second cleavage which took place in the sixteenth century the question was not entirely one of doctrine but involved more comprehensive issues. It arose primarily from the ardent desire to reform the whole life of a decadent church which had sullied and brought to dishonor the pure evangel preached by Christ and His Apostles.

And yet to many contemporaries the Protestant Reformation must have seemed to be alarmingly close to revolution. It split the unity of the medieval church which for more than a thousand years had been the sole arbiter of life and conduct, of faith and morals, and the very foundation of society. And not only so, but the Reformation ushered in an age of unrest and instability, of persecution and martyrdom and bloodshed, and a series of savage and bitter wars that devastated Europe for more than a century. How was it possible, contemporaries might ask, to extract any good thing from this devil's cauldron? And yet out of the cruel travail was born a new Europe, while the origins of modern civilization may be directly traced to the Reformation era.

Though the Protestant Reformation has influenced human life as a whole in all its various branches, it cannot be too strongly emphasized that it was primarily a religious movement.

Its true concern was God's will for men, men's relation to God, and the salvation of the human soul. Any interpretation that ignores this central fact is fundamentally and demonstrably wrong. The lodestar of the Reformers was neither economics nor politics nor even social amelioration, but religion first and last and all the time.

Nevertheless, the Reformation *did* profoundly influence human life as a whole. If it had little or no direct effect, its *indirect* effects were incalculable so that the entire world has been transformed. Generally speaking, in the field of human endeavor there are three great divisions—the economic and political, the social, and the religious. In each and all of these the influence of the Reformation is clearly discernible.

1. First, in the economic and political sphere the Protestants were everywhere more progressive than their Catholic rivals. One need only contrast the vigorous commercial life of the liberated Netherlands with the inertia of Catholic Spain, or the growing prosperity of England with the steady decline of Italy. A century ago Lord Macaulay developed this theme both in his *History of England* and in his essay on von Ranke. "It cannot be doubted," he writes, "that since the sixteenth century, the Protestant nations have made decidedly greater progress than their neighbours."[1] Under the Church of Rome, "the loveliest and most fertile provinces of Europe have . . . been sunk in poverty, in political servitude, and in intellectual torpor, while Protestant countries, once proverbial for sterility and barbarism, have been turned by skill and industry into gardens." Taking Scotland as an example, he compares it with Italy so abundantly blessed with natural advantages but lacking in human initiative. And he continues: "Whoever passes in Germany from a Roman Catholic to a Protestant principality, in Switzerland from a Roman Catholic to a Protestant canton, in Ireland from a Roman Catholic to a Protestant county, finds that he has passed from a lower to a higher grade of civilization." (The apparent exception is France, but in no Roman Catholic country has the Roman Church possessed so little authority as in France.) "On the other

side of the Atlantic the same law prevails. The Protestants of the United States have left far behind them the Roman Catholics of Mexico, Peru, and Brazil."[2]

Signs of this future progress were not lacking in the sixteenth century itself. Both prior to the Reformation and in the age succeeding it there was a strong colonizing urge among the nations of Europe. In the race for colonies Spain and Portugal were given a long initial start, but presently they were overtaken and then outdistanced by Holland, France, and England, which are still the great colonial powers in modern times. Holland and Britain are Protestant; the third power, France, again seems the exception, but once again we must remember the tenuous authority of the Roman Church in France. Here, too, the impetus given by the Reformation proved a decisive factor.

Still confining ourselves to the political sphere, we may note one further point and argue, not unreasonably, that the Reformation powerfully influenced the development of democracy. This influence was indirect, for neither Luther nor Calvin viewed with favor the thought of popular government or the democratic ideal. It has been claimed that "if democracy was the child of the Reformation, it was a child born in the extreme old age of its parent."[3] But late or early it *was* born. For one thing the Reformation brought into prominence the ordinary man. In all the lands, with unwavering heroism he endured persecution; in France, in the Netherlands, and in Scotland it was the inflexible courage and determination of the ordinary man that carried the conflict to a successful end, and not unnaturally he came to realize his intrinsic value in the community. Moreover, the Reformation by its emphasis on the priesthood of all believers made religion a thing of the people instead of, as formerly, the possession of a privileged ecclesiastical class. This in turn encouraged men to think for themselves and not to rely on priest or church, and thus was inculcated the sense of responsibility. Again, the very government of the Reformed Churches and especially the Calvinist further developed lay responsibility. There, as elders and deacons, laymen were given a voice in the management of affairs and a real share in the church's work and organization. They were appointed by the free election of their brethren, representing them in synods and church assemblies. Trained as they were in the arts of self-government, they naturally tended to apply to the state the methods they had found so effective in the administration of their churches. As members of a democratic church they were led, by an easy transition, to become believers in a democratic state, and democracy is as a fact most virile in those lands where the majority of the people are Calvinist or quasi-Calvinist—in Holland, Switzerland, Britain, and the United States. (France again seems the exception, but for the reason given above is not so in reality.) It may be justly claimed that modern democracy is one of the indirect fruits of the Reformation.

2. When we turn to the social sphere, we find that Protestantism exerted an influence equally profound and equally varied. As a cultural force it has left a permanent mark on language and literature. Luther's translation of the Bible set the standard of modern German, and a similar service to French was rendered by Calvin's *Institutes* and other writings, while in England the King James Version is not only a literary classic but has tempered the language of the whole English-speaking world. It has been said of public life in the seventeenth century that "it is hardly possible to read a speech or writing of any length without perceiving its indebtedness to the Authorised Version."[4] In literature we need only mention the impetus given by the Reformation to such classics as Milton's *Paradise Lost,* Bunyan's *Pilgrim's Progress,* and Sir Thomas Browne's *Religio Medici.*

In education, too, the Reformers played an important part. Calvin in Switzerland and Knox and Melville in Scotland emphasized the need of an educated ministry; but their educational schemes and those of the other Reformers extended far beyond this limited scope. Both Luther in Germany and Knox in Scotland desired to see the erection of schools in every city, town, and parish, free for all children to attend. It was the ideal of Melanchthon in Saxony and of Bucer at Strassburg; and in England King Edward VI is remembered as the founder of many grammar schools. It is surely symbolic of the Protestant thirst for learning that, to commemorate the relief of beleaguered Leyden in 1574, the most fitting memorial was thought to be the founding of a university. In America the Pilgrim Fathers were zealous for the spread of education in the New England colonies where it was offered free to all, especially by two laws passed by the General Court of Massachusetts in 1642 and 1647.

The Reformers, then, aimed at an educated community, but their sense of responsibility to others led them also to feel concern for their material well-being. Luther, far in advance of his times, advocated state provision for its needy citizens, while one of the first tasks Bucer took in hand at Strassburg was the organizing of an effective system of poor relief. In the Calvinist churches, too, the care of the poor was a fundamental concern, and part of the function of deacons was to deal with this very question. By the preaching of the Word, by the education of the mind, and by the care of the sick and poor, the Reformers aimed at ministering to the whole personality of man.

One of the most notable services they rendered to society was the new emphasis they placed on morality. Possibly the greatest weakness of the medieval church was its lax code of morals which had scandalized devout men long before the Reformation. A prelate might shamelessly break all the Ten Commandments and still hold the highest offices in the Catholic Church. Immorality was no bar to preferment: the medieval church was corrupt in all its members and religion and morality were completely divorced. One of the first tasks of the Reformers was to repair this sorry state of affairs and to raise the moral temperature both in the church and in society as a whole. It is true that Luther somewhat obscured the issue by his insistence on the primacy of faith and not of works. But this was no justification for sinful living. On the contrary, faith is the stimulus and motive power of the good life: as a man believes, so shall he live; and in all the lands touched by Lutheranism religion and morality marched closely hand in hand. But it was left to Calvin to emphasize the paramount necessity of the moral life. To him the Christian religion was not only a system of beliefs but a way of life, and the two were inextricably bound together. Accordingly, at Geneva we find Calvin engaged in the twofold task of instructing the people in the faith and simultaneously instituting a program of moral reform. This twofold aim is characteristic of all his work. His *Institutes of the Christian Religion* contain his massive theology and his *Ecclesiastical Ordinances* are the practical working out of that theology in the life of the church. Wherever Calvinism has taken root, both in Europe and in North America, this is the pattern that has been consistently followed. First, a confession of faith has been prepared and then a "discipline" imposed to regulate the moral life of believers. In this way Calvin laid the foundations of that moral rectitude which has endured the stress of centuries and still exerts its powerful influence on modern society.

3. The Reformation, then, has deeply affected the course of human life in all its various branches—economic and political, social and moral. But when all is said, those effects are incidental and not the essential core of the Reforming movement which, as we have already emphasized, was above all else religious. As Professor Paul Tillich has reminded us, "Protestantism is not *only* Protestantism, it is also—and first of all—Christianity." It is as simple as that. "It has never wished to be anything else, and [in Germany] the Protestant churches prefer to call themselves 'Evangelical' rather than Protestant."[5] At the same time it was more than Christianity: it was *reformed* Christianity. Moreover, reform was not confined to the Protestant Churches but was presently undertaken in the Roman Church itself. This task of reforming the church from within had been advocated by many ardent churchmen before the Reformation and might well have been taken in hand even if Luther had never broken away. But his revolt and the Reformation that followed imparted to the movement an urgency it would not otherwise have felt. In a real sense the Reformation was the direct cause of the Counter Reformation, which did so much to liberate the Roman Church from

its medieval decadence and build up the virile institution it has become in modern times.

But the Reformation was more than a reviving and purifying agent, and one of its most vital effects was to transform the whole character of popular religion and make it a more vivid reality to the ordinary man and woman. This far-reaching change was due to several factors, the first being the transcending importance of an open Bible in the hands of the people. Before the end of the fourteenth century portions of the Bible had been translated into the common tongues. But with the Reformation and its emphasis on the Bible as the authoritative Word of God and supreme rule of faith and duty, a new urge was given to Bible translation, so that within a comparatively short time translations of the Bible in the vernacular were found in all the lands touched by the Reformation. Those translations, moreover, were not the possession only of the wealthier classes of the community but were available to all. The provision of an open Bible was perhaps the greatest single contribution of the Reformation to the deepening of popular religion and in its effects was incalculable. Instead of snatching hungrily at the morsels of scripture recited in church, the ordinary man had now the whole wide range of God's Word to nourish his soul; and instead of receiving his religion at second hand through an intermediary who was not always worthy or competent, he could now listen to God speaking to him directly in the Scriptures of the Old and New Testaments. By providing an open Bible for all, the Reformers imparted to popular religion a new vividness and a new reality.

A similar effect was achieved by giving the people services of public worship conducted entirely in their own language and not in an alien tongue. Not only was the liturgy in the vernacular but congregational singing was also encouraged. Luther's own love of music amounted almost to a passion; he valued it next to the Gospel itself. The German hymnary of the Lutheran Church and the Psalters of the Calvinists, taken in conjunction with the spoken word that all could understand, again helped to make religion more real to the ordinary man.

The Reformers also influenced popular religion by encouraging family worship and the cult of the spiritual within the home. Luther constantly emphasized the importance of the home as the true field of instruction and the best school for the training of character. In Calvinist countries, too, family worship was deemed essential and its practice was widely observed. Robert Burns in one of his greatest poems, "The Cotter's Saturday Night," has immortalized this pious observance in a humble home. After a week's hard toil the family relaxes, and the Saturday evening is quite a social occasion. Friends drop in and all partake of a simple meal. And then they pause for family worship.

> "The cheerfu' supper done, wi' serious face,
>   They round the ingle [fireside] form a circle wide;
> The sire turns o'er, wi' patriarchal grace,
>   The big ha' Bible, ance his father's pride . . .
> He wales [chooses] a portion with judicious care,
> And 'Let us worship God!' he says with solemn air. . . .
> Perhaps the Christian volume is the theme
>   How guiltless blood for guilty man was shed;
> How He who bore in Heaven the second name
>   Had not on earth whereon to lay his head. . . .
> Then kneeling down to Heaven's Eternal King
>   The saint, the father, and the husband prays."

One can imagine but scarcely estimate the influence on religion of this type of simple, devout worship, especially if, as seems probable, it was widely practiced in Calvinist homes.

One task remained for the church to fulfill: if reformation was to be complete, the preaching of the Word was indispensable. Though the ordinary man had now in his hands an open Bible, the Reformers and especially Calvin believed that something more than private reading was essential. Men required guidance in the study of the Bible, and proper guidance could be given only by those ministers of religion adequately trained and duly appointed. The medieval church had been notoriously remiss in the matter of preaching, and where Rome had been weak the

Reformers determined to be strong. Protestantism has sometimes been criticized for overemphasizing the preaching ministry, but at the time of the Reformation the most clamant necessity was the need of instruction in the faith. That need has not yet passed, and one of the church's paramount duties is still the true preaching of the Word.

In all these ways, then, was religion deepened by the inspiration of the Reformers and an advance made towards a more truly spiritual ideal. It has been said that they "were interested in the long-range goal of salvation rather than in short-range efforts at improving life on earth."[6] But in a very real sense they contributed to both. Ultimately everything depends on the individual since a redeemed world is one composed of redeemed men and women. If the Protestant Reformation was instrumental in advancing personal religion, it was also, for that very reason, a means of promoting the Kingdom of God on earth.

NOTES AND ACKNOWLEDGMENTS

NOTES AND ACKNOWLEDGMENTS

Chapter 1   The Eve of the Reformation

1. Ernest Barker, *et al.*, ed., *The European Inheritance*, Vol. II, p. 74. London: Oxford University Press, 1954. By permission.

2. Stefan Zweig, *Erasmus*, p. 30. London: Cassell and Company Ltd., 1934. By permission.

3. Lord Acton, *Lectures on Modern History*, p. 81. London: Macmillan & Co., Ltd., 1952.

4. J. M. Thompson, *Lectures on Foreign History*, p. 22. Oxford: Basil Blackwell, 1947.

5. A. W. Ward, *et al.*, ed., *The Cambridge Modern History*, Vol. I, p. 633. New York: The Macmillan Company, 1902.

6. T. M. Lindsay, *A History of the Reformation*, Vol. I, p. 113. New York: Charles Scribner's Sons, 1910. By permission.

7. J. A. Froude, *Short Studies on Great Subjects*, Vol. I, pp. 53-54. New York: Scribner, Armstrong & Co., 1873.

8. W. Croft Dickinson, *John Knox's History of the Reformation in Scotland*, Vol. One, pp. xix-xx. London: Thomas Nelson and Sons Ltd., 1949. By permission.

D. Hay Fleming, *The Reformation in Scotland*, p. 128. London: Hodder & Stoughton Ltd., 1910. By permission.

9. Frederic Seebohm, *The Era of the Protestant Revolution*, p. 60. New York: Scribner, Armstrong & Co., 1874.

10. Froude, *op. cit.*, Vol. I, p. 57.

11. Henry Hart Milman, *History of Latin Christianity*, Vol. IX, p. 36. London: John Murray, 1883.

12. See G. G. Coulton, *From St. Francis to Dante*, p. 261. London: Duckworth & Co., 1908.

13. Fleming, *op. cit.*, pp. 90-92; Lindsay, *op. cit.*, Vol. II, pp. 353-354.

14. H. A. L. Fisher, *A History of Europe*, p. 356. London: Edward Arnold & Co., 1936.

15. Michael de la Bedoyere, *The Meddlesome Friar and the Wayward Pope*, p. 123. Garden City, N. Y.: Hanover House, 1958. By permission.

Chapter 2   The Reformation in Germany

1. T. M. Lindsay, *The Reformation* (Handbook), p. 8. Edinburgh: T. & T. Clark, 1923. By permission.

2. Martin Luther, *Opera*, Vol. XXXI, p. 273. (Erlangen edition.)

3. B. J. Kidd, ed., *Documents Illustrative of the Continental Reformation*, p. 18. (Translated from the Latin by the author.) Oxford: Clarendon Press, 1911. By permission.

4. The phrase is Froude's, from *Short Studies on Great Subjects*, Vol. I, p. 82.

5. See Roland H. Bainton, *Here I Stand*, p. 288. New York: Abingdon-Cokesbury Press, 1950.

6. Henry Wace and C. A. Buckheim, eds., *Luther's Primary Works*, p. 268. London: Hodder and Stoughton, 1896.

7. *Ibid.*, p. 262.

8. Lindsay, *A History of the Reformation*, Vol. I, pp. 251-252.

9. A. J. Grant, *A History of Europe: 1494-1610*, 5th edition, p. 98. London: Methuen & Co. Ltd., 1951. By permission.

10. Froude, *op. cit.*, Vol. I, pp. 91-92.

11. Thomas Carlyle, *Sartor Resartus and On Heroes, Hero-Worship, and the Heroic in History*, p. 364. London: J. M. Dent & Sons, Ltd., 1908.

12. But see Lindsay, *A History of the Reformation*, Vol. I, p. 291, note 2.

13. Grant, *op. cit.*, p. 159. For its terms see Kidd, *op. cit.*, no. 124.

14. T. R. Glover, *The Pilgrim: Essays on Religion*, p. 211. New York: George H. Doran Company, 1922. By permission.

15. T. Babington Macaulay, *Critical and Miscellaneous Essays*, Vol. III, pp. 323-324. Philadelphia: A. Hart, Late Carey & Hart, 1852.

16. But contrast Roland H. Bainton, *The Reformation of the Sixteenth Century*, p. 229: "Lutheranism is supposed to have lost all agrarian constituency after the Peasants' War, but as a matter of fact Luther's congregation at Wittenberg never ceased to be composed largely of peasants." (Boston: The Beacon Press, 1952. By permission.) This statement may well be true, but we must not underestimate Luther's personal influence on the people of Wittenberg. There the circumstances were special; and one exception does not disprove the general rule.

Chapter 3   The Anabaptists

1. Frederick J. Powicke, *Henry Barrow, Separatist (1550?-1593), and the Exiled Church of Amsterdam (1593-1622)*, p. 201. London: James Clarke & Co., 1900.

2. Edward Armstrong, *The Emperor Charles V*, Vol. II, p. 342. London: Macmillan and Co., Limited, 1902.

3. Quoted in Bainton, *The Reformation of the Sixteenth Century*, pp. 100-101.

4. Quoted in Lindsay, *A History of the Reformation*, Vol. II, p. 437.

5. Norman Sykes, *The Crisis of the Reformation*, p. 52. London: Geoffrey Bles, 1938. By permission.

6. They were contemptuously called "spirituals," and as Dr. J. S. Whale has noted, *The Protestant Tradition*, p. 200 n., "the German term of abuse for this 'pentecostal' mysticism was *Schwärmerei*, an expressive word describing what would happen if we brushed our teeth with shaving soap. It means 'swarming', 'foaming at the mouth'. It suggests, as it is meant to do, the frenzy of the epileptic or madman." (Cambridge: University Press, 1955.) By permission.

7. Quoted in Bainton, *op. cit.*, p. 102.

8. Stanislaus Hosius (1504-79), a Polish Cardinal, *Opera*, p. 202. Venice: 1573.

9. Lindsay, *op. cit.*, Vol. II, pp. 450-451; see pp. 448-449 for the amazing testimony of Conrad Braun.

10. Bainton, *op. cit.*, p. 173.

11. "*D'ailleurs l'inquisition des Pays-Bas est plus impitoyable que celle d'Espagne.*" Correspondance de Philippe II, i. 207. Quoted in John L. Motley, *The Rise of the Dutch Republic*, Vol. I, p. 341. New York: Harper & Brothers, 1883.

12. Harold J. Grimm, *The Reformation Era*, p. 273. New York: The Macmillan Company, 1954.

13. Quoted in Lindsay, *op. cit.*, Vol. II, p. 469.

14. Bainton, *op. cit.*, p. 97.

15. See Wilhelm Möller, *Lehrbuch der Kirchengeschichte*, Vol. III, p. 402 ff.

16. See also the *Twelve Articles of Christian Belief* by Balthasar Hübmaier, quoted in Henry C. Vedder, *Balthasar Hübmaier*, pp. 134 ff. New York: G. P. Putnam's Sons, 1905.

17. As regards organization, its office-bearers were deacons, elders, masters, and teachers or pastors. The brethren also met in synods.

18. For this reason they went so far as to sanction divorce (and not only for adultery), forbidding a Baptist to cohabit with a non-Baptist: separation was permissible, if not obligatory, and the Baptist was free to remarry.

19. See A. C. McGiffert, *Protestant Thought Before Kant*, p. 104. New York: Charles Scribner's Sons, 1924.

20. The Anabaptists did consecrate their infants, but this was not baptism.

21. The story is quoted in Lindsay, *op. cit.*, Vol. II, p. 439.

22. The modern Baptists also trace their roots to Calvinist traditions. Many, and possibly the majority of them, were Calvinists who acquired Anabaptist ideas. See Robert G. Torbet, *A History of the Baptists*, pp. 59-62. Philadelphia: The Judson Press, 1950.

Chapter 4   John Calvin

1. John Calvin, *Institutes of the Christian Religion*, Book III, Chapter IX, Section 2. Philadelphia: The Westminster Press, Seventh American Edition. By permission.

2. It is interesting to note that the popular party was nicknamed "Eidgenossen," "confederates," which was later corrupted into "Huguenots," a somber name in the history of French Protestantism.

3. It is not without significance that Calvin was a Picard. The people of that province were lovers of freedom; they combined "fervent enthusiasm and a cold tenacity of purpose" (see Lindsay, *A History of the Reformation*, Vol. II, p. 92). They were often anticlerical, and among them there had been many sympathizers with Wycliffe and Huss. The characteristic features of Picardy were the characteristics also of Calvin, and these became even more pronounced with the passing of the years.

4. In it he quotes from no less than fifty-three different Latin authors and from twenty-two Greek.

5. Lindsay, *op. cit.*, Vol. II, p. 99.

6. A. W. Ward, *et. al.*, ed., *The Cambridge Modern History*, Vol. II, p. 356.

7. John Calvin, *Commentary on the Book of Psalms*, p. xliii. Edinburgh: The Calvin Translation Society, 1845.

8. Whale, *The Protestant Tradition*, p. 123.

9. *The Cambridge Modern History*, Vol. II, p. 368.

10. Grant, *A History of Europe: 1494-1610*, p. 247 n.

11. Calvin, *op. cit.*, Book I, Chapter I, Section 3.

12. *Ibid.*, Book II, Chapter I, Section 8.

13. *Ibid.*, Book II, Chapters XIII-XVII.

14. *Ibid.*, Book III, Chapter XXI, Section 5.

15. McGiffert, *Protestant Thought Before Kant*, p. 87. By permission.

16. *The Cambridge Modern History*, Vol. II, p. 347.

17. Calvin, *op. cit.*, Book III, Chapter IX, Section 4.

18. *Ibid.*, Book IV, Chapter I, Section 1.

19. *Ibid.*, Book IV, Chapter XIV, Section 1.

20. *Ibid.*, Book IV, Chapter XVII, Section 10.

21. See J. A. Froude, *Short Studies on Great Subjects*, Second Series, p. 49. New York: Charles Scribner's Sons. (n.d.)

22. See Calvin, *op. cit.*, Book IV, Chapter XII, Section 1: "As the saving doctrine of Christ is the soul of the Church, so discipline forms the ligaments which connect the members together, and keep each in its proper place."

23. Grimm, *The Reformation Era*, p. 340.

24. Froude, *op. cit.*, p. 49.

25. Lindsay, *op. cit.*, Vol. II, p. 131.

26. McGiffert, *op. cit.*, p. 90.

Chapter 5   The Reformation in France

1. Quoted in Lindsay, *A History of the Reformation*, Vol. II, p. 156.
2. The name Huguenots, like their creed, probably came from Geneva, where the patriots were called "Eidgenossen" or Confederates. The name was probably first applied to the French Calvinists at Tours.
3. Fisher, *A History of Europe*, p. 568.
4. It is true that the League proclaimed the Cardinal of Bourbon, who was then in prison, as King Charles X, but he died in the following May.
5. Lindsay, *op. cit.*, Vol. II, p. 221.

Chapter 6   The Revolt in the Netherlands

1. A. W. Ward, *et. al.*, ed., *The Cambridge Modern History*, Vol. III, p. 188.
2. See Motley, *The Rise of the Dutch Republic*, Vol. I, p. 239.
3. Thompson, *Lectures on Foreign History*, p. 112.
4. Quoted by Lindsay in *A History of the Reformation*, Vol. II, p. 247.
5. Gerard Brandt, *The History of the Reformation*, Vol. I, p. 160.
6. *Ibid.*, Vol. I, pp. 261, 266.
7. Quoted in Thompson, *op. cit.*, p. 111.
8. The earliest Reformation preachers in the Netherlands were Lutherans; but Lutheranism failed to appeal to the Dutch people as a whole and was superseded first by Zwinglianism and later, and to a vastly greater extent, by Calvinism, so that eventually the Reformation in the Netherlands was Calvinist in theology, in discipline, and in church government. In the seventy years after the founding of Leyden University (1575) other seats of learning sprang into being from which flowed a succession of famous Dutch theologians. Regarding the government of the church, the distinctively Calvinist system of ministers, elders, and deacons was adopted. In 1569 an assembly of the Dutch churches was held at Emden (Germany) where it was agreed that the government of the church should be by consistories, classes, and synods. Thirteen years later a synod held at Dordrecht ratified and enlarged the articles of the Emden convention. One of its rulings was that all office-bearers of the church should sign the confession of faith, which was modeled on the confession of the French church and was known as the Belgic Confession. Lindsay *(A History of the Reformation*, Vol. II, p. 272) mentions two peculiarities pertaining to the organization of the Dutch churches. First, while they followed the method adopted by Calvinists in other lands whereby each congregation is ruled by its kirk-session or consistory, at the same time they regarded all church members residing in the same city as one congregation without special attachment to any one church. The various ministers were all ministers of the city and preached in turn in all the Reformed churches. Accordingly, in each city there was but one consistory and not several. Second, in a federated state like the United Provinces, each province enjoyed a considerable measure of independence, so that it was impossible to convene a national synod of the churches unless the provinces as a whole approved. In these circumstances each province tended to legislate in its own church affairs, and concerted action by all the churches became increasingly difficult. The disadvantages attending this practice are obvious.

Chapter 7   The Reformation in England

1. Froude, *Short Studies on Great Subjects*, Vol. I, p. 128.
2. Sir Maurice Powicke, *The Reformation in England*, 4th printing, p. 33. London: Oxford University Press, 1953. By permission.
3. Fisher, *A History of Europe*, p. 443.

4. See Lindsay, *A History of the Reformation,* Vol. II, p. 316.

5. G. M. Trevelyan, *History of England,* p. 288. London: Longmans, Green and Co. Ltd., 1926. By permission.

6. J. D. Mackie, *The Earlier Tudors,* p. 234. London: Oxford University Press, 1952. By permission.

7. See Sir Winston Churchill, *The New World: A History of the English-Speaking Peoples,* p. 31. New York: Dodd, Mead & Company, 1956.

8. The two Statutes of Praemunire (1353 and 1393).

9. For this cause were martyred Bishop Fisher, an old man of spotless character and saintly life, and Sir Thomas More, Henry's ex-chancellor, a friend of Erasmus, a man of European reputation, the greatest Englishman of his time.

10. A. D. Innes, *England Under the Tudors* (third edition), p. 143. London: Methuen & Co., Ltd., 1911.

11. Fisher, *op. cit.,* p. 518.

12. See T. M. Parker, *The English Reformation to 1558,* p. 118. London: Oxford University Press, 1950.

13. See A. W. Ward, *et al.,* ed., *The Cambridge Modern History,* Vol. II, p. 484: "It is the most conservative of all the liturgies of the Reformation; its authors wished to build upon, and not to destroy, the past."

14. It would be more accurate to say by the *majority* of worshipers. It precipitated a rising in the West Country, in Devon and Cornwall, where the people objected to the new liturgy and its English which, the Cornishmen declared, they "did not understand." Moreover, they said, the simplicity of the book made the worship of God seem "like a Christmas game." This rising hastened the fall from power of Protector Somerset, whose place at the helm was taken by the Earl of Warwick who later became the Duke of Northumberland. Somerset had been tolerant, but there was no limit to Northumberland's excess. An opportunist without principle or scruple or any real religious convictions, he threw himself into the flowing tide of Protestantism with a cynical disregard for everything except his own self-interests. He simply used the reforming movement as the most likely means of realizing his personal ambitions.

15. In his drive for a more vigorous Protestantism, even the Princess Mary was not immune. Hitherto she had been permitted to have the Latin Mass said in her own household, but now she was so persecuted and threatened that it is said her cousin the Emperor Charles V actually planned to rescue her from England by sea. (See Parker, *op. cit.,* p. 137, and *The Cambridge Modern History,* Vol. II, p. 500.) The Act of Uniformity also deprived many Romanists of their sees.

16. See Lindsay, *op. cit.,* Vol. II, p. 371.

17. Dickinson, *John Knox's History of the Reformation in Scotland,* Vol. One, p. 369.

18. *The Cambridge Modern History,* Vol. II, p. 562.

19. His text was I Corinthians 6:10: "nor revilers . . . shall inherit the kingdom of God."

20. W. B. Selbie, *English Sects: A History of Nonconformity,* p. 65. New York: Henry Holt and Company. (n.d.)

Chapter 8   The Reformation in Scotland to the Death of Knox

1. Fleming, *The Reformation in Scotland,* p. 59.

2. Sir Walter Scott, "Marmion," Canto iv, stanza 7. *The Poetical Works of Sir Walter Scott,* Vol. I. Boston: Houghton, Mifflin and Company. (n.d.)

3. Dickinson, *John Knox's History of the Reformation in Scotland,* p. xxiv.

4. His mother was a granddaughter of King James II.

5. Knox in the first book of his *History* relates the following incident (Vol. One, p. 13). At the place of execution Hamilton "gave to his servant . . . his gown, his coat, bonnet, and such like garments, saying, 'These will not profit in the fire; they will profit thee' "—surely the supreme illustration of Scottish thrift!

6. Dickinson, *op. cit.*, Vol. One, p. 14.

7. *Ibid.*, p. 18.

8. *Ibid.*, p. 69.

9. *Ibid.*, p. 86.

10. Lindsay, *A History of the Reformation*, Vol. II, p. 286.

11. Dickinson, *op. cit.*, Vol. One, p. 133.

12. *Ibid.*, Vol. Two, p. 7.

13. *Ibid.*, Vol. One, p. lxxxii.

14. It was his own conception of his mission. See his *History*, Vol. One, p. 347: "the principal comfort remained with the preachers."

15. Carlyle, *Sartor Resartus and On Heroes, Hero-Worship, and the Heroic in History*, p. 376.

16. Fleming, *op. cit.*, p. 241.

17. David Laing, *Knox*, Vol. II, pp. 263, 264. Edinburgh: The Wodrow Society, 1846-64.

18. Alex R. Macewen, *A History of the Church in Scotland*, Vol. II, p. 145. London: Hodder and Stoughton, 1918. By permission.

19. Carlyle, *op. cit.*, p. 375.

20. Lindsay, *op. cit.*, Vol. II, pp. 313-314.

Chapter 9   Our Reformation Heritage

1. Macaulay, *Critical and Miscellaneous Essays*, Vol. II, p. 493.

2. Thomas Babington Macaulay, *The History of England*, Vol. I, p. 54. Boston: Estes and Lauriat, Publishers. (n.d.)

3. Grant, *A History of Europe: 1494-1610*, p. 524.

4. Quoted in Sykes, *The Crisis of the Reformation*, p. 116.

5. Paul Tillich, *The Protestant Era*, p. 193. London: Nisbet & Co., Ltd., 1951.

6. George L. Mosse, *The Reformation*, p. 1. New York: Henry Holt and Company, 1953. By permission.

INDEX

INDEX

✠